THE ROAD TO HELL

Sidney's Way volume 1

a Five Roads to Texas novel

Written by
BRIAN PARKER

Edited by
AURORA DEWATER

Illustrated by
AJ POWERS

DISCLAIMER

This is a work of fiction. Names, characters, places and incidents are the product of the author's imagination and are used fictitiously. Any resemblance to actual events, locales, or persons, living or dead, is purely coincidental.

Notice: The views expressed herein are NOT endorsed by the United States Government, Department of Defense or Department of the Army.

COPYRIGHT

THE ROAD TO HELL

Five Roads to Texas: a Phalanx Press

Collaboration

The Five Roads to Texas world is ever
expanding. Look for more adventures from the
minds of other Phalanx Press authors on the
Five Roads' Amazon page.

Works available by Brian Parker

Five Roads to Texas
Five Roads to Texas
After the Roads

Easytown Novels
The Immorality Clause
Tears of a Clone
West End Droids & East End Dames
High Tech/Low Life: An Easytown Anthology

The Path of Ashes
A Path of Ashes
Fireside
Dark Embers

Washington, Dead City series
GNASH ~ REND ~ SEVER

Stand Alone Works
Grudge: Operation Highjump
Enduring Armageddon
Origins of the Outbreak
The Collective Protocol
Battle Damage Assessment
Zombie in the Basement
Self-Publishing the Hard Way

Plus, many more anthology contributions and short stories.

The road to hell is paved with good intentions.
~ attributed to Saint Bernard of Clairvaux

PROLOGUE

LIBERAL, KANSAS
MARCH 26TH, DAY 1

Calm down! the boy scolded himself. He was practically panting like a dog, loud enough that any of the damned loonies within five blocks would hear him and come running.

Mark was trying to get home, but he'd gotten stuck behind the grocery store, hiding from the hundreds of insane zombie-like people that chased after everything they saw. Beside him, Delanie interlocked her fingers with his. He wasn't sure if the move was for her benefit, or for his. Either way, never in a million years would he have thought he'd end up holding hands with the senior prom queen.

He'd ignored three calls from his mother this morning on his way to school and another two as he settled into his seat for first period homeroom. Then things got crazy when Emily Garland—no relation to Judy Garland from *Wizard of Oz* fame that the town was "famous" for—went insane. First, she started clawing at her skin, causing some gnarly damage to her flawless complexion, and then she attacked Mark's classmates. He was only two desks away from her and saw her tear a clump of flesh out of Mike Darnold's palm when he threw his hands up to defend himself.

The teacher, Mr. Krause, tried to restrain her, but was bitten as well. He finally got her into a full nelson and yelled for someone to contact the office. As he held onto her, Emily vomited a nasty, dark pink substance onto Josh Turner, who'd remained in his seat nearby.

It only got weirder after that. Emily wasn't the only student at Liberal High who was acting insane and biting people. Three or four *more* people, in his class alone, began acting the same way as the sophomore basketball star had, scratching and tearing at their skin. That was all it took for him to grab his bag and get out of there.

As he ran down the hall toward the front door the screams of other students who'd gone crazy reverberated off the lockers and the high ceilings. He sprinted toward the exit and the door from the Home Economics classroom burst open. Mark stopped just in time to avoid being barreled over by a boy he no longer recognized. He remembered thinking that it was odd that his mind chastised him for the sound of his sneakers squealing on the linoleum floor at a time of obvious crisis, but it'd been drilled into his brain for more than a decade to keep quiet in the hallway.

The boy who'd charged out of HomeEc fell to the floor, his body limp after he'd slammed his head into the cinder block wall when he missed the tackle. Mark leapt over the crumpled form and ran for all that he was worth. The rooms flew by as more of the crazies appeared, tearing into his former classmates. He felt a pang of remorse, his conscience urging him to stop, to try to help everyone, but he knew it was hopeless. If he stopped, he would be a victim as well.

He hit the horizontal bar that kept the school's double glass doors secure from the unwanted visitors and surged through them into the light. As he emerged into the early spring morning he realized that the chaos he'd fled inside had descended upon the outside world as well.

The scene in the parking lot was pure pandemonium. Parents who were still in the midst of dropping off children fought with attackers, both inside and out of their vehicles. Several of the busses had crashed; the one that caught his eye was high-centered three-quarters of the way up the flagpole, which was bent almost completely horizontal.

More crazies charged toward him. It wasn't only the students, but parents and administrators as well. He swerved away from the parking lot and sprinted up the road leading between the high school football field and the middle school field. He knew that he couldn't maintain the pace so he slowed slightly to avoid completely winding himself and collapsing.

A woman screamed at him as he passed her car. She'd run into the metal barriers around one of the light poles in the parking lot. The engine revved with each wave of her flailing arms as she impotently tried to reach him. The seatbelt restrained her and she didn't seem to realize that she was trapped—information that Mark filed away for future use. The car's passenger door was open. He assumed the child being dropped off had fled when the mother started acting crazy.

A quick glance behind him showed that a few people, most covered in blood and gore, were chasing after him. They were sprinting all out, going much faster than he was. He increased his pace again, intent on making it off the school grounds and then to his house that was only half a mile away, just beyond the new Walmart grocery store they'd built a few years ago.

"Hey!" a girl had yelled from near the concession stand to his left.

Mark glanced over at her. It was Delanie Swearengin, the prom queen. The sight of her disheveled hair made him slow, then run toward her. She was sitting along the fence that surrounded the football field, which was why he hadn't seen her at first. An angry, bleeding gash across her forehead told him that she must have been the passenger in the car.

"Delanie!" he huffed, out of breath.

"Where are you going?" she asked.

"Anywhere but here."

She glanced at the car he'd just passed, and then at the school before coming back to him. "Can I go with you?"

"Yeah, come on." He leaned over and extended a hand, helping her to her feet. She winced and lifted her foot off the gravel.

"I twisted my ankle."

Mark barely knew her. She was a senior and he was a sophomore. She was the prom queen, a cheerleader, and the student body president. He was a solid C student who sat in the back of the class trying to avoid being noticed. He didn't owe her anything. He could have left her.

But he didn't.

"Here you go," he said softly, ducking under her arm to help her ease the pressure on her ankle. He risked a quick glance at the parking lot. Three of the crazies were running toward them. They'd be there in seconds.

He tried to run, but her weight pulled him down, so he settled for a fast walk. "Delanie, you *have* to run. If not, we're dead. Do you understand?"

"I—" She stopped and nodded curtly, putting her foot down and hobbling quickly.

Mark increased his speed to keep up with her. Then his heart dropped into the pit of his stomach. Two more people appeared at the end of the long driveway between the two fields. Each had red splashed across the front of their chests, reminding him of Emily's projectile vomit a few minutes ago. The newcomers saw them and began screaming incoherently as they sprinted down the drive.

"Uh…" Mark cast around, weighing their options. They couldn't go back to the school or up the street. "This way!"

He led Delanie toward the middle school field. The small chain link fence would do nothing except delay the inevitable, but they were out of options with nowhere else to go. The crazies from the parking lot were twenty feet from them. It wasn't fair. He'd done everything right. He'd avoided conflict inside the school and ran, just like he'd rehearsed during all of the school shooter drills. He'd escaped into the open, out of the confined space and now…

Mark lifted the latch on the gate and pushed through it. Out of habit, he let the latch fall into place around the pole. That one simple move was what saved them.

He and Delanie stumbled and fell onto the grass inside the fence. Almost as one, the five infected lunatics hit the chain link from different directions. It rattled, but held. The top bar was neck high on all of them, so they reached over the top, trying to grasp the two teenagers. None of them attempted to use the gate or tried to climb over the fence.

"Are they—" Delanie stopped.

"Zombies?" Mark finished her question.

She tore her gaze away from the screaming lunatics. "What? No! I was gonna ask if they were sick or something." She stared hard at him for a heartbeat, and then said, "That's why I stopped. It was a stupid question. Do you think they're zombies?"

He regarded them for a moment. They certainly did seem to be intent on biting and spreading whatever they were sick with, but none of them were eating brains or intestines like they did in all the movies.

"No, I don't think they're zombies." More of them were coming from the parking lot, drawn by the hideous screeches of the five who were reaching over the fence for them. "We need to get going," he said, addressing the matter at hand. "Can you get up?"

"Yeah. I think so. Help me up."

Mark pushed himself to his feet and then leaned over, putting his hands under the girl's arms. One of his hands accidently brushed against her breast. "Hey, watch it, uh... I'm sorry, I don't know your name."

He reddened and turned his face away as he completed helping her to her feet. "Mark Mullins. We had biology together last year."

She gritted her teeth and accepted his arm around her waist. "Oh. I'm sorry, Mark. I'm just stressed out and didn't recognize you."

He wondered if that was true or if it were an excuse to appease him. He decided that it didn't really matter which, so he'd just as well believe what she said. "I get it," he replied. Using his chin, Mark gestured toward the loonies behind them. "Can you check those guys out? I can't really look, gotta watch where we're going. Are they trying to follow us?"

Delanie turned and looked behind them as he guided them onto the track around the grass field. It angled away from the high school, ending directly across the street at the Walmart Neighborhood Market that they'd built over the park that was there when he was in elementary school.

"Um, no. They're pretty much right where we left them," Delanie reported. "There's like ten of them now, all right there on the other side of the fence yelling and reaching over."

"But they aren't like, trying to follow around the outside of the fence and get us on the other side?" Mark asked incredulously.

"Nope. They look pretty focused on us and not trying to figure out another way around."

"So whatever they're sick with has either made them pretty dumb, or they're sight hunters." He grunted as Delanie's weight began to wear on him. His mom was right; he should have been getting more protein in his diet. *"Mom!"*

"What?"

"My mom," he replied, digging into his pocket with his free hand. "She tried calling me a bunch of times this morning, but I was already sitting in homeroom and Mr. Krause would have confiscated my phone if I'd answered her."

He pulled out the battered flip phone his mom had provided for him, convinced that he'd get caught up in some type of sexting scandal if he had a smart phone like every other kid in America owned. Mark deftly flipped it open, using his thumb.

"Does that thing even work?" Delanie asked.

"Yeah," he grunted in annoyance. "Of course it works. My mom just doesn't trust me to have a phone with a camera on it. She ah…" He thought of an excuse quickly before continuing. "She doesn't want me to stream a bunch of music and videos to use up all her minutes so she got me this piece of junk. It makes calls and texts, which is all I need, according to her."

"Weird. My mom would—" She stopped suddenly, limping along in silence.

"Was that her in the car?" he asked. Delanie nodded, but chose to remain silent. "I'm sorry."

"It's not your fault, James."

"Mark," he corrected her.

"Yeah, Mark. Sorry."

He dialed his mom's number from memory, which was much easier than navigating the multiple menus in the phone to reach the address book. Placing the phone to his ear, it rang several times before his mother finally picked up.

"Mark?" she croaked, sounding terrible, like she did the morning after going on a date where he knew she'd smoked and drank well into the night.

"Mom! Mom, it's me. Something crazy is happening at school. People are *biting* each other!"

"Mark..." his mother's hoarse voice drifted from the tiny speaker. "Mrs. Folgerrrrr..." She trailed off.

"Mom? What happened to Mrs. Folger?" The old woman lived next door and his mother often had coffee with her in the mornings after Mark left for school before getting ready for her shift at the Pancake House.

"Bit... Bit me," she moaned. "Mark. Not safe."

The phone clicked and went silent. He stopped, causing Delanie to look over at him. "What is it?"

"My mom says she got bit by our neighbor and that it's not safe."

He looked around. There didn't seem to be any of the loonies nearby, all of them were still back at the other end of the field, held at bay by

THE ROAD TO HELL 13

the chain link fence. He'd seen tons of zombie movies and post-apocalyptic films. The universal rule for all of them was that you needed supplies if you were going to survive. All he had with him was his school backpack and a bottle of water—not enough to do anything except delay the inevitable.

The actual Walmart, which he was sure held every kind of supply he could possibly need, was across town. That was too far to go on foot with Delanie's injured ankle, but the grocery store was right there, literally two hundred feet away. The Neighborhood Market had a small section of sporting goods equipment in addition to the standard groceries that every store offered.

"We need to go to the Neighborhood Market and get some supplies."

"Supplies? For what?" she asked.

"I don't know how long this outbreak, or whatever, is going to last. We need food and water. My mom said that my house wasn't safe and you live way out near Dorothy's House, so that's too far to go on foot."

"Wait. How do you know where I live?"

"Uh... I was at the Land of Oz one day and saw you at the house across the street," he lied, referencing the small *Wizard of Oz* attraction that the town was known for. Of course he knew where she lived. *Everyone* knew that her family owned the big house across from the attraction. Her brother had been famous for throwing the wildest parties in town before he graduated and joined the Army. "I just figured that's where you live."

She didn't comment further on it. "Okay, so we get some food and stuff, then what?"

"I don't know," Mark replied. "I mean, we could try to hole up somewhere until the police get things sorted out."

They reached the far side of the fence. There wasn't a gate to cross through this time, so he helped her over. It was delicate work to assist her without accidentally touching her butt and making their unlikely partnership even more awkward than it already was after the boob incident, but he managed to do so.

"Okay, just keep going," Mark urged as they went through the shallow ditch up to the road. They made it across the street to the entrance of the market's parking lot without incident.

Then their luck changed.

A scream, all too familiar to them now, sounded from nearby. Mark whipped his head around toward the parking lot where two or three people ran at them from the gas station in the far corner.

"Shit, let's go!" he hissed. A surge of adrenaline hit him and he lifted Delanie off her feet and onto his shoulders in a modified fireman's carry that he'd learned in gym class last year during Coach Reynold's infamous grass drills.

She protested for a moment, but then settled, likely realizing that her ankle would only hold them back. The girl was lighter than he'd expected, which allowed him to manage a half jog-walk toward the back of the building. He was relying on his earlier observation that the loonies were visual hunters, so if he could just get around the corner of the building out of sight, maybe they would have a chance.

The maniacal shrieks sounded close as they echoed off the large store's stone exterior. The idea of getting tackled from behind made him go faster and he made it around the corner.

There was a loading dock in the back. He staggered the last twenty feet, depositing Delanie on the chest-high dock before scrambling up beside her. She scooted backward toward the shadowy corner and he followed suit as the screams got closer and more frustrated.

Then he saw them.

Several bloody people staggered into view. He pressed himself into the corner, squishing Delanie in the process. He had to force himself to calm down and even his breathing so as not to hyperventilate and alert the infected to their presence. Delanie grasped his hand, lacing her fingers between his.

They tried not to move, neither one of them daring to so much as breathe. Mark, who was on the outside of Delanie, sat completely still hoping that he was right about them being visual hunters. He squeezed his eyes shut, not wanting to see when his end would come.

Their screams of rage and frustration threatened to drive him insane as they milled about behind the store. Loud thumps nearby made him flinch, expecting to feel the intense pain of teeth as they tore into his exposed flesh. It was completely unnerving to endure the thoughts of what *could* happen if they were discovered.

It seemed to last for hours, but Mark knew that it was probably only a few minutes before something caught their attention and they stormed off. The sound of their calls faded and he risked a quick peek through his tightly closed eyelids.

They were alone on the back dock.

Mark nudged Delanie, still not wanting to say anything. She looked up and he gestured toward the truck parking area with his chin. Following his direction, she watched the area of pavement that they could see for a moment, then leaned into him, her lips brushing his ear as she whispered, "We need to get behind locked doors."

He nodded enthusiastically. Being outside was a death sentence, no doubt. They stood carefully, trying to avoid making a sound. It was easier said than done as both of Mark's knees popped loudly and Delanie gave an inadvertent whimper of pain when she put pressure on her ankle that had begun to swell in the time they'd been sitting there.

Mark didn't let go of Delanie's hand, and she seemed content to leave hers in his, as they snuck carefully toward the store's back door. He considered what would happen if the door were locked, and decided that he'd cross that bridge when he came to it. Worst case scenario, they could probably open the big garage doors, but that'd definitely alert any loony in the area that they were on the loading dock.

When they were a few feet from the door, he shook his hand loose and held it up, telling Delanie to stay where she was. She nodded her understanding and waited as he tried the door.

The moment he depressed the lever, the door exploded outward, slamming into him and pushing him with the force of the blow. He became temporarily trapped in the vacant space between the door and the wall, which jutted out to accommodate the tracks for the garage doors.

Delanie's screams mingled with those of several others. The door shuddered as infected pushed their way out of the store where they'd been trapped. Dull *thuds* told the story of bodies falling off the dock and dropping the five or six feet to the ground.

He stayed behind the door, frozen in fear as Delanie's screams reached a fever pitch of pain, then stopped abruptly. Mark stared, wide-eyed through a crack between the walls of his temporary prison as the loonies out in the dock parking area stood. Fresh gore covered their faces, hands, and bodies.

He knew without a doubt that it belonged to Delanie. Her cries of pain and misery would be stamped onto his brain for the rest of his life.

Terrified screams echoed across the morning air and the infected in the parking lot loped off, drawn toward the new sounds of misery. The door jolted once more as another one of the crazies rushed out and tumbled off the dock.

The fact that more of them were coming from inside gave him pause. He'd considered trying to sneak out, but now, he wanted to wait and be sure. It didn't hurt for him to stay hidden, he reasoned with himself. People who didn't stay out of sight got— He stopped that line of thought. Delanie hadn't done anything wrong; it was just shitty luck that the loonies were piled up on the other side of the door trying to get out.

In the distance, sirens of all kinds blared as police and emergency responders did their best to quell the growing threat. Somewhere close by—maybe out at the airport—a loud explosion signaled the death of someone, maybe even a lot of people. Mingled between the sounds of crashing vehicles and screams of fear, there was the ever-present bellows of rage that seemed to be the hallmark of the crazies as they chased after people.

The time passed slowly for Mark as he leaned against the wall. He checked the time on his phone often, wishing that he had a smart phone for the real world emergency he faced. As it was, the flip phone was worthless. He could have searched online for any information about what was happening and tips on what to do and how to survive. Instead, he had a glorified alarm clock.

Once he was reasonably sure that there weren't any more of the crazies in the store, he put his dumb phone in his pocket and pushed against the door. The metal grated loudly against the concrete dock where it'd become wedged. He cringed and stopped. There were a thousand sounds marring the usual silence of Liberal, Kansas, but he was sure that *this* one would bring the infected running back toward him.

"That's stupid," he mumbled under his breath. Still, he waited another few minutes, ears straining to hear any type of response to the noise he'd made.

When nothing came, he put his shoulder into the door and shoved hard. It swung away from him quickly. He lunged to grab the handle before it slammed shut. That's all he needed was for it to close and lock him out.

Mark started to duck inside, but stopped, turning to look over the edge of the dock. He knew that he shouldn't, but he couldn't help himself. Down below, Delanie lay in a pool of her own blood. Several large wounds on her neck and face exposed the mutilated muscles, torn arteries, and the cheekbone underneath. Her mouth was twisted in a shriek of pain that had been cut off by the devastation to her throat.

It was a terrible sight. Probably the worst part was her eyes. They were fixed skyward, her blue-gray irises staring at the clouds above. Mark couldn't take it. He had to close her eyes. He owed her that little bit of dignity.

He placed his backpack in the doorframe and eased it closed slowly so it didn't lock him out. The stairs they'd missed when they came up to the loading dock were the closest way down, so he began to jog toward them.

Then a shriek of anger pierced the dock. His head snapped up. A looney was running at him full speed from the far corner of the building. He cursed and reversed course, heading back toward the door.

By the time he reached it, the infected was grasping ineffectually across the dock, trying to reach him from below. Mark considered kicking it in the head, then discarded the idea. Knowing his luck, the thing would grab his leg and he'd end up like the girl down below.

He pulled open the door and grabbed his backpack, slipping inside and letting the door close behind him.

"Sorry, Delanie," he whispered. "I'm really sorry."

He didn't know what else was in the store, so he began searching for a weapon. If he was gonna hole up in the grocery store, he had to be prepared to defend it. Off in the corner, he saw a broom and decided that it was a good start. He'd need something more dangerous in the long run, but for now it would give him a chance.

1

NEAR LIBERAL, KANSAS
FEBRUARY 10TH, DAY 320

Sidney wiped the sweat from her forehead with a towel. There wasn't as much work to do on the farm over the wintertime, so she'd recently began a workout regimen that was best described as a prison workout. She did a variety of strength building exercises in her small, ten-by-ten bedroom and then used Carmen's kids, Patricia and Miguel, as weights for stair climbing to strengthen her legs.

Her workouts had become so popular in the house that both Carmen and Sally participated in the daily ritual. They all agreed that adding cardio to the workout would be better, but with a solid six inches of snow sitting on the ground outside, the only options were running in place and shadowboxing.

Sidney had asked Jake what the odds were that they could pick up a treadmill or elliptical from Liberal, but he'd said the he didn't think it was a good idea to go on *non-essential* incursions into town, especially with the noisy Stryker or Vern's old farm truck. While Jake was officially no longer in the military, he still acted as if he were.

The former soldier and their host, Vern, were like two peas in a pod. Vern Campbell had been in the Army for seven years, with three of those years in combat in Vietnam. On his third tour, he'd been given an administrative billet in one of the headquarters down in Saigon and the old firecracker said that broke him. His assignment officer had thought he was doing Vern a favor by giving the veteran a posting away from the jungle, but he wasn't cut out for a desk job. The old man hated every day of his third tour and dropped his request for separation immediately upon his return to Fort Benning, Georgia. Then he returned to the family farm in Kansas, got married, and lived the American Dream, according to him.

"Whew," Sally said, placing a well-meaning hand on Sidney's shoulder. "That was a tough workout."

Sidney grinned. "Just wait until Jake finishes clearing the path to the barn.

Sally frowned. "Pull-ups?"

"Pull-ups," Sidney confirmed. The barn's exposed rafters made a perfect base for the metal bar she'd placed across them for pull-ups. The rolling of the bar added a degree of difficulty that she liked because it helped to strengthen her forearms as well as her back.

Lincoln's crying from her bedroom made Sidney wince. She'd hoped to get a few minutes of stretching in with the girls, something that even Katie joined in for, but now that'd have to wait. The baby was getting better about sleeping for more than an hour or two at a time, but he still needed to eat regularly.

"Here," Carmen said, handing Sidney the glass of water she'd been about to drink. "Take mine. I'll make a new one."

"Thanks," she replied, taking it and walking up the stairs quickly.

Behind her, she heard the Hispanic woman say, "I don't know how she does it. When I had my kids, I could barely get out of bed most days."

It made Sidney grin as she opened the door to her bedroom. Lincoln's wails of hunger made the smile deepen. She loved that little guy more than she ever thought possible, and couldn't believe that she'd thought about having an abortion when she first found out that she was pregnant with Lincoln Bannister's child.

Baby Lincoln was the result of being cooped up in Linc's house in Georgetown during the first several weeks of the outbreak. They'd decided to stay in DC versus making the trip to the Atlanta Safe Zone to let the worst of the disaster settle down and to allow the government time to figure out a response. Then their food supplies began to get low and they learned through intermittent Internet news that Atlanta was overrun. The CDC reestablished the safe zone in the middle of the western Texas desert near the city of El Paso. During their trip to the new safe zone, Lincoln was bitten and became infected. A man at one of the gas stations along the way killed the newly turned Lincoln and she'd made the rest of the trip alone, including a near-disastrous encounter with a hotel clerk who was intent on getting payment for the room in any way he could.

Once she was in El Paso, she learned that the FEMA camps were at capacity and had been redirected to the Army base of Fort Bliss. There, she was assigned to a camp inside the walls they were building. Within a few months, the infected penetrated the ring of defenses that the military had out in the desert and attacked the FEMA camps. It all happened so fast. The base refugee population exploded from a manageable three hundred thousand to a full four million people, all crammed into the space meant for a population a tenth of their size.

Initially, the revolts began over food and supplies, and then they were engineered as a way to shrink the refugee population. Late last summer, Sidney met Caitlyn, a soldier who offered to help her get a few pairs of clothes that could fit her ever-expanding waistline. That act of kindness had been the spark for a major revolt that ended with tens of thousands of people dead. Caitlyn introduced her to Jake, a lieutenant in the Army, and the three of them planned their escape from Fort Bliss. They stole a Stryker Infantry Fighting Vehicle and bullshitted their way through the gates into the *wilds* of Texas.

A few weeks of travel northward and they found themselves in the middle of a war between the few survivors in Liberal, Kansas. Vern's granddaughters, Sally and Katie, had been kidnapped and he'd been left for dead. Jake and Caitlyn didn't hesitate to offer to rescue them—or at least that's how she *chose* to remember Caitlyn. The soldier and her boyfriend, Eric, were killed during the girls' rescue.

With winter approaching and Sidney about to give birth, Jake asked Vern if they could stay on, at least through the spring planting season. Vern's farmhands were murdered during his granddaughters' kidnapping, so he'd graciously accepted the offer. Then Sidney gave birth to baby Lincoln a little over two months ago and now she struggled to get back into fighting shape for the day that Vern asked them to leave.

She knew they weren't safe. They never would be. The infected were everywhere, and they'd learned the terrible truth about them in an isolated New Mexico town. The creatures would do whatever they needed to do in order to survive—including eating their own.

Sidney stroked the baby's cheek as he suckled at her breast. He was her only link to the man she'd loved—a fact that she didn't realize until after he was dead. There were lots of things in her life that she'd wished she'd done differently, but the only thing she truly regretted was how she treated Lincoln in the end. He'd tried to help and keep her safe as best he could; he just didn't have the skills that their new world required. She'd been so nasty to him when she told him that she was pregnant. That interaction in the car, immediately before he was bitten would be forever stamped on her mind as a moment of shame.

Sidney wiped the tears that had gathered at the corners of her eyes, threatening to escape and trail down her nose. She couldn't do anything about the past. What was done was done. She could only try to make a difference in the lives of those who were left, and to keep her baby safe.

She glanced at the corner beside her chair. Leaned against the wall within arms' reach was a wooden closet rod with the blade from her old kitchen knife attached to it. She was comfortable with her new group of friends and survivors, but it was her responsibility to ensure Lincoln's safety and she wouldn't hesitate even a fraction of a second to defend him—against human or infected.

2

FORT BLISS MAIN CANTONEMENT AREA
FEBRUARY 10TH

"Alright, sir. That's everyone we can muster."

Jim Albrecht looked at the ragged bunch of soldiers standing in a loose semi-circle in front of the Strykers on line in the motorpool. "How many?"

"Forty-one."

He nodded at the NCO, a grizzled veteran named Sergeant First Class Turner. In an odd twist of fate, Sergeant Turner had been Lieutenant Murphy's platoon sergeant before he went AWOL, and he was more than ready to go after the deserter. "Let's see, if we go with six Strykers, that'll give us what? Twenty-three dismounts?"

"My momma always told me not to do math in public, sir. Six trucks need eighteen soldiers to drive, gun, and TC. Whatever is left over go into the back as dismounts."

Jim chuckled. "Alright, good point, Sergeant. Everything ready to go?"

"Yes, sir. Each truck has five thousand rounds for the fifty and we've loaded up ten cans of 5.56 in each. There's three snipers in that mix, so we've also got a couple cans of 7.62, but not as much as I'd like."

"Yeah, I heard the ammo point was running low on the 7.62 because we've kept the snipers busy on the wall."

"That's what they say, sir," Turner agreed without committing to the truthfulness of the statement. "Sounds like a leadership failure to me. In Able Company, we only use our snipers for extreme distances, not the shots that a regular rifleman can take. That's not the case across the division."

Jim approved of the sergeant's assessment, but he tried not to second-guess his commanders who dealt with the infected every day while he sat in an office building going to meetings and drinking coffee. It wasn't fair of him to do that to them, and he prided himself on being fair—except for the fact that he'd helped to set up Lieutenant Murphy and stage a revolt.

He shook his head. "What's wrong, sir?"

"*Hmm*?" Jim asked, feeling embarrassed that the NCO had seen him unconsciously move his head in response to his internal dialogue. "Nothing. Sorry. I was thinking about something else." He refocused on the task at hand. "Alright, we have enough Class Five to start a small war. What about everything else?"

The noncommissioned officer went down the list of their supplies. They had plenty of Class One, the Army term for food and water. The vehicles were full of fuel and each one sported six jerry cans of additional fuel—Class Three in Army lingo. That much fuel should get them between 400 to 500 miles and there were plenty of truck stops along their route. Class Five was ammo, which they'd already covered. Class Six, personal items, was up to the individual soldier, although no alcohol was permitted with the distances they were expecting to travel and the unpredictable nature of the infected. Finally, they had two medics who had full bags of Class Eight, medical supplies.

"Sounds like you've got it covered, Sergeant Turner."

"This ain't my first rodeo, sir."

"Alright, let's go talk to the troops and then head out of here."

They walked to where the soldiers stood by their vehicles, smoking and joking, although the term "smoking" was in name only since the base had run out of cigarettes months ago. When they saw the colonel approaching, they began to quiet down and he saw several people tapping others who'd sat down and fallen asleep.

"Good morning, gentlemen," Jim began, addressing them. Then he noticed two females and almost corrected himself. Thinking better of it, he continued, "Sergeant Turner tells me that we only have forty-one troopers available for duty. Two months ago, this brigade had forty-one *hundred*. That uprising practically wiped us out. But it didn't. The Ready First Brigade persevered and helped to put down the revolt in our sector.

"Iron Six has given us the opportunity to get revenge on the instigators of the uprising. As you all know, Lieutenant Murphy from Able Company was reprimanded for his actions on the night of October 8th. As punishment, he was sent to live in the camps for a month. While he was there, it's believed that he encouraged the resistance movement that led to the uprising. Two nights before the fighting began, he and Staff Sergeant Wyatt, also from Able Company, stole a Stryker and headed north. Based on several observations of Murphy with two females, a mess hall cook and a camp nurse, we believe he took some civilians from the camps with him when he went AWOL. Of course, with all the deaths, we really don't have a way of knowing whether that part is true or just an allegation." Jim wanted to be as factual as possible when dealing with his soldiers. It'd be easier to maintain the lie that covered up his shame for putting Murphy in that camp on purpose.

"What we do know is that their Blue Force Tracker pinged at a farmhouse in Tyrone, Oklahoma," he continued. "From there, it went black and satellite imagery of the area is inconclusive. To be honest, we have no idea where they've gone."

"So… How do we find them, then?" a young soldier off to his left asked.

Jim smiled. "Well, first off, we're going to Oklahoma to their last known location. Then we're going to go old school, begin looking for clues, and then searching in expanding circular patterns around their last known position. The US Army didn't always have all this high-tech gadgetry that we have now. We'll dismount and find tire tracks, .50 cal bullet casings, whatever we can to identify where they went next."

"Yeah, but isn't it possible that they just turned off the BFT, or removed it before traveling to Canada or something?" the soldier pressed.

"Watch your tone, Private," Sergeant Turner growled.

"No, it's all right, Sergeant. Private *ah…*" He squinted to see the name tape attached to the front of the kid's vest. "Private Stout has a good point. We don't know what we don't know. You're right, they could be long gone by now, but I'm willing to bet that Lieutenant Murphy and Sergeant Wyatt are still in Tyrone—maybe even at that farmhouse."

"Sir, I've got a question," a corporal asked.

"Go ahead."

"I was on Lieutenant Murphy's first mission to the Sam's Club. I was his gunner, actually. There were thousands of infected that swarmed toward the sound of those helicopter engines. What about them? We're pretty damn good at killing them from up on the wall where they can't get to us, but once we go out there, on their level… I don't know."

"You're right, Corporal Jones. The infected will outnumber us a hundred-to-one, maybe more. But that's their *only* advantage. They can't think. They can't plan. They don't do anything except attack sound and light. Now, I know I just said that we don't have to rely on our technology to find Lieutenant Murphy, but that's only partially right. We all have NODs and thermals, every one of you were issued suppressors for your M-4s for this mission, as well as the thicker uniforms, Kevlar gloves, and knee and elbow pads. What do the infected have? Teeth and fingernails. That's it. We'll be okay against them as long as we," he held up his fingers and began counting, "one, use the equipment that we have, and two, work together as a group. No Lone Ranger bullshit."

Jim looked around the group once again. "Any more questions?"

"Hey, sir. One more."

Jim looked back to the corporal who said he'd been Murphy's gunner. "Yeah?"

"Do you expect us to kill Lieutenant Murphy and Sergeant Wyatt?"

Jim shook his head. "No, son. I wouldn't ask that of you. Now, obviously, everyone has the right to defend themselves if it comes to that, but the ultimate goal is to bring them back to Fort Bliss peacefully for their trial and to recover the missing Stryker." He paused. "Does that make sense?"

"Yes, sir. Thank you." The soldier kicked at the gravel and Jim could tell that he had another question.

"What is it, Corporal?"

"Well, sir. I know we're in the shit here at Fort Bliss, fighting the infected every day—and the refugees too—but... Is it true about the Norks?"

"What?" Jim asked, taken aback by the question.

"I have a buddy who works up at the Division Headquarters. Told me the North Koreans have troops here in the States. Is that true?"

"I have literally no idea what you're talking about," Jim replied truthfully. "Why would there be North Korean troops?"

"My buddy said they're here as a UN force or something. He's not entirely sure."

Jim organized his thoughts before replying. "I'll have to ask once we get back, Corporal Jones. That's the first I've heard about Koreans, but to be honest, I'm skeptical. This outbreak is worldwide, an extinction level event. They would need to be fighting in their homeland, not sending troops over here." He held up his hands. "I'm not saying your friend is lying to you, it's just not likely. But I promise that I'll follow up when we return." Jones nodded and stared at the ground.

"Any more?" Jim waited a moment, trying to look every soldier in the eye to give them the opportunity to speak. Finally, he said, "Okay then. Let's mount up and head north."

"You heard the Colonel," Sergeant Turner bellowed hoarsely. "Let's get loaded up and ready to move. I want asses in seats, ready to go in two minutes."

Jim grinned, despite the odd question from Jones. He missed being on the line with the infantrymen like Sergeant Turner. *Well, looks like your old ass is gonna get to experience it again for a little while.*

3

LIBERAL, KANSAS
FEBRUARY 11TH

Jake Murphy crouched beside a dumpster as the group of infected moved past his position. They looked terrible, not much more than skin and bones. Dark grey and black patches of skin on their fingertips, noses, and ears revealed areas ravaged by frostbite over the course of the mild southern Kansas winter. The infected were alive, if you could call it that, and their flesh responded to the elements. He wondered what the damn things further north, where the weather got *really* nasty, would look like.

Snow fell from the clouds, blanketing the town in a carpet of new powder and furthering the perpetual silence that had descended upon the world after the rise of the infected. The girls back at the farm were sick of the snow, but Jake liked it. In truth, it made things a little easier for him on days like today.

Sidney's baby, Lincoln, was healthy—too healthy. He screamed constantly because he was hungry for more milk. Carmen said it might be that Sidney wasn't producing enough to satisfy the kid, so the task fell to Jake to head into Liberal, the town nearest the Campbell farm, to find formula and more diapers. The snow helped him to see if the infected were in the area.

Of course, he couldn't rely solely on the snow technique. It helped, but he had the thermals on his M-2010 sniper rifle to check out the area before moving. The infected had changed their tactics somewhat since winter set in. They were much more active in the daytime now than they were in the summer, when they primarily moved at night. He guessed that it must have something to do with not being able to properly regulate their body temperatures, but biology hadn't been one of his strongest subjects at West Point.

When he was sure the group he'd spotted was out of sight, he eased his way out from behind the dumpster and peered after them. They were long gone, so he checked the surroundings once more before continuing. His target was the Walmart Neighborhood Market across the street from the Kansas National Guard Armory on 7th Street. He hoped the smaller store, which was much closer than the Supercenter across town, would have everything he needed. He didn't feel like trudging an extra two miles—and then back—through the heart of town. Liberal wasn't a big city by any means, but the city limit sign he passed coming from the Campbell farm said there were 20,525 people living there.

That was a whole lot of the infected that he'd rather not encounter.

He glanced at the armory, wondering for the hundredth time since he'd learned of the small building what types of supplies they had inside. He knew there was probably an arms room full of M-4s, but doubted there was any ammunition for them since there were regulations against storing ammo with weapons in military buildings. When he'd gone AWOL from Fort Bliss, they'd brought a lot of ammunition with them, but he could always use more. The silenced rifles he had fired standard 5.56mm ammo. The silencer made shots much quieter than an unsuppressed rifle, but Jake needed to find a supply of subsonic ammunition to make them truly quiet.

There weren't any signs saying what type of unit the armory used to house, but a row of heavy equipment transport trucks out back in the motor pool made him assume it was a transportation company—nice to know if he needed a big ass truck and had enough time to figure out which batteries still held a charge. In truth, it probably wasn't worth the hassle. The loud vehicle would bring the infected screaming in from all directions.

Jake made his way quickly across the street and down through a ditch to the back of the Neighborhood Market. He crouched beside another dumpster, assessing the area. Vern said that they'd never hit up the store for supplies, even though it was the closest one to the farm besides the gas station that they frequented. The infected had been far too prevalent in the area to try to make it into town before winter set in.

The back dock was clear, so he sprinted across the open space between the dumpster and the elevated platform. As he neared the dock, a small, desiccated female corpse lay on the pavement, her face frozen in the pain of her death. Seeing the female's body jogged his memory of the last time he'd been at a loading dock. He'd been in Midland, Texas sling loading tractor trailers full of food from a Sam's Club when Sergeant Orroro was bitten. The NCO gathered everyone's grenades, assuring them that he'd take as many of the infected with him as he could. As far as Jake knew, the man never blew himself up because they'd left before any explosions occurred.

Not the time, man, he chastised himself. He could think about the people who'd passed on and all of those he left behind when he was back at the farm. Doing so out here was a sure-fire way to get himself killed. The infected didn't give humans a second chance. One slip up and you were done for.

Jake slid along the platform until he came to the back door. He turned the handle downward and pulled. The door didn't budge. He placed a foot against the wall and tried to heave it open. The door was still stuck, making him think that it was locked from the inside.

"Dammit," the soldier muttered under his breath. He did not want to be outside any more than was absolutely necessary, but now, going in the back door was not an option.

He eased down off the back dock, using the heavy rubber trailer bumpers to help himself down without making too much noise. The snow fell thicker now, obscuring his ability to see farther than twenty or thirty feet, so he lifted his goggles up onto his helmet and brought up his rifle, pressing his eye into the scope's rubber cup to seal out the light.

Scanning the direction the larger group of infected had gone, he determined that the way was still clear. When he turned toward the south, though, a solitary heat signature illuminated inside the reticle pattern. He pulled his eye away and tilted the rifle at an angle, aiming down the iron sights he'd mounted offset from the thermal scope. He had no way of knowing whether the heat signature was an infected, an animal, or a human seeking shelter.

Jake's unaided eyes couldn't see anything but snow. He pressed himself against the building and used the thermals again. The white shape of a human appeared roughly where he'd last seen it, illuminated against the gray background. It was still a hundred meters away, so he turned slowly, scanning the surrounding area once again. He didn't need to get rolled up from behind while he was focused on the one potential threat.

Nothing presented itself, so he returned to the figure. It had gotten closer, but was taking its time, walking upright, unafraid of detection. That made up his mind. It was an infected. A human wouldn't be out for a Sunday stroll.

He slid back around the corner and pressed the goggles onto his eyes once more. Then he dropped the M-4, letting it hang loose from the sling around his neck. He had a suppressor on the weapon, but it still made noise when fired. Jake wasn't sure how far the sound would travel with the current weather conditions, but he sure as hell wasn't willing to risk his life to find out.

Unsnapping the nylon sheath on his tactical vest, he slipped the seven-inch K-BAR blade free and pressed his back against the wall. Ideally, the infected would wander off in another direction, but that wasn't how things usually played out. It was following the others, their footprints already beginning to fade under the falling snow.

As he waited, the pervasive silence weighed heavily on him. At Fort Bliss, there was always noise, whether it was vehicles or people. Here, on the southern border of Kansas, it was deathly silent. The infected remained mute until they found prey, and all of their prey was either dead or turned.

Jake was the only thing on the menu this morning.

A ragged intake of air followed by a wet, raspy exhale alerted him that the infected was closing rapidly. It sounded like the thing had fluid in its lungs, probably pneumonia. It appeared around the corner and he tensed. The creature walked past him without turning its head. It was completely nude, like so many of them that he'd seen over the months of fighting. In the summer, they'd removed their clothing to help cool their bodies, he wondered if they had enough mental clarity to realize they needed to wear some type of clothing against the chill.

Jake considered simply letting it pass. Given the sounds it made and the lack of clothing, the thing would probably die from exposure before too long anyways. He could simply let nature take its course.

He couldn't do that, though. Leaving the infected only extended the problem. He had no illusions about clearing the city, but each one he killed was one less that couldn't wander into the farmland beyond and attack his friends.

Jake pushed himself off the wall with his free hand. The momentum carried him up to the infected quickly and he clamped a leather-gloved hand over the thing's mouth and nose. The knife snaked under its flailing arms and he angled it up under the ribcage, plunging it home. The infected didn't react to being stabbed, it continued to try to grab at him, while biting into his fingers.

He was conscious of the position he'd put himself in, so he dragged the infected back to the shelter of the loading dock as he pushed the knife away from both of them and then brought it inward once more. Then again. And again.

Jake had no idea how many times he stabbed the infected, but he managed to pierce its heart with one of his thrusts. Its movements quickened for a moment and then ceased completely. Still, he held onto it, not wanting to let the thing go before he was sure it was dead. He didn't need it alerting any of its brethren that he was there.

After several long heartbeats, he dropped the creature softly to the ground. For good measure, he pressed the knife through its ear, puncturing the brain. There was no recovery from that. Lifting the infected's arm, he placed the blade of the K-BAR into its armpit, and then pressed the skin close, cleaning the blade as he slid it out.

He quickly sheathed the knife and grabbed his rifle's pistol grip to bring it up. Another thermal scan of the surrounding area through the drifting snow told him that he was alone once more.

"Alright," he breathed softly. "Time to find out who locked that door."

Jake moved slowly out of the loading dock and went around the side of the building. He kept his eye glued to the thermal as he advanced steadily. The grass underneath the snow was thick, but manageable as he made sure that every footfall landed solidly on the ground. The Neighborhood Market wasn't nearly as large as a Supercenter, probably a quarter of the size if he were to guess, so it didn't take him long to reach the front of the store.

After scanning for infected, he made his way to the front entrance. What he saw there made him drop to the ground. He looked carefully for any booby-traps nearby, but didn't see anything. Someone was definitely holed up inside the grocery store.

The carts were lined up in three rows in front of the doors. The two rows nearest to the glass doors were side-by-side directly blocking the doors, adding about six feet of standoff distance from anyone inside. The third row of carts was fifteen feet beyond the first two and formed a semi-circle around the doorway, with either end against the building. Three bodies lay in the open area between the carts in different states of decay. None of them looked like recent kills.

"It's a goddamned kill box," he mumbled into the snow beneath him.

Whoever had set it up was obviously prepared to defend their home and had done so on a few occasions. Jake considered what he knew of the town, which was only what Vern and the girls had told him, pointing out a few locations on a map. There were likely other grocery stores and pharmacies nearby, but he sure as heck didn't know where they were and didn't like being on foot in the heart of an infected city.

He got up slowly and made his way to the outer ring of shopping carts. Whoever had put them together did a damn good job of it. The way they were interlocked, there was no pulling them apart or moving them outward; the only way through them was to go over the top. Jake grimaced as the carts made a lot of noise while he clamored over them into the kill box.

He looked around sheepishly, wondering if the infected that'd tramped by the back dock were far enough away that they hadn't heard the noise. It didn't take him long to figure out as the screams echoed across the parking lot.

"Fuck," he grumbled, rushing toward the next row of carts.

The glass doors slid open a few inches and a green metal broomstick appeared. The large kitchen knife taped to the end with silver duct tape made him stop and raise his hands.

"Whoa now. I'm human," he breathed quickly.

"Who else is with you?" a muffled voice asked, the end of the makeshift spear wavering. From the height of the person holding the weapon, Jake guessed it was either a woman or a kid.

"No one. I'm just trying to get a few things for my group."

The spear dipped. "You have a group?"

The screams of the infected began to solidify as they got closer, the sound no longer bouncing off of structures further away.

"Can I come in? It's gonna get nasty out here soon."

"Give me your rifle."

"No way."

"Then you aren't coming in here."

"Come on, kid. This is—" A body slamming into the shopping cart ring startled him and he spun, bringing the rifle up. Using the iron sights, he snapped a muffled round into the chest of an infected only fifteen feet away. More of them were running across the parking lot, slipping on the snow-covered asphalt.

"Oh, fuck this," Jake said, turning. His hand darted out, grasping the broom handle below the knife, and jerked the weapon from the defender's hands.

"Hey!"

Jake dropped the spear and hopped up awkwardly onto the shopping cart barricade. Scooting his butt across the wire mesh, he made it to the door then forced them open. "Shut up and let me work, kid."

The top of the barricade made a steady platform for his elbows as he leaned into his rifle and began to fire at the nearby group. The shopping carts did a good job at keeping the infected at bay long enough for him to dispatch the threats. Only one made it up to the top of the first row. It didn't make it into the kill zone.

Jake quickly lost count of the number of infected that he shot. He had to change magazines twice, so that was sixty-plus rounds used up—ammunition that he could ill afford to spare. When the immediate area looked clear, he ducked back inside the store and slammed the doors shut.

"Lock! How do these lock?"

The youth looked at him dumbly from behind a homemade mask cut from a beanie cap. "You just killed like a hundred of those things."

"We'll talk later," Jake said. "Do you know how the doors lock?"

The kid stepped forward and twisted a deadbolt that Jake hadn't seen. "I can't reach it, but up top, there's a bolt. Push that."

Jake pushed the bolt on one of the doors upward, slamming it home. Beyond the glass, he could see more of the infected entering the parking lot from wherever they'd been. He grabbed the kid's arm and pulled him sideways, out of the line of sight of the doors.

"Hey!" Jake clamped a hand over the kid's mouth and shook his head violently. He released him slowly then brought his index finger up to his pursed lips, indicating that they needed to be quiet.

Outside, the screams of the infected intensified as they got closer. Several of the shopping carts rattled. They'd reached the first barrier.

Jake switched magazines, careful to hold the empty one as he dropped it to avoid further noise. He leaned close to the kid. "How secure is this place?"

The youth shrugged. "Kept you out," he whispered.

"Smartass."

The jangle of the shopping carts brought his eyes back to the doorway. The handles began to hit the glass and he frowned, wondering if Walmart had sprung for the shatter resistant glass or if they'd gone cheap out here in Bumfuck, Kansas. Hands beat against the doors as the unnerving screams of hundreds of the infected reverberated through the building.

"We need to move to the back of the store," he said into the kid's ear. "Do you have any weapons?"

"Duh. Come on."

The youth got up and moved away from the entrance. He turned down an aisle leading into the darkness. Jake followed him, resisting the urge to slide his night vision monocular down over his eye. If the kid could navigate his way to the back unaided, then so could he.

He bumped into the back of the kid, who'd stopped. "It's right here," he said, pushing gently on a set of double doors.

When they were through them and into the stockroom, Jake asked, "Any way to secure those doors?"

"Not that I know of. We could pile boxes in front of them, but they swing both ways, so it's kind of pointless."

"*Hmpf,*" he grunted. "What's your name, kid?"

The youth pulled the mask from his face. "Mark."

"Nice to meet you," he said, holding out a hand for the kid to shake. "My name's Jake. How old are you, Mark?"

"Fifteen. I'll be sixteen in March."

"Only a month then."

"A *month*?" He sounded surprised. "I thought it was like November or maybe December."

"Nope. It's the tenth or eleventh of February. I'm not sure which, but I'm supposed to get my girlfriend something nice for Valentine's Day."

"*Girlfriend*? There are more people out there?"

Jake nodded, then cursed since the kid couldn't see him in the darkness. "We live on a farm about five miles outside of town. There are, let's see…" He counted everyone off on his fingers. "There are nine of us."

"Wow. I ain't seen another normal person in probably three or four months."

"Really? I would have thought it was longer than that."

"I used to see these two guys every couple of weeks, driving around like a bunch of idiots with the crazies chasing them, but I never let them know I was here. I was pretty sure they'd have just killed me and been done with it."

"The Cullens," Jake surmised.

"No idea," Mark stated. "I never saw 'em before all of this went down."

"Well, if it was the Cullen brothers, then you were right for staying hidden from them. They were definitely not good people."

"What do you mean by they *weren't* good people?"

"They're dead," he responded flatly.

"You kill 'em?"

Jake flipped down his monocular and powered it on. "You sure ask a lot of questions." He stood and walked around the building's exterior wall until he came to the back door. A metal hex wrench dangled from a chain attached to the push bar. That's why the back door had been locked. He pushed against it without hitting the bar. It was secure.

"Okay," Jake said when he returned to where Mark leaned against the wall. "I'm gonna go back out there and try to see what I can see. Stay back here."

"You ain't my— Never mind. Okay, I'll stay put."

Jake grinned in spite of himself. The kid was a teenager. It was natural to want to challenge authority at that age. He remembered himself as a teen. Young, dumb, and full of cum, he would have taken on the world. The fact that the kid had survived this long on his own, especially since he'd seen the Cullen brothers on several occasions, meant that he was a survivor.

And now Jake felt responsible for him.

He snuck through the doors into the front of the store, slinking low along the back wall until he was at the aisle that led directly to the front doors. He flipped his monocular up, then lifted his rifle to peer through the thermal scope at the doors. A mass of writhing, angry infected were outside, but they were no longer pounding on the doors.

Jake observed them for several minutes before deciding that it was pointless. They were quickly losing interest and already beginning to wander away. None of the ones out there had actually seen him. They'd been drawn by the screams of the ones he killed. The fact that they didn't even recognize their dead as anything more than part of the landscape was disturbing. He knew they'd become cannibals out in the desert, but figured that they had *some* level of awareness of each other.

Since he was stuck for a while, he decided to collect up the items he'd came into town to get before returning to the back of the store. He flipped down his night vision once more and wandered over to the baby products aisle. He was clueless as to what type of formula to get, but he figured it was better to get all of one brand instead of a bunch of different ones, so he pulled out the empty duffle bag from his backpack and crammed six of the plastic containers into the empty pack, then grabbed two more for good measure. He pulled diapers from their oversized boxes and put them into the duffle bag still sealed in tight plastic wrap. The original packaging would have taken up too much room.

He'd gotten a large assortment of diapers and a few toys for Carmen's children when Mark cleared his throat softly behind him. "Shit, kid! You 'bout scared the piss out of me."

"I waited back there for you. But when I come out here, you're just looting?"

"I'm not looting. I told you, I had to come to town to get supplies."

Mark thrust his chin out. "Somebody have a baby?"

"How the hell can you see in the dark?"

He shrugged. "I don't know. I'm just used to it, I guess."

Jake regarded Mark through his monocular. "Getting this formula and the diapers is the only reason I came into town. I figured we have some time to kill while the infected wander around out there. This way, my gear is ready to go and I can leave as soon as I see a break."

"You're gonna leave me here?"

"I hadn't thought about it, really," Jake admitted. "Must be tough being here all alone, huh?"

"Yeah…" The kid trailed off. Jake knew the signs. He'd heard variations of the same story a hundred times over.

"You lose someone?"

He nodded. "My mom. I guess my dad too, but he wasn't really in my life, so I don't know what happened to him." He paused and then continued. "There was a girl too. We didn't really know each other that well, but I might have gotten her killed when we were coming here."

Jake thought about the body in the back dock. "The girl outside?" he prompted.

Mark nodded. "Yeah. She got attacked when I opened the back door to the grocery store. A bunch of them freaks ran out and knocked her off the platform. I couldn't get to her before they'd killed her."

The soldier nodded. "At least they killed her instead of turning her into one of them, okay? That's a much worse fate than death." He thought about it for a second before going further. "You can come with me if you want to, but it's not my farm, so Old Man Campbell would have to be the one who decides whether you can stay or not."

"You think he'd turn me away? 'Cause if you do, I'm not even gonna bother leaving. I've got everything I need in here to last me a long time."

"I think he'd let you stay. I haven't talked it over with my friends yet, but we were originally only supposed to stay with him through the spring planting, then move north. If that's still what they want to do, then that will just leave Mr. Campbell and his two granddaughters."

"Granddaughters?"

"*Heh*," Jake chuckled, knowing full well what the teenage boy was thinking. With practically zero prospects of ever having a girlfriend again, the idea that there were multiple women—of any age— nearby must have been extremely appealing. "Yeah,

Katie and Sally. They're a few years older than you. College girls."

The stupid grin on his face grew wider, giving him an eerie appearance through Jake's green night vision monocular.

Jake sighed and zipped his duffle bag. "Okay, Mark. I got what I came here for. Looks like we're gonna be staying a while. This store have any beer in it?"

"Yeah, it's over this way," he replied, waving an arm. "I got rid of all the dairy products down the bathroom drain, but it still smells bad over there, so I try to avoid it whenever I can."

"No worries." He saw a case of Bud Light sitting open and half the contents missing. "You been drinking?"

Mark shrugged. "What else am I gonna do to pass the time?"

"You wanna grab a beer or two?"

"You ain't mad?"

"No. Why would I be? You're not my kid. Besides, when I was sixteen, I was sneaking vodka from my mom's bottle and refilling it with water."

"That's a pretty neat trick."

"Eh, not really," Jake admitted. "After a few times doing that, it was easy to tell that I'd taken it. Water just doesn't have the same taste as alcohol, y'know?"

"I never had it before," Mark confessed.

"It's okay. I prefer whiskey though," Jake said, easing the pop top on a can of beer in an effort to make as little noise as possible. "So, what should we drink to?"

"How about getting out of here safely?"

Jake smiled and tapped his can of room temperature beer against Mark's. "To girls, then."

"What? I didn't…"

Jake chuckled softly before taking a long pull from the beer. If he had a white light, he'd probably have seen the teenager's flushed cheeks. Instead, he just saw the same washed out green that everything in his world was reduced to right now.

4

BRAZILIAN HIGHLANDS
RAINFOREST, BRAZIL
FEBRUARY 11TH

"We have a breach!" a diminutive man shouted across the security station in his native tongue.

The earpiece of Major Taavi Shaikh, the Iranian commander of the lab's security detachment, translated what the Korean scientist said in real time, but the technology wasn't required as the red strobe lights protruding from the ceiling were already turning. Mere seconds later, the ear-shattering wails of the facility's alarms began to wail.

"Turn that off!" Taavi hissed, gesturing toward the klaxons and the lights. "We have a simple breach. Follow protocol and we will contain it. If we announce to the entire jungle that we're here, every one of the Cursed will come to us and there will be no hope."

The watch officer, a lowly 3rd lieutenant named Khavari that had only been an officer in the Iranian Army for two months prior to this assignment, nodded dumbly and began pushing buttons to silence the alarms.

It wasn't going well. The sirens continued to blare, surely echoing across the jungle to bring more of the Cursed to their location.

"The rest of you, put on your riot gear and go to the maintenance entrance," the major ordered all of the security personnel who stood nearby, waiting to be told what to do. His frown turned to a slight smile as the men rushed to their lockers, obedient as dogs. They knew what was at stake with their families' lives. They would stop this breach and secure the facility like they had dozens of times before.

"Sir," the lieutenant said, bringing Taavi's attention back to him. He pointed to first one monitor, and then another. "I'm not sure if—"

"Quiet, you fool," Taavi barked. "Let me see."

He leaned down over the security console. What had initially appeared to be a small group of the Cursed had swelled to hundreds. The mixture of local villagers and former Red Cross aid workers tore into every non-infected person they stumbled across in the facility. "Allah protect us," Taavi muttered, his false bravado falling away.

He began shouting orders to his men. The facility's security element was a mixture of North Korean and Iranian soldiers who were trained in subterranean warfare and knew what to do. Of the sixty he'd started with, fifty-six remained after four of them had committed suicide.

His hurried through the preparations for combat, sliding into well-worn riot gear and helmets. Having been the ones to infect the local villages, these men were used to the carnage that the Cursed wreaked. They'd seen how quickly the tide could turn if even a single man was not one hundred percent focused and lost his footing.

Taavi grimaced as he strapped on his own gear. The facility had never suffered a large-scale breach before. His men would protect it, as they'd done countless times when a few of the Cursed slipped past the outer perimeter. The major wondered what the breach meant for the long-term tenability of the labs in the jungle that had relied on secrecy for so long.

Finally, the lieutenant found the correct button and stopped the sirens from wailing, but there was no cure for the spinning red lights overhead. The only way to stop those was to cut power to the entire facility.

"Call the Facilitator," he ordered the lieutenant sitting at the console. The man was pale, as if a djinn had inhabited him. Shaikh knew that the lieutenant did not have the bite-proof riot gear that the security elements did. His only hope of survival was to hide behind locked doors while the security forces cleared the facility. The only doors that could hope to stop the Cursed were the exterior ones, and one of those was flung wide, fallen off its hinges.

"Y—yes, sir," the lieutenant stammered.

By the time the young man held the phone out for Taavi, he was fully dressed in all of his gear and the first of his men were already rushing out the door toward the maintenance bays. He accepted the phone, glancing at the monitors as he did so. The Cursed were already at the doors of the maintenance section, tearing at them to get into the rest of the facility. It was only a matter of time.

"Hello? This is Major Shaikh."

From the other end of the line, a sleep-hoarse voice said, "*This is Sari. What is wrong?*"

"We have a breach, Facilitator. The Cursed have made it through the outside perimeter and we've lost the maintenance bays. I estimate..." He glanced at the monitors again. "I estimate twelve hundred of them inside the facility."

"That many? What of the specimens?"

Shaikh's eyes wandered to the *other* set of monitors, the ones that his men usually tried to avoid watching as the scientists conducted their experiments, carrying on the work of madmen such as the Nazi doctor Josef Mengele and the Japanese Surgeon General Shirō Ishii of the infamous Unit 731. The facility's scientists had perfected the work of those men and the Cursed were a part of what they'd released upon the world. Taavi hated everything the scientists had created, but understood that the spread of the disease globally must have been Allah's will. If He did not approve, then it would not have happened.

The monitors showed patients in various states, most visibly excited, running around their cells to smash into the cinder block walls or standing at the bars, shaking and biting at them like animals in a zoo. They would not escape. The cages were too well constructed.

In addition to the raving lunatics, several other patients seemed to remain calm, staring dazedly at the walls as they sat on their blanket. He'd learned through the weekly report to the council that the scientists believed those patients were the furthest along. Naturally immune, they'd been experimented upon to find a blocking agent for the curse, one that could be administered to the armies before they invaded the United States.

"For now, the patient wing is secure, Facilitator," Taavi spoke firmly into the receiver. "I do not know how much longer that will be the case."

"Why do you say that?"

"The doors from the maintenance facility will not hold against the pressure of so many bodies. They will be torn from their hinges from the push alone."

"Why wouldn't they just go away?"

Shaikh smirked. It was painfully obvious to him that the Facilitator had never been around the Cursed. "It took a long time to get the facility's alarms turned off. Those klaxons that some idiot installed worked the local population into a frenzy. More are coming even as we speak, Facilitator. They *will* breach the main facility and all the research will be lost."

There was a moment of silence on the line before Hamid Abdullah Sari spoke once more. *"I must call Kasra Amol. She will make the decision about what you are to do with Site 53. I will call back in three minutes."*

The phone clicked dead and Shaikh handed the receiver to the lieutenant. "He will call back in a few minutes. You must answer it."

"Where are you going, sir?"

"With my men," the commander answered. "I have my handheld. Once the Facilitator calls with instructions, you may reach me there."

"Uh… Yes, sir," the man replied, standing and following after the major.

"Lieutenant?"

"Yes, sir?"

"Do not even think about locking this door behind me. If any of my men need to retreat from the Cursed, they will come here first. Understand?"

"Yes, sir. The door will remain unlocked."

"Good," Shaikh answered as he shouldered his way through the door into the corridor beyond. Behind him, he heard the lock click into place faintly.

After a year and a half underground, he knew the facility's layout by heart and could navigate to the maintenance area blindfolded. At the moment, however, gunfire echoed down the halls, guiding him toward the fight. The exposed rock of the walls managed to both deaden and redirect the sharp reports from the rifles, temporarily disorienting him.

The bare earth and rock walls of the facility's hallways were in stark contrast to the antiseptic white walls, floors, and ceilings of the scientific labs in the films that Taavi used to watch at the cinema as a youth. The engineers who built the lab did so with the purpose of speed and secrecy, not aesthetics. He turned toward the maintenance bays and began a slow jog. Anything faster and he risked becoming overheated or exhausted in the three-fourths of a kilometer between the security office and the outer doors of maintenance.

He made it less than half of that distance before the first of his men appeared. They stood in a line across the hallway, shoulder to shoulder, braced against the press of bodies assaulting them. The first row of his men acted as a wall, pushing back against the Cursed, while the next row stabbed between them into the crowd with long poles. It was similar to the Greek Phalanx of old, primitive, but highly effective against this type of enemy. Behind them, more of his men fired their rifles at head-height into the crowd. They were killing the Cursed by the scores inside the facility.

And yet, they were losing the battle.

He knew immediately that there would be no return from this incident. Shaikh wondered briefly if there was a way to draw them back outside through sound somehow, but knew it was a fool's errand. The facility and all of the labs here were lost.

His radio crackled and he lifted it to his lips. "Yes?" he demanded.

"*Sir, it's—*"

"I know who it is, dammit. What did the Facilitator say?"

"*He said that Kasra Amol directed you to hold the labs. You are to secure the breach and save the work that the council has spent a decade perfecting.*"

Typical, Shaikh thought. *The dogs were safe back in Tehran while I am here, on the front lines of the battle. They direct me to hold what they have built, but I can't.* He depressed the transmit button on the radio, holding it near his lips. Slowly, he released the button and dug the small nub of an antenna into his forehead in frustration.

"*Major Shaikh?*" the lieutenant asked over the radio.

Taavi sighed heavily. If he tried to keep the facility open, *all* would be lost, that much was plain to see. Those fools in Tehran did not see what he did.

Already, his men were being forced backward from sheer numbers. It was only a matter of time before their steroid-riddled muscles gave way to exhaustion. They would all die and all of the work would be lost anyways.

However, if he were to save the most promising subjects and take the hard drives, all would not be lost. He could deliver the prize to the council and snatch victory from the proverbial jaws of defeat. The council would understand the position he was in once he could explain it to them.

"Lieutenant Khavari," he said, once more pressing the transmit button on the radio.

"Yes, sir?"

"Announce over the speakers that Site 53 is overrun and it is to be abandoned."

"Sir?"

"No questions, Lieutenant. I am in charge of security for this station and I have made my determination based on facts on the ground. Are you writing down what I am telling you to say?"

"Yes, sir."

"Good. Have the pilots prep the airplane. Tell the scientists to secure their lab notes and computer hard drives. There is no time for personal effects. Sedate and transport the test subjects who are the best candidates for success. All others are to be abandoned. Finally, tell the security forces to keep fighting, but to make their way slowly to the hangar. They must allow enough time for the scientists to clear the facility." Shaikh checked his watch. "We will go wheels up in fifteen minutes."

He paused, letting the man write everything down. When he felt that sufficient time had passed, he said, "Read it back to me." Once the young officer had done so, Shaikh continued, "Good. Make the announcement and follow the instructions as well. Record the video footage showing that the facility is overrun and bring those disks with you to the aircraft. That is the most important task, Khavari. Without proof that we had to abandon the facility, the council will have our heads on a spike. Do you understand?"

"*Yes, sir.*"

"I will see you in a few minutes. Allāhu Akbar."

"*Allāhu Akbar.*"

The press of the bodies in the hallway in front of him was too close to use his sidearm, so Shaikh pulled a long, slightly curved knife called a peshkabz from his belt and reversed his grip on the handle. The flat edge of the blade ran along his forearm with the point toward his elbow. Holding his knife this way would allow him to react quickly to the Cursed who emerged from around a corner on his way to the labs.

He didn't have to wait long to test his skills with the Persian fighting knife. A man, nude except for one sock, bowled into him when he ran in front of an opening that led to the barracks rooms. Shaikh only had enough time to lift his arms when he saw the creature out of the corner of his eye. The blade sunk to the hilt in the soft flesh of its abdomen as he fell sideways with the man on top, riding him to the ground. Teeth grated against the hardened shoulder protector and Shaikh wrenched the knife upward. The razor sharp blade sliced through the skin, spilling gore onto his gloved hand.

As the facility's chief of security, Taavi Shaikh had witnessed the transmission methods that the Cursed employed. They bit once or twice, and then vomited onto their victims, so it wasn't a surprise when the creature's mouth opened wide. He twisted and placed his foot against the man's chin, then shoved hard.

A pink frothy mix of blood and fluids erupted against the wall. Shaikh left the boot in place and jerked at the peshkabz to free it. He had to push several times against the creature's neck to get the leverage he needed to slide the blade away. Performing an awkward sit up, he slid his fist along his shin and slashed across his attacker's jugular. It fell away, the lifeblood pumping rapidly from its failing body.

Shaikh breathed deeply as he rolled onto his stomach. Pushing himself to all fours, and then to his feet, he made his way toward the labs. *Allah be praised that I avoided infection*, he thought.

…*For now.*

Taavi's stomach lurched as the ancient C-130 bounced down the facility's short dirt runway before the pilot jerked the plane skyward to avoid the jungle below. Strapped into the seats along the fuselage, the major couldn't see the trees, but he'd watched the old cargo planes taking off and landing often enough to know that they were mere meters below the landing gear.

He looked up and down the length of the aircraft as the hasty piles of hard drives, paperwork, backpacks, and even the occasional suitcase tumbled toward the rear ramp. There was nothing to be done about it until the pilots leveled off. If they'd had more time, they may have been able to secure everything under cargo netting, but the Cursed hadn't afforded them that luxury. The security forces had collapsed only eight or nine minutes after his announcement and the pilots had to take off immediately.

The rapid collapse of the security forces meant that only one of the test subjects made it onto the plane. He was a white man, an American as far as they knew. The man had been captured during an attempted raid on the facility just a week before the council unleashed hell upon the entire planet. He'd proven to be naturally immune to the curse, and according to the scientists who studied him, his body was surprisingly resilient to experimentation. It was sheer luck that they'd been able to get *that* subject onto the plane. The rest were still strapped to the gurneys where they'd been lined up, ready to load when the Cursed came pouring through the hangar doors and the pilots began moving to the runway. Shaikh had sprinted to catch the taxiing aircraft, otherwise he'd be trapped at the facility, like the others.

He grimaced at the thought. Every one of his men had been left behind to die.

The group on the plane was a sorry bunch. Shaikh recognized two or three of the scientists, a nurse, and Lieutenant Khavari but no more. Out of the hundred and twelve personnel that the facility roster listed just this morning, only eight men sat in the back of the C-130. He assumed the entire crew of five Air Force personnel were aboard, but didn't have a way of knowing that right now.

The numbers wouldn't matter to the council, only the results.

The plane leveled out and several of the scientists unbuckled to retrieve their work. Shaikh unlatched his harness as well and staggered toward the front of the plane. His stomach was still in knots over the combination of physical exertion and the rough takeoff, but he needed to talk to the pilots about their destination.

The cockpit was controlled chaos as the four men inside fiddled with buttons, plotted courses on paper maps, and checked so many gauges that he could never know what they all meant.

"Who is the pilot in charge here?" Shaikh demanded, elevating his voice to be heard over the loud thrumming of the C-130's four large engines.

"I am the lead pilot," said the man in the seat on the right. He wore the three stars of an Air Force first lieutenant on his shoulder epaulets.

"I'm Major Taavi Shaikh. Until we took off, I was the chief of the facility's security forces. Now that we're airborne—"

"Allāhu Akbar," the pilot said, which the others repeated quickly. None of them appeared to look up from what they were doing.

Taavi followed suit. "Allāhu Akbar. I am the highest ranking soldier on board. Now that we're airborne." Another round of God is the Greatest made its way across the cockpit. When all were finished, he continued. "We need to find a destination. How much fuel do you have?"

"We have full tanks. We can make three thousand, eight hundred kilometers."

"Where does that get us?" Shaikh asked.

"Lieutenant Rafati is the navigator, sir. He's plotting our options now."

Shaikh cast his eyes around the cockpit until he saw the nametag for the lieutenant. "We need to head toward America."

"Sir?" the young officer blanched.

"We have forces there—or at least our allies do. The Koreans have troops on the mainland that can help us."

The navigator gulped, then overlay a sheet of thin, almost transparent paper on top of a map. He drew an arc from a point on the map that Shaikh assumed was representative of where they were currently located.

"We can make it to Mexico City!" he announced excitedly.

The absurdity of the man's statement made Shaikh laugh. It was a great, rumbling belly laugh. He couldn't contain himself and his laughter echoed throughout the cockpit.

"Sir?" Lieutenant Rafati asked.

It took him a moment to stop laughing. When he did, he had to wipe away tears from his eyes. "Mexico City? You want to go to Mexico City?"

"It is the largest city within safe distance of our fuel range."

"And it is the most populous city on the planet," Shaikh stated. "We just barely survived—"

"Allāhu Akbar," the crew all shouted together.

"Allāhu Akbar," Shaikh agreed. "There were only a couple thousand of the Cursed in that jungle. Mexico City has a population of twenty million people. That means there's *twenty million* of the Cursed."

"Uh…"

"Exactly, Lieutenant. We need to find a small airfield that is far from major population centers where we can stop to get fuel and then make the second leg into America."

"Yes, sir." The lieutenant leaned down over his map and paperwork, and began to look closely at the map. He went through several options, writing names on the paper, and then cross-referencing a printed manual that he'd pulled from a shelf. Each time he looked up the name in the book, he'd cross it off and pore over the map once more.

Finally, the navigator shouted out, "That's it!"

Shaikh's eyes narrowed. "What have you found?"

"The, ah… *Aeródromo de Palma Sola*," he said, stumbling over the Spanish title. "The Palma Sola Airport. It looks to be about three kilometers from a small town. Improved runway long enough for the C-130 to land…" He trailed off as he scanned the paragraph. "And the manual says they maintain a large supply of both regular gasoline for small aircraft, and the Mexican government keeps s supply of jet fuel onsite for emergency use since it is near the coast."

Shaikh leaned down, looking at where the lieutenant's finger pointed. He said it was near the coast, but it was actually *on* the coast. The narrow strip of land between the airport and the Caribbean Sea was maybe around five hundred meters wide. "Okay, plot a course to there. We will get directions from the council about where we are to go after that."

The navigator ducked his chin and Shaikh turned to exit the cockpit. "Yes, sir," the navigator said from behind him.

He stopped and turned back to the fourth man in the cockpit, another junior officer. Pointing to his ear, Shaikh said, "I need a place to make a phone call. Where is the most quiet place onboard?"

The man looked at him for a moment, obviously trying to decide if the major was making a joke. "There is nowhere on the aircraft that is any less quiet than the cockpit."

Shaikh shook his head. "Too loud in here. There is nowhere else?"

"No, sir. This aircraft was built for functionality. There isn't even a proper toilet on board."

Shaikh grimaced. He did not want the flight crew to hear his conversation with the Facilitator. He was certain that given enough time, he would be able to convince the man that it was necessary to abandon the laboratory facility. But that would take much discussion on his part and for now, everyone on the plane except for Lieutenant Khavari believed that the council had ordered the evacuation. Shaikh would need to ensure that the man never spoke of the betrayal.

"Thank you. I will return to the cargo area to make my phone call." He left the small cockpit, pulling the door closed behind him. He sat down on the nearest canvas bench seat and fished out his satellite phone.

The major sighed before selecting the first number from the two stored in the phone's memory. The other was for his wife at home in Iran. There would be time to call her once they were on the ground in Mexico. He pressed the green connection button and placed the phone to his ear, and inserted his index finger into the opposite ear.

The Facilitator answered on the first ring. "*Yes?*"

"Facilitator," Shaikh spoke loudly into the lower end of the phone. "It is Major Shaikh."

"*I know,*" the man answered. "*What is that noise? Where are you?*"

"I am aboard the lab's cargo plane, sir."

"*Why are you on the plane?*" Sari hissed. "*My instructions were clear that you were to hold the facility.*"

"The Cursed overran the entire compound. My men were all killed trying to delay them. We—"

"*What of the research?*"

Shaikh gulped. "We were able to save one patient, most of the hard drives and notes, and including the airplane's crew, a total of fourteen people."

"*One patient!*" the Facilitator screeched. "*You abandoned Site 53 and only secured* one *patient?*"

"Sir, there were thousands of the Cursed inside the building. We barely escaped with anything. The pilots didn't even close the ramp before they began their taxi down the runway."

"*And yet* you *managed to find your way onto the plane,*" the Facilitator accused.

"I was overseeing the hasty evacuation. I—"

"*You are a failure! We were conducting important research in Brazil. Research on immunity and vaccinations…all lost because you could not keep the facility secure.*" There was a momentary pause where Shaikh considered defending himself, but the Facilitator's voice returned. "*I warned you of the price of failure. Your wife and children—*"

"Don't you touch them," Taavi barked, abandoning the weak, placating manner that he'd affected for this conversation.

"*Bring them here.*" There was the muffled sound of a woman's scream and his heart sank.

"Please, Facilitator. Don't do this. They are innocent."

"*Your spawn must never walk the earth.*" The sound of two gunshots was impossibly loud over the roar of the aircraft's engines. The woman, his wife if the Facilitator was to be believed, screamed a long, anguished wail. It was the sound of a mother forced to watch her children murdered in front of her. Shaikh's eyes shot wide and he removed his finger from his ear to cover his mouth. Tears flowed freely down his cheeks as he thought of little Sohail, only three, and Yasmin, his desert flower… She was five. His children, his very reason for being, were taken from him.

"*You are a failure. Your family line is now also a failure. Your whore of a wife will be used up by my men until she is dead.*"

Shaikh pulled the phone from his ear and pressed the red button to disconnect the call. He leaned forward, burying his face in his hands as great sobs of pain wracked his entire body.

He didn't know how long he cried, but finally he wiped at his face, rubbing the snot and tears away. He looked at the digital compass on his watch. It was blurry, so he screwed his fists into his eyes until the tears cleared. When he determined which way was east, he knelt on the floor and prayed. He prayed the *Salat al-Janazah*, the prayer for the dead. He knew that his family's bodies would never be given a proper Muslim burial, but the prayer was the only thing he could do at this time.

When he finished, he used the sleeve of his shirt to clean his face. He'd heard that the Koreans were setting up bases on the west coast of America, in California, but ironically, he did not know about the Iranian military's plans. They were more cautious than the Koreans and so he did not know where they would be to strike back at them—for *that* is what he'd decided must happen. He would avenge his family's death and his own honor, whatever the cost.

Shaikh stood and returned to the cockpit. He burst through the door, saying, "Allāhu Akbar, the council has given us a place to go."

"Allāhu Akbar," the men replied.

"Where are we to go after we receive fuel, sir?" the navigator asked.

"The Koreans are in the west and we are in the east," he stated, making the assumption that simple logistics would determine the eventual invasion location for the Iranian Army. "The Army has not yet invaded, so we are to wait for word of their arrival."

"So we are to go west, then?" the navigator asked.

"No. Find us a landing spot in the middle, somewhere that we can go either east or west after further information is obtained. Use the same search parameters as before: a small airport, no large cities nearby, and fuel to refill the plane."

The navigator nodded and began to work. "Assuming we are able to fill the bird's tanks in Mexico..." Once again, the protractor arced across the paper and he began referencing his manual. It took considerably longer than finding a suitable airfield in Mexico since the United States was much more populated, but he finally read the name of an airport off the map.

"What about the Liberal Mid-America Regional Airport?"

"Mid-America?" Shaikh asked. "It sounds like a good option. Where is that?"

"In Liberal, Kansas, sir."

"Kansas? What is Kansas?"

"It is a province of the United States," the navigator replied. "Near Texas."

Shaikh grinned. He knew of Texas. "That's good. Plot a follow-on course to this province. Once we get there, we'll await further instructions."

He turned and left the cockpit once again. Getting to America was the first step in his revenge. Next would be finding a way to make it back to Iran so he could murder the Facilitator and destroy the council.

5

NEAR SANTA ROSA, NEW MEXICO
FEBRUARY 11TH

"Say again?" Jim Albrecht said into the microphone integrated in his combat vehicle crewman's helmet. His hearing had still not recovered fully from all of the nearby gunfire during the revolt. He probably had permanent damage to his eardrums to match his shoulder injury, but he felt like a fool going to the doctor for such trivial matters when thousands of people had gunshot wounds and other terrible injuries caused in the fighting.

"Sir, Truck Five is almost out of fuel again," Sergeant Turner's voice came over the radio. *"We need to stop to see why they're using so much gas."*

Jim cursed under his breath. Truck Five had nearly run dry on fuel earlier in the day, only their second day out of Fort Bliss. All the other trucks still had over half a tank of gas, so the truck running low twice in one day meant there was a problem with the vehicle's fuel system. Major General Bhagat's orders had been to bring all the trucks back, but the colonel wasn't sure that was going to be an option.

He zoomed in on the Stryker's Blue Force Tracker. There was a town only about two miles away. They'd likely be able to find a garage where the mechanic could look at the fuel lines and see what was going on. Jim keyed his mic. "Okay, Sergeant. We're on the outskirts of a town called Santa Rosa. We'll look for a garage there."

"Roger, sir."

They coasted into Santa Rosa, New Mexico and were immediately set upon by the infected. Jim ordered each of his trucks to button up, meaning to close all the hatches and fight from the safety of the vehicles. The sudden movement as he dropped down jarred his wounded shoulder, sending waves of nausea through him.

He watched the weapons station monitors as his gunner, Corporal Jones, stitched the oncoming infected full of holes. The kid was good. *No wonder he was Murphy's gunner*, the colonel thought. They'd taken Top Gun at the brigade's last gunnery table before the outbreak.

"Great job, Jones."

"Thank you, sir."

Jim rotated his optic and was surprised to see two of the infected immediately in front of it, climbing onto the truck. "Goddammit," he muttered. Into the radio, he said, "All Ready First elements, this is Ready Six. There are infected climbing on the trucks. Do not open up until you've coordinated with the trucks to your left and right to pick any of them off. Over."

A chorus of responses came as the other five truck commanders responded to Jim's order. All the Strykers began maneuvering, turning slowly in circles in front of their wingman to ensure there were none of the infected clinging to the side, waiting to jump the first soldier who popped his head out of a hatch. About halfway through this maneuver, Truck Five ran out of gas.

"Goddammit," Jim muttered, ensuring that his mic was switched off. "Of course it couldn't be easy." He'd hoped to find a serviceable garage in which to fix the fuel issue, but now they would have to tow the piece of crap to a garage.

Into his microphone, he ordered the crew from Truck Five to load into another vehicle while they explored the little town. He didn't tell them to cross-level ammo or food because he was not prepared to abandon the vehicle—yet.

They stayed buttoned up as they reconnoitered Santa Rosa. Jim checked out the cached webpage about the city, finding out that there'd been a pre-outbreak population of 2,800 people. Best guess, they'd only encountered a third of them so far; there were plenty more infected to ruin their day if they weren't careful.

Colorful signs proclaiming that the town was part of the original Route 66 stood out starkly against the drab backdrop of the desert surrounding them. There was even a large billboard claiming the city was **"World-famous for our massive Blue Hole!"** and **"Divers welcome!"** Their sign didn't make a lot of sense to him until he zoomed the Stryker's optics in on it. The massive blue hole, as they called it, looked like a small lake that went down deep into the desert floor. It reminded him of the cenotes down in Mexico, which were just deep sinkholes filled with water. Now, it was probably filled with the bodies of infected who'd wandered in and drowned.

They cruised past the billboard and Jim took in the surrounding area, with its single story homes and businesses. There were very few two-story houses, and only the churches seemed to be taller than the average ranch home. He couldn't imagine the city on the edge of the desert was very green to begin with, but the winter turned what little had been growing there into the dull brown of hibernation. With the exception of a few scattered cedar trees here and there, the skeletal remains of trees locked in winter's long embrace reminded him of death.

Jim hadn't thought about it before, but the realization that he hadn't seen a single stray dog or cat in town made him pay closer attention to their surroundings as they drove. Evidence of the town's demise was everywhere. Dried blood smears along the walls of homes, bodies that lay where they'd fallen, and fires that had burned unchecked across several buildings told the same story that had been repeated tens of thousands of times across America.

Santa Rosa was a dead town full of dead people.

"Ready Six, this is Apache One-Niner."

Jim sighed at Sergeant Turner's use of his old Able Company call sign. He hadn't officially designated the man as his temporary sergeant major, but the NCO was the highest ranking noncom left in the entire brigade. He'd have to talk to him privately once they stopped.

"This is Ready Six. Over."

"Hey, sir. We found a garage over on the east side of town, out beyond the downtown area."

Over the radio, he could hear the steady staccato of machine gun fire. "How bad are the infected in the area?"

"Same as everywhere, sir. Moderate. We're killing 'em, but more will follow the sound of gunfire."

That was the problem with fighting the infected. As Lieutenant Murphy had tried unsuccessfully to demonstrate, the creatures were attracted to sound and visual stimuli. The more noise they made killing infected, the more the infected would be drawn to the sounds of the guns, which is why Fort Bliss was still fighting a steady stream of infected almost a year after the outbreak. There was just too much noise and the base's lights shined like a beacon in the night.

"Roger, acknowledged. What's the address of the garage?" Sergeant Turner gave him the location of Bozo's Garage on Historic Route 66.

"Got it," Jim said. "Truck Two, this is Ready Six."

"Yes, sir?"

"Follow me back to Truck Five. We'll hook her up and tow her to the garage."

"Roger, sir."

"Guidons. Guidons. Guidons. This is Ready Six," Jim said, using the term to get everyone to pay attention on the radio. When the four other trucks acknowledged him, he gave everyone the order to stop searching for a garage and head over to the address that Sergeant Turner had given. They were to set up a defensive perimeter around the garage and clear out everything that was no longer human while he and his wingman drove back to get Truck Five where they'd left it when it ran out of fuel.

There were only a few infected milling around the area when Jim's two trucks arrived. They dispatched them quickly and his men went about the process of hooking up the tow bar to one of the pintles on the front of the disabled Stryker. Everything seemed to be going fine until Corporal Jones was attacked.

Jim was in the TC hatch on his Stryker, watching the surrounding area as the men worked below. There was an unholy wail near the back of the Truck Five—different from the frenzied screams of the infected. He whipped his head around, the M-4 rifle in his hands following in what seemed like slow motion.

A soldier was on his knees, screaming in pain as two others pulled an infected from him. Jim aimed through the ACOG scope on his rifle, but didn't fire for fear of hitting his men. He saw one of the two soldiers who'd pulled the infected off the other bash its head in with the butt of his rifle, then slice its throat with a large knife.

Jim scanned the surrounding area quickly before turning back. "What happened?" he demanded.

The soldier who'd been attacked rolled on the ground, clutching the back of his leg. "There was one back here by the wheels, sir. We thought it was dead with all the bullet holes in it."

"Did it break the skin?"

The soldiers tried to calm the writhing man down, but there was no consoling him. A bloody smear on the back of his thigh told Jim that the infected had bitten hard enough to break the skin.

"Goddammit," Jim muttered, glancing around the area to insure there weren't any more live infected before he climbed out of the hatch and worked his way down the front slope of his Stryker. He jogged quickly back to the soldiers, standing around the injured man. When he got there, he saw it was Corporal Jones, his gunner.

"Fuck, Jones," he said. "Hey. *Hey!* Stop it, Jones. You need to calm down."

He waited, examining the nearby buildings nervously. This was exactly how units got rolled up early on. They would become focused on one injured soldier and the infected would tear them up when they weren't looking.

Jim knelt beside the gunner. "Look, man. That infected that bit you went through your pants. You're fine. It tore your skin because of the pressure, there's no way that thing's body fluids got into your wound."

Corporal Jones stopped squirming and looked to the colonel. "You think so, sir?"

"I'm positive, Corporal. It takes blood or saliva from an infected getting into a cut. There's no way that it made it past your uniform."

Jones smiled widely and accepted Jim's outstretched hand to help him up. He limped back to the first truck with his arm over the colonel's shoulder. When they got there, Jim had the gunner drop his trousers and examined the wound.

"You're goddamned lucky, Corporal."

Jones twisted around awkwardly, trying to see the back of his leg while standing with his pants around his ankles. "I can't… I can't see it, sir. Is it bad?"

A long oval of red, swollen skin showed where the infected's teeth had clasped onto the soldier's leg, biting hard through the material. There was no blood though. "That blood on your clothes must have been from the infected. It didn't even break the skin. You'll be sore as hell for a few days, but otherwise, you should be good to go."

"Really?"

"Really," Jim affirmed. "Now switch out your trousers and clean that goop off of them before getting back to work. Better safe than sorry."

"Yes, sir," Corporal Jones replied, leaning down to untie his boots.

Jim shook his head as he clamored back up the front slope of his Stryker to the TC hatch. That had been a close call. The loss of any soldier out of his small element would be catastrophic, but Jones in particular. The colonel didn't harbor any illusions that bringing Lieutenant Murphy in would be an easy task. If he was still alive, he'd had months to prepare his position. The corporal knew Murphy very well, having spent countless hours together in the cramped confines of the infantry fighting vehicle. If this was going to end without a lot of bloodshed, then Jones was his best bet.

Regardless of what the division commander directed, Jim Albrecht wasn't about to kill that boy in cold blood.

6

NEAR LIBERAL, KANSAS
FEBRUARY 12TH

Sidney pulled the curtains in the kitchen aside once again, staring at the road beyond the driveway. It was just as empty as it had been all morning long.

"You might as well sit down and have some eggs, Miss Sidney," Vern said. "The girls risked their lives on that ice to go out and gather them this morning and then cooked 'em up for you. Don't you go and waste their time."

She sighed and turned back to the table where everyone—*almost* everyone—was sitting down for breakfast. "I'm not trying to be rude, Vern. I'm worried about Jake. I sent him into town for baby formula and he's not back yet. I'm worried that something—"

"Now don't you go gettin' that in your head," he chided her. "Jake volunteered to go into town and get supplies that a member of our *group* needed. Without that formula, Lincoln may not make it, and I ain't about to let one of our people suffer needlessly." He grumbled from behind his mustache. "*Hmpf.* We needed supplies and he went into town. That's the end of discussion on the subject."

Sidney accepted the scoop of eggs and sliver of cornbread that Sally offered her without comment. She ate in silence as Vern and his granddaughters discussed the day's chores that needed to be done before the snow fell even harder than it currently was. February was famously brutal on the Plains for snowstorms and they had no idea if, or when, the weather would get worse.

Finally, after listening to them for a few minutes, Sidney put her fork down. "I'm going to go find him," she declared.

"What?" Carmen said, jerking her head back.

She glanced at Jake's girlfriend, or whatever the term would be these days for the two of them. The woman looked genuinely surprised at what Sidney had said. "He's gotten himself into some kind of trouble, I just know it. And, he's in trouble because of me and Lincoln. You may be able to live with something like that on your conscience, Vern, but I can't."

"And just what in the Good Lord's name do you think you're gonna do about it, Sidney?" Vern demanded. "That boy's an Army Ranger. He's been trained for this sort of work."

"Nobody was trained to face this," she countered, waving her hand toward the window where she'd watched for his return. "He went into town on my urging. Now he's in trouble and I'm going to go get him."

"What about Lincoln?" Sally asked.

She turned her fiery gaze on the oldest of Vern's granddaughters. "I'm going to have to leave him here. He has enough formula for a week or so, can one of you girls watch him for me?"

"Wait a minute—" Vern started, but was interrupted by Carmen.

"I'll watch him." She fretted with her napkin for a moment before saying, "It should be me going, though. Not you."

"You know that you're not cut out for what has to be done, Carmen."

"And you are?" Vern laughed. "Girl, this world is—"

He was cut off again as Sidney slapped the table. "I'm going and that's final. I'll wear all white and blend in with the snow as much as possible. The infected won't be able to tell that I'm there."

"Ha!" he scoffed. "And what will you do if they do see you?"

"Then I'll kill them," she replied calmly. "I may be small, but I'm not a fucking—"

"Please," Vern said. He was a devout Baptist and hated cursing in his presence.

"Sorry," she amended before continuing. "I'm not a victim, Vern. I'm not going to let a good man possibly die because I was too afraid to go after him and help out. I'm not letting that rest on my conscience."

"I'm coming too," Sally said.

"Oh, for Pete's sake," Vern grumbled. "You aren't going anywhere, Sally. I forbid it."

"You can't make me stay here, Grandpa."

"I can and I will, young lady."

"I'm not so young anymore," she retorted. "I can make my own choices." She held up her hand to quiet the old man. "No, hear me out. Sidney's right about their eyesight being terrible—worse now than it was at first. Wearing all white may be the perfect disguise against the snowy backdrop. Plus, having a partner with her makes her a whole lot less vulnerable since we can watch each other's back. Sending her out there alone is dangerous, but the two of us together can make it to that Neighborhood Market that he was planning on going to and then come back here once we get an idea of what happened to him. It should only take a few hours."

Vern looked back and forth between the two women. He knew his granddaughter too well to know that she wouldn't back down once she set her mind to something, even if it *was* dangerous. No amount of arguing or protesting on his part would change that girl's mind.

"You're going to give me an ulcer," he grumbled.

"Does that mean you approve of me going?"

"No, it means I can't stop you." He pushed up from the table and picked up one of the M-4 rifles that had belonged to the two soldiers that Jake brought with him. Those two got themselves killed trying to rescue his granddaughters and Jake had come near enough to joining them.

He handed the rifle over to her. "That boy had better be in a heap of trouble and need your help instead of sleepin' off a drunk somewhere because he finally got some alcohol in him."

Sally accepted the rifle and checked the chamber like he taught her. Then she used the sling to put it on her shoulder. Everyone, including old Vern himself, had drilled extensively with the shorter, more maneuverable weapons over the course of the winter and it looked like Sally had taken those drills seriously.

"It's 9:15 according to Mickey," he grumbled, referring to the cheap digital watch that had replaced his old wind-up Mickey Mouse watch ten years ago. "You girls need to get ready and be prepared to get out of here by ten. That'll give you two or three hours to town, no more than an hour or two looking for that darn boy, and then two or three more hours for the return trip."

The women nodded and Sidney turned to follow Sally out of the kitchen. Vern grabbed her arm. "You keep my grandbaby safe, y'hear? I've seen what she's capable of, but I don't know about you yet. If you run into trouble, just stay low, the infected will most likely walk right past you."

"I'm not going looking for a fight, Vern."

"Yeah, but one may come looking for *you*. Keep that ego of yours in check. The world is a dangerous place, but not everyone is out to get you, and you sure as heck can't take it on alone. Your baby will be here waiting for you to get back. You get me?"

Sidney stared hard at him for a moment. Was that a veiled threat against Lincoln if Sally got hurt or was she reading way too much into the old man's advice? She'd vowed to herself that she wouldn't be a victim ever again, and that had meant being a hard-nosed bitch at times, but Vern was right. She could carry out her mission without starting a fight. She didn't have to face every problem head-on. There was a lot of truth to the old sports axiom that sometimes the best offense was a good defense.

She nodded her chin curtly. "I'll keep us in the shadows and let the small threats pass by without starting a fight."

"Good," he replied, releasing her elbow. "There are a bunch of old bedsheets in that big chest in the attic. Sally knows where it is. Use those to help camouflage you in the snow."

She leaned down to pick up the other M-4 and checked the chamber and safety as well. "Thank you," she said, forcing herself to be polite to the man who may, or may not, have threatened her child. She still wasn't sure if he had or not, but she sure as hell would be on guard around him from now on.

She glanced back to Carmen. "Thank you for watching Lincoln. Can you watch after Rick James too? I know you don't like him, but—"

"*Shhh!* Of course I'll watch them," the nurse replied.

Sidney stared at Vern as she said, "That's one less thing I'll have to worry about. Good to know that we've got support back here."

She didn't give him the opportunity to respond. She had a mission to do. Sitting around here arguing wasn't going to help her accomplish it. It was time to go.

NEAR TYRONE, OKLAHOMA
FEBRUARY 12TH

"Say again, Truck Six?" Jim Albrecht had heard what the soldier reported, but wanted to be sure. It was simply too far-fetched to be accurate.

"*I say again,*" the young sergeant's voice came over the radio. "*A non-US fast mover of unknown type just flew across the horizon behind us.*"

He stood up taller in the TC hatch and turned around to look behind the column down the road. He was in the middle of a simple road march column in Truck Three, with about seventy meters between trucks. Truck Six was in the back of the five vehicle column pulling rear security after they'd left Truck Five in the garage back at Santa Rosa. The rear truck had the responsibility of watching behind them to ensure that no infected snuck up and attacked the group each time that they slowed down to maneuver around obstacles in the road and when they stopped, like now.

Jim toggled the push-to-talk switch on his CVC helmet. "Are you sure it was a non-US jet?" Corporal Jones' question about North Korean troops on the morning they left Fort Bliss swam up from the recesses of his mind.

"Yes, sir. I'm an aircraft enthusiast. Was gonna apply to the Air Force Academy before I got my girlfriend pregnant." Jim grimaced as everyone in the column could hear what the kid was saying. He'd have to talk to him about discretion. *"I know every aircraft that the Air Force and Navy uses, plus a lot of our allies. If I were a betting man, I'd say that was a Russian-made MiG-29."*

"Okay, thanks for the head's up, Truck Six." Jim paused a moment and then put out a net call for all the truck commanders, "Guidons. Guidons. Guidons. This is Ready Six. I'm sure all of you monitored Truck Six's transmission about seeing a foreign jet. I'll reach out to Division to see what I can learn.

"In the meantime, keep an eye out. But, this doesn't change our mission. We are in position to hit the target house now. As discussed, drivers, TCs and gunners will stay with the trucks. Everyone else will dismount and move through the cornfield to the target. Acknowledge."

He waited until all the trucks had replied and then told Sergeant First Class Turner to meet him at his truck in four minutes. He figured that amount of time should give the grizzled infantryman enough time to get everyone online and ready to attack toward the last known position of Lieutenant Murphy's Stryker vehicle. In all honesty, Jim had zero idea of what to expect at their objective.

They had satellite photos of the farmhouse and barn from the pre-outbreak timeframe, but that was coming up on at least a year old, possibly more. Any type of improvement to the land, or fortifications that the residents—or Lieutenant Murphy—had made would be a surprise to them. It was of the utmost importance that they go in slow and deliberate without alerting the occupants of their presence.

The threat didn't end with the residents of the house. The infected that they'd seen in the area appeared to be well fed, possibly from all the old corn and wildlife in the area. The cornfields that had been planted in the spring when the outbreak occurred grew wild and unharvested, the kernels drying up. Deer, quail, squirrels, and rabbits had been seen in abundance and it was all Jim could do to keep his soldiers from shooting one of them in order to supplement their diets of MREs and bottled water.

Soon enough, he told himself. They were only minutes away from actioning on their target. If Murphy's merry band of deserters weren't at the farmhouse, Jim's mission would be over. Without giant signs saying exactly where they'd gone, there was no way to find them, regardless of what he'd told his soldiers the other day before they left Fort Bliss.

He'd never admit to the men and women under his command that he secretly hoped they came up with a dry hole at the farmhouse. The more he thought about the position that he'd put Murphy in by placing him in that refugee camp, the more Jim believed that the kid had no other options available to him. He deserted an army that had already abandoned him.

Jim toggled the radio a bit and tried to reach the base operations cell back at Fort Bliss. Even with perfect conditions, pre-outbreak, the military radios using satellites to pass data would have been a long shot. Now, with an unknown number of satellites down for maintenance, or that had simply fallen out of the sky when their orbiting pattern had decayed, the military radios were useless beyond line of sight.

He grunted and pulled the satellite phone that he'd been given for emergency use only from his pocket. Jim wasn't sure if it was going to work either. The Division Signal Officer had assured him that military satellites remained aloft, but the lack of standard radio comms disproved that assertion.

It rang twice and then the general's aide, Lieutenant Freddy MacArthur, answered. *"First Armored Division Commanding General's office, Lieutenant MacArthur speaking. How may I help you, sir or ma'am?"*

"Freddy Mac!" Jim replied, genuinely glad that the phone worked. "This is Colonel Albrecht. Is Iron Six available?"

"I'm sorry, sir. He's not. He's on a SVTC with the president right now."

Jim was impressed. If the division commander, Major General Bhagat, was in a Secret Video Teleconference with the president, then maybe there was some good news about a cure or at least a way ahead. As far as Jim knew, they hadn't heard much from their civilian leadership since the outbreak, so it was a welcome change to how things had been going.

"That's good to hear," Jim said. "Hey, you're in all the CG's meetings, do you know anything about non-US aircraft in US airspace? We believe that we've seen an aircraft, possibly a Russian MiG-29."

"Russian?" the lieutenant asked. *"That's weird. They were hit just as badly as us. You sure it wasn't—"* He stopped talking for a moment. *"I'm sorry, sir. I don't know anything about foreign aircraft."*

"Freddy, you know something. What is it?"

"Sir, I'm not authorized to discuss it."

"We've already heard the rumors down here. What's the real story?"

"I'm sorry, sir. I can't—"

"Bullshit, Freddy. You know me. I was the one that recommended you for the CG's aide position. I wouldn't be asking you if I didn't have a need to know. I'm operating completely alone out here, without any type of communication with Higher since we rolled out the gates." He dropped his voice so anyone within earshot of him couldn't hear. "What the fuck is going on, Lieutenant?"

"Wait one, sir." There was a rustling of clothing and then Jim thought he could hear a door open, then shut. Finally, the lieutenant returned. *"Sir, it's fucked up. UN forces are operating inside the US. There have been reports of firefights between the Koreans and civilians. It's—"*

"Wait," Jim said, stopping him. "Koreans? That rumor is true?"

"I don't know which rumor you heard, sir. There are a lot of them going around. North Korea—and Iran—have troops on the ground here. Almost every UN troop-contributing nation was hit hard by outbreaks in their own countries. North Korea and Iran volunteered to provide military and humanitarian support and the UN Security Council accepted it. They had to."

"What the hell?"

"*Like I said, there have been reports about gunfights between US civilians and the NORKs—uh, I mean North Koreans.*"

"How long have you known about this?" Jim demanded.

"*A couple of months, sir. The CG was gonna talk to all the brigade commanders and then the uprisings happened, then it seemed like everything was O.B.E. and it sort of fell off the radar.*"

"So instead of dealing with this, he has me chasing a damn deserter all across the Great Plains?"

"*The general feels very strongly about desertion because of our tenuous position here at Bliss and he also thinks that Jake Murphy caused the uprisings, so he's on the CG's shit list twice over.*"

"In other words, shut up and color," Jim mumbled. He was disliking his division commander more and more.

"*I'm sorry, sir. But the general is adamant that you recover the Stryker and that Murphy is brought to justice.*"

Jim nodded, then rolled his eyes since the action couldn't be seen over the phone. "Okay. So until I get a change of mission, I'll carry on with attempting to find and apprehend Murphy."

"Yes, sir. Do you have a SITREP that you'd like me to pass on to the CG?"

He considered his words carefully before replying, "Tell Major General Bhagat that we've reached the last known location of Lieutenant Murphy's Stryker. We are in our assembly area now and are preparing to move to the target location on foot. I also want you to be sure to tell him that we've observed foreign fast movers operating overhead near the Oklahoma-Kansas border and have established an air guard to protect our vehicles. Maybe if he hears that we are reacting to foreign troops on US soil, he'll actually share some information with us so we don't *accidentally* shoot down a United Nations jet."

"Sir, I—"

"No worries, Freddy. I'll keep what you told me close to my chest. The general will never know that you told me. Thank you for being honest with me, son."

"Roger, sir. Thank you." Freddy Mac sounded truly relieved, which prompted Jim to wonder just what in the hell was going on at the division

headquarters. Purposefully keeping operational intelligence from men in the field was a major leadership failure. Bhagat was playing a deadly game and he sure as hell didn't appreciate being one of the pawns.

"Alright, Freddy Mac. You keep your head down." He paused and then said, "Don't hesitate to call me if something else major is in the works, okay?"

"I'll try to, sir."

He ended the call and walked back toward where the dismounts were preparing to go through the cornfield toward the farmhouse. The news about the United Nations being supplemented by North Koreans and Iranians was disturbing, to say the least, but the fact that those *UN* soldiers were now operating on US soil was mind boggling. They'd been enemy nations less than a year ago, now they were here on a peacekeeping mission.

It also sounded suspicious as fuck.

The world of international politics was certainly strange and outside of Jim's realm of expertise, but something about the entire ordeal stank. If they were here for humanitarian reasons, why was the Fort Bliss Safe Zone still isolated and running out of food? Why was Bhagat keeping their presence a secret? Hell, having that knowledge a few months ago meant that the uprisings could have been stopped. Almost two hundred thousand dead, double that for wounded who would either die from wounds or heal on their own since the base had run out of medical supplies to render aid. Those people rioted over *food*, and information that there was an international humanitarian mission might have prevented it.

Jim shook his head in disgust. He was starting to understand why Murphy had chosen to desert. He sighed and placed his helmet back on his head. He'd have plenty of time to think about things later. For now, he had a mission.

"Alright, Ready First troopers," he said as he addressed the assembled dismounts. "Let's go and get this over with."

8

LIBERAL, KANSAS
FEBRUARY 12TH

Jake woke from the nap he'd taken on the bed of paper towels. It wasn't the most comfortable place to sleep, but it beat the cold concrete floor. He glanced at his watch, it was a little past one in the afternoon. He'd been able to steal an hour of rest. He concentrated and could still hear the infected outside.

He'd been gone from the farm for about thirty hours now. They were probably worried for him. He wished there was a way to contact them, but phones didn't work anymore and they didn't have any type of long-range radio, so he'd have to get over it since there was nothing he could do right now. It would stay that way until the infected found something else interesting to chase after so he and Mark could slip away.

He heard movement on the next aisle over where the kid lounged on his bed made from bags of dog food and small pet beds. Jake had thought the kid was crazy, but the dog food was surprisingly comfortable as the pellets shifted into place and formed to your body.

"Hey," he whispered.

"Yeah?" Mark replied, his voice hushed as well.

"How long before they clear out and go looking for something else?"

"The last time they swarmed the building like that was a month or two ago, while the trees across the parking lot still had leaves. It took them four or five days to go away, and I think that was only because something made them leave."

"Thanks," he mumbled and stood, stretching his arms above his head. "I'm gonna go sneak a better look through the doors."

"Be careful, man. I think they forgot that we're in here and are just too dumb to leave yet."

Jake nodded, but didn't' reply. He sure as heck didn't want to get noticed by the infected. They'd lost interest as far as he could tell, so he didn't want to arouse them. Most of the day before had been nerve-wracking as a couple of them pounded against the doors while others walked into the shopping carts. Several times, he'd mistaken the grating of the metal carts together as the doors opening and sprang into action to repel the intruders.

He went to the darkest part of the store, away from the front doors and then hooked around the aisle so he was in line with them. Bringing his weapon's scope up to his face, he scanned through the glass. There were still the same two loonies—as Mark called them—within the circle of shopping carts, but they were no longer looking through the windows into the store. Now, they faced out, positioned against the dull grey metal carts. He elevated the rifle, scanning into the parking lot. There wasn't any sign of the other infected outside the defensive ring.

If they were lucky, the damn things had gone chasing a squirrel or something.

Jake considered his options about what to do with the two at the front. On the one hand, he could keep waiting and hope that they went away. It would take something mighty enticing to make them crawl over the barrier again, so he dismissed that one. He could try to sneak out the back door, but there was no way of seeing what was out there. The solid metal door was useful for keeping out the infected, but made observation of the backside of the building terrible. The same went for the sides of the building, and there were no skylights in this one to try to climb through.

That left the front of the building and taking out the two infected. He didn't think it would be that difficult to do, Mark had killed at least three of them through the door at varying times. His suppressed M-4 would make quick work of the infected if he shot them through the glass, but doing so would basically ensure that the store had to be abandoned and he wasn't ready to give it up just yet, so he was going to need to open the doors.

Jake knew that getting bitten by one of the infected lunging at him when he opened the door was a real risk if he allowed himself to become overconfident. Getting cocky about your skills is how you got dead. Easy as that.

He crept forward, alternating his gaze between the infected outside and the floor to make sure that he didn't accidentally kick something and make noise. It was remarkable that Mark had been able to survive alone all this time, but he'd done a shit job of keeping the garbage from used food containers cleaned up.

When he reached the end of the aisle, he slid sideways, so he was at angle to the doors and shielded by the last of the registers. He verified that the parking lot was empty and saw movement across the street. *Familiar* movement.

"Oh, what the hell?" he muttered.

He looked through his scope again and, incredibly, saw Sidney and Sally drop into the ditch. They must have decided to come looking for him when he didn't show up this morning at the farm. There wasn't a way to signal them that he was fine, without—*shit!*

He dove behind cover as the girls opened fire on the two infected. Glass tinkled to the ground and rounds passed overhead, slamming into the glass doors of the freezer section.

"What's happening?" Mark whispered loudly from the end of an aisle.

The smell of rotten food began to permeate the store as the rancid air inside the freezers was released. It was terrible, worse, Jake thought, than the rotting corpses outside. At least the gasses from those released into the atmosphere gradually. That hadn't happened in the freezers, it had built up into a noxious mixture that threatened to turn his stomach.

"Ugh," Jake groaned, swallowing the bile that had risen in the back of his throat. "My friends are shooting the infected outside."

"They are? Aren't they gonna bring back more of them?"

Another burst of gunfire peppered the freezers. "They wouldn't if they learned to fucking aim," he grumbled. "We have suppressed rifles, not totally silent, but good enough that the weapons themselves shouldn't attract any attention."

"What about all the broken glass?" Mark hissed.

"Yeah, well…"

"Jake!" a woman whispered loudly from outside the front doors. "Jake, are you in there?"

He risked a quick glance over the counter and then stood when he saw the girls had reached the ring of shopping carts. "Yeah," he replied. "Stop shooting!"

"Okay," Sidney said as Sally faced outward, covering the parking lot.

Jake shuffled over to the doors and unlocked them, then stepped outside. He examined the two infected, making sure they were dead before looking up at Sidney. "What are you guys doing here?"

"We came to get you. Is everything alright?"

He wanted to say something sarcastic, but chose to hold his tongue. "Yeah. Thanks. I got stuck in here yesterday when a mob of them came from nowhere."

"Are you ready to go?" Sidney asked. "It took more bullets than we thought it would to kill those two. I think the noise might attract some more of them."

"No shit," he muttered under his breath, deciding that the girls needed more marksmanship practice once they got back to the farm. "Yeah, hold on, let me grab my bag."

"Ok... Should we come inside?"

"No!" Jake hissed. "Those carts are loud as hell, all rusted together. That's how I got trapped in here yesterday." She nodded in understanding, resting a hand on the ring of carts. "Two minutes," he continued.

He turned to see Mark's silhouette nearby, seemingly transfixed by the fact that there were other people. Jake snapped his fingers. "Hey! Time to go. Get your bag that you packed yesterday. I'm gonna get mine and then we're out of here."

"Oh, uh... Okay." The kid disappeared down the pet food aisle and Jake went to the paper products aisle where he'd slept. He lifted the heavier backpack onto his back and then picked up the duffle that he'd stuffed with the lighter diapers. He did a quick 360 to ensure that he didn't leave anything behind and then groaned. He'd almost left his helmet—and more importantly, his NVGs—on the shelf.

"*That* would have been a costly mistake," he mumbled, fitting the helmet onto his head. He did a second search, more thoroughly this time, conscious that he'd almost left one of the most important pieces of gear he owned, besides the suppressor for his weapon.

When he was sure there was nothing there, he walked quickly to the front of the store. Mark already waited there for him, his backpack filled with food, water and candy. There were probably better things that the kid could have packed, but Jake didn't check on his bag, that was his responsibility.

"Ready?"

Mark nodded. "I've been ready to leave this place for months."

"Okay. Let's go introduce you to the girls."

9

NEAR TYRONE, OKLAHOMA
FEBRUARY 12TH

They crept through the field toward the old farmhouse as quietly as the dried cornstalks would allow. It was slow going, each move carefully calculated to produce as little sound as possible. From the moment they entered the fields, they'd been aware of infected in and amongst the corn. Every so often, a small *pfft* sound would announce the discharge of a suppressed rifle nearby.

The half-mile trek, upright at first, then crawling across the frozen ground as they got closer, was excruciating for every one of the dismounted infantrymen, but none were as abused as the brigade commander. Jim Albrecht's shoulder ached as he crawled, the movements made more miserable by the awkward position that he had to put his body into in order to move while he kept an eye out for infected.

He wasn't leading the formation, or commanding any of his elements. Jim's world was reduced down to the half a foot on either side of him between the rows of dried out corn stalks and the twenty or thirty feet that he could see in front of him down the row. He had to trust that his soldiers would do as they were trained to do for the movement to the objective.

As he crawled, Jim's mind wandered to the conversation he'd had with Freddy Mac. The kid had sounded scared shitless, he even had to go into what sounded like a broom closet to pass along the information about the Koreans and Iranians—the so-called "United Nations troops". What was Bhagat's endgame? Why was the division commander keeping the information secret? Jim knew, or thought he knew, that New York City still held firm and that several smaller military installations across the US were secured against the infected, but could they withstand these invaders as well—if that's even what they were.

He clutched at the thought. Why did he automatically assume that the North Koreans and the Iranians, enemies of the US before the outbreak, were still enemies? Wasn't humanity fighting for its very existence against the infected? Maybe they were genuinely trying to help.

Yeah, right, Jim laughed to himself. *Those fuckers are involved somehow. They have to be.* He could suspend reality long enough to believe that the North Koreans were isolated from the rest of the world, what with few international flights and heavily-defended, relatively short international borders, but the Iranians? No way. They had major commercial travel routes through their country *and* lengthy land borders with other countries in the Middle East. If Iraq, Afghanistan, Pakistan, and Turkey, just to name the larger countries surrounding it, had been hit hard, then without prior knowledge of the infection, there was no way the Iranians could have survived intact.

But the real question was, were they responsible? Was the sudden worldwide outbreak an attack against the West?

It was a sobering thought. They'd been too busy trying to survive, with too little thought as to what—or who—was the cause, let alone how to pay them back. Did that mean that Major General Bhagat was somehow involved as well, or was he following orders to hold the line at Fort Bliss and not get involved with the international fight?

The dried cornstalks beside his body shook and rattled, then spread wide as an infected staggered into view. Jim rolled away from it as the thing began to scream, lunging toward him. He had just enough time to bring his rifle up to block the infected from falling on top of him.

The skeletal weight of the thing, which must have been a man at one time, pressed down on Jim. Only the rifle across his chest held the creature at bay. Ropes of sinewy muscle, shrunken due to starvation, strained against his hasty barrier. It clawed at him as it snapped its jaws and bellowed its hatred. Its teeth clattered against one another and the unmistakable smell of body odor and feces assaulted Jim's nostrils.

He couldn't let it—

The infected vomited a pink, bubbly froth directly onto him, coating his face and chest. The taste of copper filled his mouth as the fluid bypassed his gritted teeth, causing him to retch. The rifle gave way slightly with his involuntary reaction and he had to focus on the fight or risk getting bitten as well.

Jim winced as the fluid stung his eyes. The viscous liquid sought every pathway into his body, to spread the pathogens of the infection. He struggled against the creature. It shouldn't have been that difficult, it was nothing but skin and bones, but the singlemindedness of its attack made it more than enough of a match for Jim. He kicked ineffectually with his knee, trying a move he'd done several times during the mandatory Army combatives courses that he'd had to attend. It did nothing to the infected except to temporarily interrupt its screams as air was forced from its lungs.

"Hold on, sir," someone whispered harshly.

He pushed with his rifle against the thing's mass. Suddenly the pressure let up as an arm wrapped around the infected's neck and began to pull it off of him. Through blurred eyes, he saw his gunner's face appear around the back of the infected. Corporal Jones grimaced as he strained against the creature, attempting to choke the life out of it.

Jim sat up, pulling his combat knife from its sheath as he did so. He thrust the knife into the thing's distended abdomen. Noxious gases escaped through the jagged hole and the colonel pulled his knife away, then stabbed again and again. Intestines fell from the creature and still it struggled against Jones, trying to reach him.

Blood and gore flowed down Jim's arm, sliding into his uniform sleeve, then continuing down to his armpit. Half-digested corn spilled from its stomach and fell all around the soldier. Gradually, the infected stopped struggling. The combination of choking and blood loss was finally enough to stop it.

Jim's stomach lurched and he leaned to the side, throwing up. The contents of his stomach ran dry and he began to spit up yellow bile. He was dimly aware of weapons fire around him, but he was powerless to stop the vomiting.

"Sir, what's your—" Sergeant Turner stopped and Jim looked up to see him kneeling over him. Turner looked him up and down, then called softly, "Medic!"

Jim wiped at his mouth with a bloody sleeve. He knew he was a goner. He'd swallowed the infected fucker's vomit and it had gotten into his eyes. That was how the infection passed rapidly without the need to bite.

"I don't need a medic. I'm done."

"Uh, sir, you know what they say. Like one in a couple hundred people are immune—"

Jim laughed bitterly. "More like one in a couple of thousand, Sergeant." He sighed and sat forward, intending to push himself to his feet. Sergeant Turner shuffled backward and started to bring his rifle up. "Calm your tits. I ain't turned yet. Still got a few hours—more than enough time to raid that house and apprehend Lieutenant Murphy."

"You sure that's a good idea, sir?"

Jim continued his movement to ease up onto his knees. "Yeah. I'm not going to die in vain. I'm going to—" He paused to spit out the bile in his mouth. "I'm going to finish my mission before I go out."

Two more muffled shots sounded, reminding Jim that they were not out of the woods. "We're continuing mission, Sergeant Turner. You keep a close eye on me, if I start showing the signs... Well, you know what to do. Until then, we're gonna stick to the plan."

Turner regarded him for a moment before nodding curtly. "Yes, sir. We should only be about a hundred meters, maybe a hundred-fifty meters from the edge of this cornfield."

Jim wiped at his face, clearing away the putrid mixture of the infected's vomit and his own. Would his family even know what happened to him or would he be written off as just another nameless casualty in this endless war? When he'd agreed to go on this mission, the thought of becoming infected had never crossed his mind. He was a colonel in the United States Army. He was supposed to have been several echelons removed from the front line; all of that running and gunning was reserved for the younger soldiers. Well, here he was, cold, battered, exhausted, and handed a death sentence.

Life was shit. Feeling sorry for himself wouldn't change any of the facts. The only thing he could control was how he went out and the legacy that he left for his family and his soldiers.

"Hey, Sergeant Turner," he croaked.

"Yes, sir?"

"I never wrote one of those letters to my family that I know a lot of you guys carry around with you. I never thought I'd need one." The NCO nodded in understanding, but didn't say anything. "So I... When it's time for me to go, give me a couple of minutes if you can. I want to write it and send it back to them with you."

"I can do that, sir."

"There's also something else."

"We need to get moving, sir," the NCO said, obviously wanting to skip the colonel's melodramatics. "More infected are gonna be headed our way after that one was yelling its head off."

"Yeah," Jim agreed. "Indulge me. I talked to the CG's aide before we came into the field. It's the last number in the sat phone. General Bhagat is hiding the truth from us." Sergeant Turner's eyebrows shot up above his sunglasses. "Corporal Jones was right. The North Koreans and the Iranians have troops here in—" He had to stop as he retched, the taste of bile assaulting his mouth once more.

"The Koreans and Iranians are here in the States," Jim continued. "That was probably a MiG that Sergeant Chen saw."

"Are they behind the infection?"

Jim shook his head. "Lieutenant MacArthur didn't know that. He only said that there are foreign troops operating freely on US soil, part of a UN contingent, and that their nations hadn't been affected by the infection. I think they may be behind all this, but... Well, that's not my fight anymore."

"What am I supposed to do with this information, sir?"

"I don't know. It's just... I just wanted someone else to know about it."

"Yes, sir. I'll think about it on the drive back to Fort Bliss."

Turner's statement made Jim's heart leap into his chest. He wouldn't be making that return trip back to the base where his family was safe behind the walls. "There's one more thing."

Sergeant Turner sighed, obviously done talking to the dying colonel. "What is it, sir?" There was a half-hearted scream of frustration from an infected nearby that was cut short by the muffled report of a rifle.

"Bhagat sent Lieutenant Murphy to the refugee camp on purpose. He wanted another riot that would reduce the population. I don't think he meant for it to be as bad as it was—especially not the burning of the food storage facility—but it was a calculated move. Don't trust him."

Sergeant Turner shook his head. "Fucking officers. Goddammit, what the hell?" He stopped and appeared to refocus on Jim. "You knew about that, too?"

"After the fact, yeah."

"And you kept it secret. The lieutenant was right. All of this…" He composed himself and set his jaw.

"I've been working through it on the trip up here," Jim said. "I think that's why Bhagat is so fired up for us to get Murphy. He's the only one left who can say that putting him down in that refugee camp was meant to start a riot—well, after me, but, you know… Bhagat doesn't want any loose ends."

"Come on, sir. Feeling sorry for yourself ain't gonna change a damn thing. We have a mission to complete."

Jim agreed. He'd let Bhagat manipulate that kid—he'd even been the one to deliver the sentence. It wasn't right. Bringing in Lieutenant Murphy unharmed just got a whole lot more important in his mind. If they could bring down Bhagat and get the word out about the Iranians and North Koreans, then maybe the people at Fort Bliss would have a chance at survival.

The colonel rolled onto his stomach and began to crawl forward once more. Behind him, he could hear Sergeant Turner following close by. The discomfort of doing a high crawl as a forty-six year old man that Jim had experienced before was dulled. He felt the pain, but more than anything, he felt a burning desire to be near his wife and kids one more time. He wouldn't get it. Depending on how quickly his body reacted to the infection, he'd be dead somewhere in the next twelve to twenty-four hours.

The life of a fucking soldier.

It took less than ten minutes for all of Jim's dismounts to arrive at the edge of the cornfield. Out of the close confines of the cornrows, the snow swirled in a beautiful arc across his vision. He'd always loved the snow.

Jim looked through a small pair of binoculars that he'd bought for hunting originally, but always took them with him to the field because they folded and fit into a pouch on his tactical vest. The farmhouse appeared abandoned.

Several decomposing corpses littered the gravel driveway leading to the two-story white farmhouse. The front door was open and what looked to be about a hundred large-caliber bullet holes riddled the building's exterior, beginning on the first floor and then concentrated around a window on the second floor. "Looks like Murphy shot up the place with the Stryker's .50 cal," Jim whispered to Sergeant Turner beside him.

"Ten-to-one there was a sniper in that room upstairs," the sergeant replied.

Jim continued to scan the area. Two rows of fencing guarded a pathway from the house to a large, faded red barn with an old grain silo next to it. From his vantage point, it looked like all the doors on the barn were closed. Directly outside the barn was a horse trailer filled with bodies. Arms and heads stuck through the openings in the trailer's sides. None of them were moving.

"What the fuck is that?" Jim muttered, attempting to hand the binoculars to the NCO, who declined. "Oh yeah," he replied, remembering that the bloody vomit was still on his face.

"Looks like somebody captured a whole bunch of infected in that trailer, then left 'em to starve," Sergeant Turner said.

Another rifle report reminded Jim that they needed to move. "I think this place is abandoned."

"Looks like it. We gonna check it out or just go back to the trucks?"

Jim didn't answer. Instead, he pushed himself to his feet and staggered onto the gravel. His knees protested the movement after crawling for so long, but he willed himself forward. He heard the crunch of more gravel behind him as the others followed his lead.

Not far off the road leading to the farm, one of the soldiers found a scattering of spent .50 caliber casings in the snow, confirming Jim's assumption about Murphy lighting the place up with the Stryker. *But why?*

He supposed he'd never know. He advanced on the house rapidly, stepping on the old wooden porch steps as lightly as possible. Jim didn't have anything to fear, he was already a dead man, so he entered the house.

More bodies inside told him of a fight through the house. These were mostly nude or covered in a small tattering of fabric, meaning they were the infected. A kitchen to the left of the foyer was empty, so he went back across the hall to a bedroom. There, the remains of a very fat body with giant holes in its chest and abdomen told him the Stryker had killed him—or her, he supposed. It was difficult to tell.

Jim heard his soldiers searching the back of the house, so he left the bedroom and went up the stairs. At the top, immediately to the left was the room that had been hit by the .50 cal. He walked in and found a man with two or three small caliber bullet holes in his upper body and massive damage to his legs. He guessed the .50 cal had hit the guy low and then someone came in to finish the job.

Jim used the end of his rifle to lift the man's head from his shoulders, turning it so he could see the face. It *wasn't* Lieutenant Murphy. Besides all the infected, there were two bodies inside the farmhouse, neither of which were the lieutenant. What had he been doing here?

A quick search of the upstairs yielded nothing so he walked back down to the first floor. He endured several uneasy glances from the soldiers he found there, which he ignored and tried to assure them with a confident smile. Walking toward the back of the house, he met Sergeant Turner returning down the fence line from the barn.

"Anything?"

"We found a lot of weird homemade shit that looks like they were torturing people. Can't tell if it was infected or non-infected, though."

"Any clues about Lieutenant Murphy or the soldiers with him?"

"Not a damned thing, sir. They hit this house, wiped everyone out and then took off. No idea where to."

Jim grunted in frustration. He looked through the windows toward the cornfield beyond the barn as Sergeant Turner called the trucks on his radio to bring them up.

They hadn't found Murphy or the other soldiers. There was no Stryker hidden in the barn. They didn't even know where Murphy had gone after getting into the firefight here.

It was all for nothing. He'd been given a death sentence, for nothing. Such was the life of a fucking soldier.

10

NEAR LIBERAL, KANSAS
FEBRUARY 12TH

Jake plodded along behind the girls and Mark, taking up the rear of their small group. The way he'd come from the farm, directly up Hatcher Road, was blocked by a large group of infected. They seemed to be pretty worked up about something, but the small group of survivors had no idea what it could have been, so Sally suggested they swing out onto Highway 54, head south for about two miles and then take one of the side roads north toward the Campbell's farm.

He'd agreed since he didn't know the area nearly as well as she did. He'd gained most of his knowledge outside the farm's immediate surroundings through map reconnaissance. Sally had spent almost every summer in the town. He had to trust that she knew a few ways home that he didn't.

He glanced over his shoulder once again, checking the road behind them for any signs that they'd picked up a trail. As he started to turn around, something caught his eye to the south. Jake stopped and stared. There was a plane — *two* planes! — flying toward them on the horizon.

"Hey, guys, look!" he called, pointing toward the aircraft.

The others turned to where he pointed as the shape of the planes became clearer. Jake had seen the jets from Holloman Air Force Base flying attack missions around El Paso for months, but he'd never seen anything like the ones coming toward them. Now he knew why the infected in town were all riled up.

Something in the back of his brain screamed out to him in warning.

Jake shouted, "Get down!" Now was not the time to whisper like they always did when they were outside. He threw himself off the road, landing in the ditch. The others hesitated for a moment before following suit.

"What is it?" Sidney asked. "Are you afraid they're going to try to—"

The roar of jet engines cut her off as they passed overhead, less than a hundred feet above them. Jake looked up, there was a flag that he didn't recognize and what appeared to be the depiction of an explosion painted in red on the tail of the second aircraft. *That's not good*, he thought.

He stood and looked northward in the direction the planes had gone. They split apart and then circled back around. "Oh shit, guys. I think they saw us," he said.

"Then maybe we're saved?" Sally offered.

"Get back down," Jake ordered. "Those aren't US aircraft."

"What do you mean?" Sidney asked. "Why wouldn't they be US warplanes?"

The planes passed overhead once again. This time, one of them continued southward while the other turned only a short distance away. Jake watched in horror as it lined up on them. They were sitting ducks in the ditch. A strafing run from above on their position would kill them all instantly. Jake turned, frantically searching for some type of cover, but there was none.

Before he could turn back, the plane passed overhead, lower this time than it had been before. He slid his hands up under his helmet and clamped them over his ears. It was so loud that he thought his brain would burst.

Then it was past them and the sound of the engine changed. Jake risked a glance to the north and saw the jet continuing lower with its landing gear down. "That thing's landing," he told the others.

"Jake, what's going on?" Sidney asked.

He glanced at the girls, then at Mark. "I don't know, but I have to find out."

"What do you mean you have to find out?" Sally asked, bewildered.

"I have to find out why there are Chinese or Russian—" He stopped. That wasn't right, the old Soviets had used a red star, but the Russians had their flag painted on the tail fins of their jets, he'd learned that at the Infantry Officers' Basic Course. The red starburst emblem that he'd seen was odd. "I don't know who they are, to be honest. But they aren't American, that's for sure. I need to go to that airport to figure it out."

"Even if you do, what good is it gonna do us?" Sally pressed.

The second jet roared overhead along the same path that the first had taken, causing the four of them to duck lower into the ground once more. When it was past them, Jake said, "If it's something completely crazy, I can always call the Army back in El Paso. I have all the commo equipment in the Stryker turned off and unplugged, but it won't take long to turn it all on and get in contact with somebody to tell them what I saw."

"Jake, you're not a soldier anymore," Sidney reminded him. "You don't—"

"I may have turned my back on the Army because they were completely fucking wrong in what they were doing, but my oath to the nation will never expire. There is no reason, and I mean like *zero*, that a couple of foreign jets should be flying over Oklahoma and then landing at a local airport."

Sidney studied his face for a moment and then nodded. "There's no talking you out of this, is there?"

"No, so don't even try."

She held up her hands, letting the M-4 dangle on its sling across her chest. "I'm not trying to convince you otherwise, Jake."

"Good," he replied, lifting the duffle bag's strap over his head and letting it fall into the snow. "Do you guys think you can carry these two bags?" The large backpack tumbled to the ground as well, hitting the duffle and falling sideways. It made more noise than Jake had intended.

"What do you mean?" Sally interjected. "We came to get *you*. We're not gonna just let you go off by yourself."

Jake ground his teeth in frustration. "Thank you for helping me out of the grocery store. This is entirely different. I need to do a military-style recon so I can observe without being seen. Having three additional bodies is not going to help."

"Hey, man. I don't want to go," Mark said. "I was comfortable in my little Walmart and then you came along, telling me about all the nice stuff that your group has on the farm. Now I want to go there, not running all over the countryside with the loonies chasing after me."

Jake nodded. "Okay, so that makes it easy then. You girls take Mark to the farm and I'll run up to the airport for a quick look, then come home after I figure out who the heck they are."

"No way," Sidney replied. "You need somebody watching your back."

I can't believe I'm dealing with this, Jake thought. The others didn't need to be out here any longer.

"What I *need* is for you to go back to the farm and let me do what I've been trained to do. I'm an Army Ranger. I've been trained to sneak around without being seen."

"Fat lot of good that did you back at the Neighborhood Market," Sally scoffed.

He grinned. "I deserved that. Please, Sidney, go back to the farm with Mark and all these supplies that we picked up for Lincoln. The three of you can be back in less than an hour. I'm only gonna go up to the airport, snoop around a bit from a distance, and then head back home. Should only be a couple of hours behind you."

"Jake, please…" Sidney started and then stopped. Jake wasn't really sure where they were in their friendship anymore. He was clearly with Carmen, but at the same time, there was an undeniable attraction between him and Sidney. Hell, she'd left her baby at the farm to come and rescue him; clearly there was more than just friendship there.

"Sidney, I'll be safe," he assured her. "Any sign of trouble and I'll fade into the fields."

The two women exchanged glances, both staring at one another for a long moment before Sidney finally broke eye contact. She nodded and said, "Damn you, Jake. You better keep yourself hidden.

Find out whatever it is that you need to know so badly and then get the hell out of there. Do you hear me?"

"Yeah, I— Hey!" She surprised him by wrapping her arms around him. He hugged her back until she pushed him away.

"Get going," Sidney said. "We've been standing here too long and need to get moving."

He gave Sally a quick hug, then shook Mark's hand. "Listen to these two. They're survivors, like you. They know a thing or two about the infected and what to do out here in the open that you didn't learn from dealing with them while you were holed up. Okay?"

"Yeah, of course, Jake," the boy replied. "Take care of yourself, alright?"

"Yeah," Jake replied, looking beyond Mark to Sidney. She'd turned her body and stared intently southwest along the length of the road they'd followed. "Don't forget these two bags," he said to the three of them. "That's why we're out here. See everyone in a couple of hours."

He didn't wait for any more conversation. Instead, he turned back the way they'd come and headed toward the last road they'd passed. He knew from the sign before the exit that it led to the airport, so all he had to do was follow that for a ways before slipping into the fields alongside the road a half mile or so from the airport. Then, he'd figure out what to do based on what he saw there.

In all likelihood, he'd mistaken the star on the tail fin as they flew by overhead and it was a couple of US Air Force guys trying to refuel their jets. But if it wasn't, then he wasn't sure what he'd do.

One thing he did know: He was a Ranger, and the Regiment's motto was *Sua Sponte*, which was Latin for 'Of their own accord'. He was the only man on the ground here and it was his responsibility to determine if there was a threat to the United States by a foreign power. If they were a threat, then he'd have to stop them the same way he stopped the infected. Permanently.

"Rangers lead the way," he whispered to himself, tightening his grip on the rifle. "*Sua* fucking *Sponte*."

11

NEAR LIBERAL, KANSAS
FEBRUARY 12TH

Jake picked his way around the wreckage of a plane. The medium-sized aircraft must have crashed on approach or take off. He wasn't an aviation guy, but it looked like it was one of those commuter planes that transport passengers from the small regional airports like the one here in Liberal to the larger hubs. He saw several skeletons, picked clean by nature after so many months and wondered briefly who any of them had been.

He left his unanswered questions, and the dead who prompted them, behind. About two hundred feet beyond the wreckage was the fence that ran around the airport. He jogged to it, bent over at the waist to take advantage of the tall grasses that'd grown through the chain link.

He'd arrived at the south end of the runway in a little less than an hour after he split up from the girls and Mark. Looking through the fence, he saw that the paved airstrip stretched out for thousands of feet, running north-south. From where he was, he could see the jets where they'd parked near the hangars. Beyond them, a larger cargo-type plane with propellers that looked similar to a C-130 was nestled close to the terminal. Other than determining for sure that they weren't US planes, he was unable to tell anything about them from this distance. He was going to need to change his angle of sight or try to get closer so he could get details.

He glanced left and right. To the left, the fence continued westward for a couple hundred feet and then turned northward to run the length of the runway. To the right, it ran for about a hundred yards, then turned northeast, angling toward the terminal and the parking lot.

Jake decided to go right and slid along the fence toward the terminal. He had to watch the surrounding countryside for infected and inside the fence for whomever it was who'd landed. He knew the cargo planes could handle rough terrain airstrips, but not the jets. They would have required ground support to clear away debris on the runway and make sure there weren't any infected inside the fence line. The ground crew also meant that they might have security patrolling the perimeter, so he'd need to be doubly cautious.

He was getting closer to where he could see something of what was going on around the terminal. The cockpits of both jets were open, their glass canopies angled up from the fuselage and reflecting the poor winter sun. Several figures ran from the terminal and Jake stopped. *That's it, the pilots are dead,* he thought.

Then, the figures lifted ladders into place alongside the cockpit. The people he'd thought were infected surging forward to attack the pilots were actually ground crew. Confirming that there was a military presence just a few miles from the farm had been his primary reason for coming out to the airport. Now that he had his answer, he considered just leaving and returning to the farm to talk things over with Vern, but the old veteran would want more intel than what he'd already gathered.

The pilots climbed down and walked quickly to the terminal while the ground crew unreeled hoses for fuel and whatever else they did as they scurried around the aircraft. Jake watched the pilots intently until they disappeared inside and then the ground crew, trying to determine who they were and what they were doing here in Kansas. Besides what could only be described as *tan* skin, he couldn't see well enough to determine much of anything. Snatches of conversation reached him, carried on the wind blowing from the north. It was definitely not English, though he had no idea what language it was.

He turned his attention to the jets. Like the conversation, he was convinced that they were not US aircraft. They were painted a mottled tan and green color, whereas the Air Force and Marines pretty much just used gray paint these days. Each plane had two vertical stabilizing fins set wide apart. They looked similar to the F-15s that he'd seen dropping ordnance around Fort Bliss, but there was something about them that made him think they weren't the same type of aircraft.

There was a flag of some type, with three horizontal lines. He couldn't make out the color of the top bar, but the middle was white and the bottom one was red. What he'd thought was a starburst decal on one of the vertical fins was actually a lion's face and mane, painted in red. There was also a bullseye painted along the side, with presumably the same national flag colors since the red was in the middle, surrounded by a white circle, and… *Is that green*? he wondered as the sun peeked through the clouds above.

Jake stared hard and decided that it was a green ring around the bullseye. The colors were green, white, and red. He knew that was a clue that should trigger some sort of reaction from him, but it didn't. He'd been a terrible Social Studies student in high school and hadn't done much more than the required history and economics classes at West Point.

Damn, I was a shitty student, he mused.

The distant sounds of engines reached his ear. He cocked his head, trying to determine which way it was coming from. It was impossible to tell which direction the noise originated from. As he listened intently, he also heard the echoes of screaming: Inhuman, incoherent, rage-filled screams.

The infected had heard the jets landing, and now they were coming to destroy them.

I can't believe that he sent me away like that, Sidney fumed. She'd risked her life—and Sally's—to go after Jake that morning. Hell, if they hadn't gone after him, he'd probably still be stuck inside the grocery store.

"*Ugh*," she sighed aloud.

A hand fell onto her shoulder from behind. "Jake?" Sally asked.

"Yeah. He's such an ass."

"It isn't gonna make things any easier," Sally said, "but you've gotta tell him how you feel."

Sidney stopped on the road, turning to the younger woman. "I don't know what you mean," she lied.

Sally *harrumphed*, then looked at Mark. "Oh, come on, Sidney. Everyone knows, even Carmen."

"Knows what?" she asked, turning her head back toward the west in their direction of travel.

Sally cocked her hip and placed a hand on her side. "Are we really gonna do this? Everyone knows that you like Jake, but he's with Carmen."

The kid, Mark, threw up his hands. "Are you kidding me?" he whispered harshly. "Jake has *two* women in love with him?"

"You shut you goddamned mouth, kid," Sidney said. "I don't love that moron. I like him since he's like the only guy around who hasn't tried to kill me or rape me, but I sure as hell am not in love with him."

"O...kay," Mark replied. "That's a kind of messed up way to look at life."

"Nobody asked you about your opinion," Sidney barked. "I mean, how old are you anyways, like twelve?"

"Fifteen," he said, looking down and kicking at the asphalt.

"Fifteen? I was working forty hours a week and dating college guys by the time I was your age, so don't try to tell me about *your* view of the world. Got it?"

He nodded and Sidney refocused on Sally. "I'm not going to tell him shit, and I'm not going to ruin my relationship with Carmen. She's the best friend that I could have ever hoped for in this fucked up world."

Sally locked eyes with her, not backing down. "I still think you should tell him how you feel."

Sidney grimaced, then looked westward once more. "We need to get going if we want to make the turn before it gets dark and the infected start creeping around."

The college girl pushed past her, leading the way toward the turnoff from the highway. "You know as well as I do that they don't hunt very well at night. We're in more danger right now than we would be in an hour."

They walked along the highway, Sally leading, with Mark in the middle and Sidney bringing up the rear of their little group. She had a lot of stuff to work out, and inviting a man into her life was certainly not anywhere in her plans—even if she was attracted to Jake Murphy.

The turn to the Campbell farm came soon enough, thankfully, without seeing any infected along the highway. The number of creatures in the area had thinned to begin with, likely from starvation, but Sidney wondered if those jets flying all over the place had drawn more of them away. They were fairly stupid and easy to avoid once you figured out what triggered them, and noise definitely triggered them.

They'd gone less than twenty feet down the side road when Sally held up a hand, using the hand and arm signals that Jake had taught them to say "freeze" without speaking. Mark stopped alongside Sidney and she held a finger to her lips, telling him to be quiet.

Sally's head tilted slightly as she strained to listen. Then Sidney heard it too, the rumble of engines coming from the west.

"Get down!" Sally hissed, pointing to the shallow ditch alongside the road. They dove to the ground and waited.

It wasn't long before five large, eight-wheeled tan vehicles rumbled by, spaced about half a football field apart between the trucks. Each one bore a very large weapon of some type up top. Sidney glanced at Sally. "Are those ours?"

"I don't know," the younger woman admitted. "Maybe? I mean, they look kind of like what Jake has stowed away inside the barn, but I'm not sure. Don't Army vehicles have a big white star on them or something?"

Sidney shrugged. She'd seen a few war movies, but didn't remember anything about big white stars. She wished that she'd paid closer attention to the Army trucks and such when she was in the refugee camp, or even when she rode in one for several days as they fled Fort Bliss. The vehicles were big and tan, she didn't think she'd ever have to try to distinguish between different kinds of Army trucks, so she didn't commit the stuff to memory. If they were American vehicles, wouldn't they have US flags painted on the side?

"Who cares that they aren't American?" Mark asked. "I want to know why they didn't stop to help us."

"We're hiding from them, kid," Sidney replied. "We don't know who they are, but I bet you *that's* why there aren't any infected out and about. They're all chasing after those loud trucks and the jets."

"So, what are we gonna do about it, then?" Mark pressed. "I mean, there are people in those trucks— non-infected people. Surely they want to help us, right?"

"I don't think so," Sally answered. "We had a run in with a couple of non-infected people a few months ago that almost cost me and my sister our lives. They killed my mom before Jake rescued us. I think we should go back to the farm like we told him we'd do. At the very least, we could tell my Grandpa and he can decide what to do about them."

Sidney looked up the highway to where the trucks were still visible in the distance. "I think they're going to the airport too."

"So, what does that mean?" Mark asked, exhaustion becoming evident in his voice.

He needed sleep. They *all* needed sleep, Sidney decided. The stress was getting to them. The combination of their earlier firefight at the Walmart, traveling down the highway that they'd dubbed the Highway of Death after hearing one of Vern Campbell's war stories about a bunch of trucks lined up on a road and destroyed by US airplanes, and the constant vigilance because of the threat of the infected was getting to them.

"I think it means we need to get back to the safety of the farm," Sally said.

Sidney nodded. "I agree with you. There's been a lot of activity around here in the past twenty-four hours—and I'm not sure that's good. Until we can figure out what's happening, it's best to lay low and wait for Jake to come back with his report of what's happening at the airport."

"Uh, guys?" Mark's voice trembled. "Are you any good with those rifles?"

Sidney looked beyond the other two toward where Mark pointed. Several infected, maybe as many as twenty, had appeared on the horizon from the direction that the trucks had come from. They were running, then walking, then running again.

"Dammit," Sidney hissed. "They're following the trucks, but they've lost sight of them, so they don't know what to do."

"If those trucks don't start making a lot of noise, then probably half of those things are gonna turn up this road and end up at the farm," Sally concluded.

It was true, Sidney thought. Now that the infected had lost sight of what they were chasing, they'd flow wherever the terrain allowed them to go with the least restrictions. Most of them would probably continue down the highway, but some of them might turn and head down the turn off toward the farm.

"We should kill them," Sidney announced.

"Are you... Are you sure?" Sally asked.

"Yeah. If we want to keep the farm safe, then we need to take them out."

Sally held up her hand, extending her fingers sideways like Jake had taught them to measure distance. "I think it's about three hundred, three-fifty."

Sidney mimicked the farm girl's measurements. "Yeah, about that. I count twenty-three infected. Should we wait until they get closer or try to take them now?"

The younger girl looked up the road toward the farm, then rolled onto her side. She pulled several magazines from her pocket and tossed them on the snow beside her. "I can hit them from here," she said, laying back on her stomach and bringing the suppressed rifle into her shoulder.

She didn't wait for Sidney to respond before she began firing. "Uh, you missed," Mark said after her first shot.

"Shut up. I was just getting my aim point," Sally said, firing another round that found its mark in the stomach of an infected.

Sidney lined up the reticle center mass on an infected that was in the lead of the group. She began to apply pressure to the trigger, but stopped and adjusted her aim up several notches so that the crosshairs intersected *above* the creature's head, and then she squeezed the trigger.

A bright red blossom of fluid appeared as her round punctured the infected's jaw and punched through the back of its throat. "Good shot," Sally commented, squeezing her trigger once more.

The infected fell one by one. The dumb beasts didn't even realize that they were being murdered from afar.

12

NEAR LIBERAL, KANSAS
FEBRUARY 12TH

He could feel it moving inside of him, working its way through his veins to transform his body. Within the first two hours after the infected had vomited its filth onto him, he'd felt weak and tired, like he was coming down with the flu. Those feelings had since left him, leaving him with a numb sensation all over.

As he rode in the TC hatch of the Stryker, he contemplated his fate. It wasn't often that a man knew with certainty when they would die. The feelings of foreboding before a so-called suicide mission may have been similar, but Jim had never experienced anything like that during all his years in the Army. He knew, with certainty now, that he would be dead soon. It wouldn't be by his own hand, he could never do that. Instead, one of the soldiers in the vehicle below, or in one of the other trucks, would end his life with a bullet to the back of his head.

He'd had illusions of being immune at first, regardless of what he'd told Sergeant Turner. Every one of them had a shot at being immune, right? The government scientists who'd been working on a cure at the hospital were all dead. They'd died early on in the outbreak during some type of bizarre shootout between the Homeland guys and an unknown faction. Since then, the base only had normal MDs, doctors who were adept at patching up the wounded, but not at scientific research. All attempts to identify a cure—or what made people immune for that matter—were postponed indefinitely.

The infection moved through his body like a living thing. He could feel it, as if it were a worm, traveling the length of his veins and arteries, leaving a thickening substance in its wake. *That* was the strangest sensation out of all of them. Jim could feel his veins becoming harder, the infection coagulating the blood inside his body, hardening it against the damage that all infected were prone to receive over their remaining time on earth.

Jim Albrecht was becoming one of them.

He pushed the transmit button on his CVC helmet's microphone. "Truck One, this is Ready Six," he said, startled at how terrible his voice sounded over the integrated speakers. The taste of blood in his mouth caused him to wipe at his lips. His sleeve came away with a line of dark red. His gums were starting to bleed.

"This is Truck One," the TC of the lead vehicle replied. Jim was having a hard time remembering the kid's name.

"What's..." He stopped. What was he going to ask again? He thought back to the events of earlier in the day when they'd raided the empty farmhouse and found evidence that the lieutenant had killed the monsters who'd lived there. The monsters were the two men, not the infected they'd tortured. When the trucks returned, to pick them up, two jets flew by less than a mile away. *That's right.*

"What's the ETA to the airport?" Jim asked. There was a pause as the man on the other end checked his computer-thing—*Blue Force Tracker!* Jim reminded himself, struggling to keep it together.

"Looks like about half a mile to the turn off that we identified, then another mile to the vehicle collection point."

Jim nodded. They'd made a plan to turn off of the highway and send the lead truck forward to ensure the way was clear. Once he determined they weren't walking into a trap or that the area wasn't infested with the infected, the rest of the trucks would roll forward and they'd dismount. It was only about half a mile to the airport from the collection point.

He could feel himself slipping away. How long had it been since he'd become infected? Was it six hours now? He looked at the watch on his wrist. It was probably closer to seven.

"Uh… Truck One," Jim said. "When you get to the turn, hold up for me. I'm coming with you."

"Say again, Ready Six?"

"I'm altering the plan. I'm going to move forward with your elment—I mean *element*." He'd begun screwing up words when spoken aloud too. *Dammit.*

"Roger, sir. We're…ah, we're at the turn now."

Jim switched to the vehicle internal channel. He couldn't remember the driver's name. *Damn.* "Driver, pull up alongside Truck One and drop the ramp. Change of plans. I'm going with the lead vehicle."

"Yes, sir," the driver replied.

Jim didn't bother to watch where the driver went as he felt the Stryker increase speed. Instead, he disconnected his CVC helmet from the communications system and began the process of crawling down through the cupola, made harder than usual due to his deteriorating health. The driver began lowering the ramp before the vehicle had come to a complete stop. *Must want me out of his truck pretty bad*, he chuckled to himself.

Jim switched his CVC helmet for his Kevlar and grabbed his M-4 from its place in the rack before exiting the Stryker. He considered bringing his rucksack, but decided against it. He'd already written his letter to Jill and the kids. He'd lamented in the letter that he'd never see Alex hit that home run, or watch Ella cheering on the sidelines of her high school football team. It was probably the hardest when he mentioned the baby, little Eric, who was only one, still learning to walk without falling.

All that's in the past, now, he chided himself. *Only thing I can do now is try to make a difference for the future of our nation.*

Jim turned away from the rucksack that contained the letter and walked tiredly to the waiting truck. He walked up the open ramp and sat down on a bench. The soldier beside him shifted over several inches, and then stood, switching sides of the vehicle to leave him alone on the seat. "I ain't gonna bite you, son," he grunted.

"Not yet, sir," the soldier replied. "But you'll try to pretty soon."

"*Heh*," he chuckled, watching the ramp close. The watery daylight outside that had flooded the interior of the Stryker was replaced incrementally by the red lighting inside. "I guess you're right about that. For now, though, I won't bite you. Deal?"

"Yes, sir."

The ramp locked into place and the truck lurched forward. Jim momentarily lost muscle control, his helmet slapped against the ramp at the back of the vehicle as they moved out.

"Uh, sir?"

He focused his eyes in the dim red lighting. Across from him was a female soldier, one of only two in the entire force. She'd been the one to ask the question. "Yeah, Specialist? What is it?"

"I don't mean to pry, sir. But what does it feel like? You know, the infection."

He considered yelling at her for her insensitivity. Then he considered ignoring her stupid, selfish question. Finally, he just decided that she was curious because his fate awaited them all, and each minute they spent beyond the walls, the higher the probability that they'd end up like him became.

"It hurts," he whispered, barely audible over the steady thrum of the engine and the sounds of the four axles churning below as they turned the vehicle's eight massive wheels. "I can feel it moving inside my body, like a thickness in my blood—I don't know how else to describe it. I have a fever and I'm thirsty—all the time." He couldn't remember the word that meant the same thing. "I drank five or six canteens, but haven't peed since I became infected. My thoughts are still clear," he lied, "but the words coming out of my mouth get jumbled. It's like...like I'm beginning to get Alzheimer's or something."

"That sounds pretty terrible."

Jim smiled and then quickly covered his teeth with his lips. He didn't want the soldiers in the back of the Stryker to see how far along his infection had advanced. He still had the belief that if he saw the jets at the airport, then he could somehow get the information to Higher and they'd be able to do something about the foreign invaders.

"It is," he replied.

"And sad," the woman continued. "I'm sorry it happened to you, sir."

He nodded his head, but didn't reply. The truck began to slow down and then stopped. Above them, the Stryker's .50 caliber machine gun completed two full rotations as the gunner checked for infected. When he was satisfied that nothing was in the immediate area, the TC had the driver shut off the engine and lower the ramp.

Jim was up and moving before any of the others. He'd already decided that he'd take point, even if he hadn't communicated that to anyone else. He was infected and the only thing that he had to look forward to was death.

"Let's go!" Jim ordered harshly. The two soldiers from the back of the Stryker followed him, along with the TC, the sergeant whose name he couldn't remember. "I don't have much time left, but I'm gonna make it count."

"Roger, sir. I'll take point," the sergeant answered.

"No. I've got point, Sergeant. If I catch a bullet, it's no big loss anymore."

He didn't wait for an answer. Instead, he took off at a brisk walk up the gravel road toward the airport. They were supposed to be about a half of a mile away, so he wasn't concerned with moving tactically, yet. Once they got closer, he'd move off the road and try to creep along the ditch, although he didn't think it would make much of a difference. There were no trees of substance along the road. The only cover available was the occasional bush that had somehow managed to grow in the Plains.

The distance closed rapidly and he could see the fence line. Jim checked behind him to ensure the others were with him. Even from almost a half of a mile away, the Stryker stood out starkly against the horizon. The lines of sight made it nearly impossible for any type of element to go unnoticed if anyone was watching.

They moved the last little distance in the ditch as he'd planned. They were perhaps two hundred feet from the fence when the sounds of the infected began to echo across the landscape. He froze.

"That's coming from that town over there," the sergeant said, pointing toward the cluster of buildings a mile or two away.

"They must have heard the jets land and are coming to investigate," Jim surmised. There was nowhere to hide. "Let's move up to the fence line. That tall grass will offer us some concealment."

By the time they reached it, the shadows were beginning to lengthen with the approaching dusk. The sounds of the infected closing in on the airfield had gotten much louder. They'd closed the distance faster than he'd expected. "Down! Get down!" he ordered, indicating the grass.

The soldiers did as he ordered while he crouched and looked through the fence toward the jets. The two planes were MiGs alright. Each sported a green, white, and red flag. *Iranians.*

"Those are Iranian jets," he whispered to the soldiers. "What the fuck are Iranians doing here?"

"Sir, you need to get down. You're exposed," the sergeant urged.

"Nah. I'm *infected*, Sergeant." He glanced toward the Stryker in the distance. His vision was blurry, so he wiped at them. More blood. "I don't care about being seen by the infected; I'm one of them now."

Gunfire erupted from the terminal building. Jim couldn't see any muzzle flashes, so he assumed that the Iranians were firing from the front side of the building. He looked down at the soldiers and said, "I need you to get back to Sergeant Turner. Tell him that the jets are Iranian. He'll know who to contact at division with the information."

The female he'd spoken to earlier blanched. "What are you planning to do, sir?"

He smiled sadly. "I'm going to kill me some Iranians. Those bastards inside that building aren't the ones who did all this, but they're all I've got."

"Did all of what?" she asked.

Jim pointed to his eyes and the blood leaking from his tear ducts. "They're the cause of the infection. They're the ones who attacked us with this shit."

"Wait," the soldier said, rising up from the tall grass along the fence line. "You're saying that it was an attack and not a biological mutation like they told us? And that you *kept* it from us?"

"I only found out this morning when I called division," he grunted. "We followed through with our mission, and I got fucked. I don't want the same thing to happen to the rest of you. Take the information back to Turner and get the fuck out of here."

Jim didn't wait for her to respond. Instead, he staggered along the fence toward the wreckage of a small plane that had taken out part of the fence when it crashed. Ahead of him, the steady staccato of gunfire mingled with the insane screams of the infected. Behind him, the two soldiers who'd taken cover in the grass were already picking their way through the roadside ditch to return to their vehicle.

Jake Murphy cleared the wreckage as the gunfire from the terminal building began to increase. He estimated that he was about six or seven football fields away from where the two foreign jets were parked near the terminal. It was too far to run all kitted up like he was, so he settled for a light jog, taking advantage of the fact that all of the ground crew he'd seen earlier were now fighting the incoming infected.

He wondered if he was being foolish and slowed after only running for about fifty feet. He'd determined that there were foreign planes on the ground at the airport and that they had a support staff holed up in the terminal. What more did he expect to find out? Getting himself trapped inside the fence while hundreds of infected surrounded the perimeter was not a smart thing to do.

His feet stopped shuffling forward and he stopped altogether, considering whether he should return to the farm and let these foreigners do whatever the hell they were doing. He didn't need to get himself killed. The sound of feet scraping against metal at the wreckage behind him made Jake spin, crouch, and bring his rifle up to fire.

"Whoa, there!" a voice rasped in English. The sun was barely peeking over the western horizon, its light at the perfect angle to blind him and hide the face of the new arrival.

Jake allowed the muzzle of the rifle to dip slightly. The infected didn't speak, and as far as he knew, the foreigners he came to spy on didn't speak unaccented English. After months of not seeing anyone besides the Campbells around Liberal, the town was becoming absolutely crowded in the last two days. First, he'd stumbled across Mark, then discovered the foreigners here at the airport, and now this newcomer sneaking up behind him. *What the hell is happening?*

"Who are you?" Jake demanded in a harsh whisper.

"I'm here with the US Army," the stranger said.

"Bullshit. The closest functional Army base is Fort Bliss, down in El Paso."

"That's not exactly true…Lieutenant Murphy."

Jake's head snapped back like he'd been flicked hard by one of his buddies in the middle of his forehead. "Step closer where I can see you."

"I don't want to startle you," the newcomer said without moving toward him. "Jake, it's me, Colonel Albrecht."

The ground seemed to open up underneath Jake. The man's build was about right, but the voice was different than he remembered. It'd been a long time, though, and he'd only been around the man a handful of times, so his memory could be wrong. What decided it for him was the name. Albrecht wasn't a common name, so it had to be him. He'd never expected to see his former brigade commander again, and the feelings of anger, even hatred that he'd harbored for the man welled up, threatening to overwhelm him.

"Tell me why I shouldn't just shoot you right now," Jake demanded, allowing his voice to edge dangerously toward a shout.

"Jake, we don't have a lot of time," Colonel Albrecht said. "I know that we did wrong by you, believe me, I know that now. There's no excuse for what I allowed to happen—no, for what I *did* to you by putting you in that situation."

Jake brought his rifle up again. Something was off in the man's mannerisms. The Colonel Albrecht he knew would have been up in his face almost immediately. "I said, come closer, *sir*." He added that last part out of habit, but he harbored no illusions that he would ever take an order from this man again.

He saw the colonel's hands rise up, his silhouette dark against the sun behind him. "Jake, I want you to know something before I come closer."

The gunfire at the terminal was becoming sporadic as the defenders must have been either running low on ammo, or taking casualties. "Oh yeah? What's that?"

"I'm infected," the older man admitted.

"What?"

"I've got a few hours before I turn, but there ain't shit anyone can do for me."

Jake looked over his shoulder at the terminal before advancing toward Albrecht. He was covered in blood, both from himself and what appeared to be from others. Fresh rivulets of the dark fluid ran from his eyes along his cheeks and dripped from his chin.

Jake doubted that the colonel actually had the few hours left that he thought he did.

"Sir, what are you doing here?"

The man laughed. "It's funny meeting you here, Jake. I came to arrest you."

"*What?*" Jake replied, truly shocked. Why would anyone try to arrest him for going AWOL with the world gone to shit around them?

"I've been working through it. Bhagat needs a fall guy. You're it."

"Bhagat? The division commander?" He looked over his shoulder once more. The firing had stopped completely.

"Same same," the colonel nodded, sending drops of blood cascading down his chest. "I found out this morning—before I became infected looking for you—that he knew about the Iranians and North Koreans. That he purposefully kept that information from us."

The flag he'd seen on the tail fin of the jet flashed in Jake's mind. The green, white, and red flag that he didn't recognize must have been Iranian. "What did he know about, sir?"

Human screams from the terminal told Jake that the infected had made it inside. "We need to get under cover where they can't see us," Jake said. "We can leave after dark. That crashed plane should provide sufficient cover."

They retreated to a section of the plane's hull that was still relatively intact. Colonel Albrecht leaned heavily against a broken window. "I'm gonna be honest with you, Jake. I'm not gonna make it to wherever you're holed up. You know that. You've been out here for a lot longer than I have. But I still have a few hours left."

Jake eyed him again. "I don't think so, sir. Maybe an hour, two tops."

The older man nodded. "I like your honesty. Always have. After we didn't find you at the farmhouse, we didn't—"

"You went to the farm?" Jake asked. "Is everyone alright?"

Albrecht stared at him. "There was nobody there. Lots of dead infected, but they were dead for a long time."

Jake's mind worked to piece together what the colonel was saying. His mind was slipping as the infection ravaged inside of him, but saying everyone at the farm was dead for a long time didn't make any sense. *Wait.* "Sir, did the farmhouse have a weird fence running between the house and a big barn?"

"Yeah."

"Lots of .50 caliber bullet holes everywhere?"

"Mmm hmm. Last place your...BFT pinged."

"You went to the Cullen's house," he said, breathing a sigh of relief. "I never bothered to fire up the comms system after Sergeant Wyatt and Private Dickerson were killed; there wasn't any need to since it was just me. I just drove the Stryker back to the Campbell farm."

"Oh!" He pointed down the dirt road that Jake had traveled earlier. "Five Strykers... Go there. Wait for me. I need to try to find a survive—survive—a prisoner," he amended when he couldn't say the word.

"You have five Strykers, here?" Jake asked incredulously.

Albrecht grinned. "Bhagat really wants you dead."

"That bastard."

"I got infected at the farm. We were going to start random searches when we saw the planes flying overhead. We came here to figure out what the Iranians—or the North... North..."

"Koreans?" Jake offered.

"That's it. I came to see what they were doing in the America."

Red flags went up in Jake's mind. The colonel was losing it. He shifted slightly, putting a broken airline chair between them and positioning his rifle so the seat back wouldn't get in the way. "That's why I came here too, sir."

Albrecht nodded again. "I don't have much time. I think I can go up to the infected now. Give me a chance to capture one of those... One of the bad guys."

Bad guys? Oh shit, he's losing it. "Do you have any more information about why they're here?"

His former brigade commander gestured weakly at the terminal. "They caused it. I don't have proof, but they're the only ones who weren't attacked... Now, they're here. You...you do the math."

The older man stopped talking and stared intently at the wall for a moment. "*Sir!*"

"Hmm?"

"Sir, are you good to go?"

The colonel didn't answer. Instead, he pushed past him, making Jake grab for his rifle because he thought the man had turned completely. Albrecht stumbled past him without acknowledging him further and headed toward the terminal.

13

NEAR LIBERAL, KANSAS
FEBRUARY 12TH

Jim staggered toward an open doorway that led into the building in front of him. His mind was fuzzy. He couldn't remember how he'd gotten there. There was snow all around, but he didn't seem cold. He didn't feel the wind that blew the snow along the pavement. Had he been drinking?

Somehow, despite his lack of knowing where he was or how he'd gotten there, Jim knew that it wasn't because of drinking alcohol. He was supposed to be doing something important, but beyond running into that lieutenant, he couldn't remember what it was. He held a rifle, which made sense, and... He stopped and raised his left hand. In it, he clutched a double set of zip ties. They looked like they could be used as handcuffs.

That's it! he shouted inside his head. He was supposed to try to capture one of the bad guys. Were they Iraqis? That sounded right. He'd fought against Iraqi insurgents most of his time in the Army, so that was probably what he was doing. He had to capture somebody, but for the life of him, he couldn't remember who the high value target was.

What is wrong with me? Jim wondered. He couldn't remember getting assigned the mission, but he knew it was his to complete. His lack of comprehension and ability to remember any details were disturbing. He was married, with a kid—no, two kids. Wait. He had *three* children. How was that so hard to remember? He was a career Army soldier. There was a mission to capture someone... Someone else, who was it?

The memory hit him hard. "Shit," he muttered aloud. "I'm infected." He was supposed to go into the building and see if he could capture one of the Iraqis— *Iranians*, Jim corrected himself. He was going inside because the infected wouldn't attack him since he was already infected.

The memories brought a level of clarity for Jim. His vision, while still blurry, seemed to clear enough that he recognized the open door on the back of the building. He made his way toward it at a slightly faster pace than a brisk walk.

When he arrived at the doorway, he saw that it opened into a long hallway. Shadows bounced wildly off the walls at the far end and sounds echoed toward him. Intermittent crazed shrieks punctuated the steady, rapid panting of the infected, as they searched for prey.

Jim stepped into the building and swallowed the hard lump in his throat. His mouth was extremely dry. He didn't know for sure that the infected wouldn't attack him. It was more of a feeling that he had, but it wasn't a solid bet.

He checked his rifle. There was a magazine in it, and he didn't remember firing it—not that it meant anything, since he could have shot the damn thing two minutes ago and not remembered it.

The doorway at the far end of the hall darkened and Jim brought the rifle up. He fired a round directly into the creature's chest, the weapon kicked against his shoulder as the suppressed report reverberated off the close walls. The man staggered and fell.

The intermittent screams became a consistent wail as many voices picked up the cry. The *suppressed* shot had been too loud.

Sounds of flesh hitting chairs, tripping over potted plants, and bouncing off counters reached him. Even if they didn't attack, the press of bodies in the hallway would keep him from doing anything. He knew that he needed to get into the main room or his mission was over.

Jim began walking quickly, staggering forward. The wails of the infected became louder, more confusing and disorienting to him. He screamed in response as he emerged through the doorway. He wasn't sure if he shouted in defiance of the others or if his brain was responding to their calls.

There were many more infected in the building than he'd thought there would be. There must have been hundreds of the creatures in the main terminal, and they were all coming directly at him.

Jim gritted his teeth and braced himself for the impact. It never came.

The mob broke around him, not cleanly as several errant arms hit him accidentally as their owners streamed by him and knocked him sideways, but it was enough that he knew he'd be fine—until he died from the infection.

He walked away from the hallway, further into the terminal. Several of the windows closest to the town were broken and covered in blood. Emaciated bodies lay impaled on the glass and more were scattered both inside and outside of the building. The infected had paid dearly for their entrance into the terminal.

The soldier's eyes roved across the terminal floor. Bodies of soldiers wearing tan camouflage patterned uniforms were mingled with the bodies of infected. They'd been torn to pieces. Oddly, there was what appeared to be an overturned stretcher, the kind like they used in ambulances. The presence of the stretcher itself wasn't odd, since there were probably thousands of those things lying around as first responders attempted to work on the wounded in the first couple of days during the initial outbreak.

The odd part was that the sheets on the stretcher appeared fresh, completely white and undisturbed, except for a few wrinkles where it had held a patient at one point. He filed the image away into his growing mental folder that he'd labeled "What the Fuck?" and continued searching.

Jim stumbled around, and in some cases over the mounds of dead, following what appeared to be a trail of dead deeper into the facility. He made his way through the defunct security area into the recesses of the building. It was already hard enough to see through his blurred vision, but the near total darkness made it nearly impossible to see beyond the ends of his outstretched hands.

He remembered that he had a small flashlight attached to his vest and fumbled with it. The process took several seconds as his fingers refused to cooperate. He screamed his frustration, the action making his vocal chords strain and his throat raw. Finally, he pulled it from the pouch, wincing at the sound of the Velcro separating.

When he turned the flashlight on, he found himself in another hallway. This one was substantially less crowded than the main terminal with only two of the infected wandering aimlessly in the dark. Jim wondered what the others would do if he killed these two. Would they smell the blood and come running, or would they simply go about their business without even noticing the deaths?

"Does it matter?" he grunted loudly, eliciting an excited response from the nearest of the infected. It looked in his direction, toward the sound of his voice, but it didn't appear to be looking at him. It was as if the creature looked through him. *Strange fuckers*, he thought, careful not to let himself utter it aloud.

He yelled a challenge to the infected. They responded by screaming back at him, unsure what he'd seen and whether they should follow him. He pulled the combat knife from its sheath, remembering that he'd used it only a few hours ago to kill the infected bastard that had pinned him to the ground. He didn't hesitate. Walking up to the nearest infected, he wrapped a hand around its mouth and sliced its neck open. Hot blood spurted onto his forearm as he held onto it until its movements ceased. Then he dropped the body.

He flashed the light, clicking the button to check the position of the other one. It hadn't really moved too much, it was still standing there, waiting for something to attract its attention. Jim smiled at his newfound knowledge that the infected were completely oblivious to one another's death, but then realized that it didn't matter what he learned if he didn't get back outside and tell Whatshisname.

The second creature went down as easily as the first and Jim used the flashlight to ensure that there were no more of them in this section. When he was satisfied, he followed the trail of dead infected. He hadn't seen any of the other soldiers in a while, so whoever was left was a damn good shot.

As he walked, he became aware of a scratching noise. It was hard to tell how far away the sound originated from since the hallway made everything echo strangely. He walked on, no longer afraid of being attacked by the infected, and turned a corner to a dead end.

Four more infected stood in front of him, pawing at a closed doorway. They twisted around at the sight of his flashlight, but none of them attacked. One stumbled toward him while the others turned back to the doorway and resumed their hopeless efforts to open the door.

That'll be me in a couple hours, he thought, making himself angry. "This is bullshit," he shouted, once more making the infected turn. Jim buried the combat knife up to the hilt in the nearest one's chin, stabbing into its brain. Then the bloodlust took him and he let himself be consumed by it.

"They're going to get through," Grady warned his newfound companion.

The man looked at him in confusion and the operator pantomimed the devils breaking through the doorway. He adjusted his grip on the broken broom handle, a weapon more suited for the close fighting that he anticipated than the empty AK leaned against the corner. The soldier beside him passed the strange dagger he held from one hand to the other as he wiped sweat from his palms, despite the chill in the air.

Grady Harper didn't know who the man was, or how he'd even gotten to wherever they were. There hadn't been a lot of time for discussion. The last thing he remembered was a village in South America, somewhere in Brazil. Havoc diverted his team from an operation in North Korea after they reported seeing evidence of human experiments taking place in one of the tunnel complexes they'd infiltrated. The drugged up super-freaks in Brazil had attacked his team and he remembered people getting killed, but not who. Then he got...separated? Ambushed? That part was still fuzzy as well.

Grady had awoken to the sound of gunfire, here in an airport. He'd been strapped down to a table or hospital gurney. Men in strange uniforms were firing AKs at others who didn't care about taking cover or getting shot. They appeared to be similar to the crazies he'd seen in Brazil. And they were losing the battle.

He'd screamed for them to untie him, to give him a gun. One of them finally did, and they'd fought a retreat back to this closet. Now they were out of ammo and out of time.

"What's your name?" Grady asked the tall man beside him. Again, the man shook his head, not understanding. Grady put a hand on his bare chest and said, "Grady. Grady Harper."

The soldier nodded and mimicked his actions. "Taavi," he said, smiling through his close-cropped beard.

"Taavi? Do you speak English?" It was a dumb question, but he had to ask. It was hard to see in the dim lighting, but he thought the man's face twisted into a grimace for a moment. Then, Taavi shook his head no. "We need to sit tight and wait for these things to go away," Grady said.

The scratching at the door continued for a long time, the creatures outside never seemed to get bored. Every once in a while, one of them would jiggle the handle, but Grady suspected it was more a matter of them accidentally touching it instead of actually trying to open the door with it.

He tried to make small talk with the soldier, but it was hopeless, the man didn't know any English and didn't seem smart enough to carry on a conversation with hand signals, so Grady settled against the wash basin at the back of the closet to think.

He still had no clue where he was or how he'd gotten there, and his memories were spotty at best. He didn't know what happened to his team, Hannah, Baz, Knasovich—*actually*, he remembered the sniper getting his throat ripped out, so there was one of them that he knew about. Rob Carmike had been with Alex when it happened and called it over the team net, but what happened to the communications expert or Chris McCormick, their mechanic, he had no clue. The Brit, Simon, never made it out of Japan—he'd turned after being bitten in Korea.

There were flashes of memories, fleeting, confusing images of him being in a small, brightly lit room and needles. Lots of needles. He remembered moving around the room at times, at others, he was strapped to a table, like he'd been here in this building. None of it made any sense to him.

Taavi's uniform bore a symbol he'd never seen before and when Grady pointed to it, the man whispered something very quickly. He'd done a lot of time in Iraq and Afghanistan, even picked up a little bit of the language here and there, but nothing the soldier said sounded even remotely familiar.

As he was trying to puzzle out the mystery of how the two of them had ended up in the closet, the scratching outside abruptly stopped. "That's different," he mumbled, pushing away from the sink.

About thirty seconds later, the door handle jiggled once more, making Grady jump. He grinned in spite of himself then lowered the broom handle to chest level as he crouched. An errant thought occurred to him as the movement stretched the muscles in his calves. He had to have only been out of action for a couple of days, otherwise, he'd have experienced muscle atrophy, the wasting away of the body after being sedated for a long time.

That fact gave him hope that he'd be able to find his team once he got out of his current predicament. Once he found them, he was going to Texas to get his daughter, Lucy, from Kim and take her somewhere safe until he could figure out what was going on.

The door swung outward, revealing another of the creatures. Grady paused before he struck to examine the thing since it hadn't tried to attack him. It was covered in blood and gore, the clothing across its chest and arms was dark and glistened in the light cast off from a discarded flashlight. Blood oozed from its eyes and the mouth opened and shut oddly.

"Bad...guys?" the thing croaked.

The crazies didn't talk, Grady remembered that much. This one wore a US Army uniform and held a large combat knife in one hand. The other twitched rapidly. An M-4 with an oversized suppressor dangled from a sling across his body. Grady wasn't sure what the guy's story was, but he was a goner, that much was evident.

"I'm Grady Harper, with the Havoc Group," he said, not offering the man a hand.

The older man's eyes seemed to focus on him and he shook his head slightly. "I'm... Colonel Jim. Need to find... A bad guy."

"Bad guy?" Grady whispered. "What the hell are you talking about?"

The colonel pointed at Taavi. "Need to take back." The officer struggled with his words. The infection that he carried was almost complete. "UN not friends."

"UN?" Grady felt stupid. He was lost in the sauce and wondered if he was dreaming. That *had* to be it. He was drunk and passed out somewhere, maybe even in his Petworth apartment, and he'd dreamed this whole stupid scenario. *Time to wake up*, he told himself.

A scream echoed down the hallway, followed by another. The creatures had returned. "How do we get out of here?"

"I came through...terminal."

Grady glanced beyond the colonel. He'd only seen the large room and then the hallway. If the soldier said he came through the terminal, then it made sense that they were in an airport. He hated not being able to remember what the hell had happened to him.

"Okay, let's go, Taavi," he said, tugging at the foreign man's sleeve. "You coming?" he asked the bloodied colonel.

They ran, quickly passing by the hallway that they'd came down when they'd gotten themselves trapped in the closet. The inhuman sounds drifted from somewhere down that passage, so Grady thought it was best to avoid it. The colonel screamed, making Grady jump and whirl around, broomstick in hand. The man fired three rounds down the hallway.

He was panting heavily, even though they'd only run for fifty meters.

"Go," the colonel's voice came out dry and raspy.

Their route took them around a corner and along a corridor made of floor-to-ceiling glass windows that overlooked a runway. There was a C-130 outside, looming large. It was parked dangerously close to the building, the nose almost touching the glass. Beyond it were two small fighter jets of a make that Grady had never seen before.

As he went, he wondered just what the hell was happening. The colonel was obviously pretty fucked up, but what did that mean? Had he been through a fight or was he infected with whatever the villagers in Brazil and the others in the terminal had?

They reached the end of the glass wall and the hallway opened up to another small waiting area. It was a dead end except for the door leading to the runway. "This way!" Grady hissed, sprinting to the door and depressing the handle.

Thankfully it opened, revealing a set of covered stairs leading to the tarmac below. "No," the colonel said. "I'm done."

Grady turned around to see the man standing in the center of the hallway. "What?"

He tapped himself on the chest. "Infected."

"No shit, man. Let's go."

"No," the other man repeated. Screams bounced down the glass wall hallway. The others were almost there. "Outside…fence. Lieutenant Murphy." He pointed at Taavi. "Give him…bad guy."

Grady's head swam with questions that he didn't have time to ask. He settled on the most pertinent one. "There's a lieutenant at the fence waiting for us?"

Colonel Albrecht nodded and smiled. Blood glistened on his teeth. "Yes. At crash." He lifted his rifle over his shoulder. "Take…this."

Grady rushed over and grasped the suppressed M-4. "You don't have to do this, Colonel."

"I'm dead…already. Go."

Taavi tugged at his sleeve, the tall man was obviously ready to leave. "Fuck it. Go with God, Colonel," he said, then whirled around. Four quick steps and they were through the door, then bounding down the steps to the ground below.

When they emerged from the covered stairway the cold hit him like a ton of bricks. The wind howled, tearing into his exposed skin as heavy snowflakes eddied around them. Where the hell were they? As far as he remembered it was March, maybe even April if he'd been out of it for a couple of weeks. And he was supposed to be in *Brazil*.

Grady looked around. The colonel had said there was a soldier waiting for him at the fence and something about a crash. He couldn't see a fence anywhere through the swirling snow. Several gunshots rang out from the terminal and in his peripheral vision he saw the muzzle flash through the glass windows above. He turned to look up.

The colonel stood there, arms extended holding a pistol. He fired at point blank range into the scores of the crazies that had surrounded him, and then dropped the magazine, calmly inserting another. They paid him no mind, as if they didn't even see him. He fired again and again until the slide locked back once again.

Grady watched in fascination as the colonel shoved the bloody, diseased creatures away roughly, making his way to the glass windows. He looked down at them and pointed beyond the C-130, telling them that they needed to go that way. Grady nodded, watching as the older man inserted a single bullet into the chamber of his pistol with shaking hands.

Colonel Albrecht placed the gun against his temple and Grady screamed for him to stop, waving his arms above his head. The crazies inside saw his movements and began beating wildly on the glass, their screams muted.

Once more, Taavi tugged on his sleeve. He was right, the door leading out of the terminal opened outward with a push bar handle. All it would take was for one of the crazies to bump into it and they'd be able to get out as well.

Albrecht's eyes focused on Grady and he pulled the gun away from his temple, then placed it under his chin and squeezed the trigger.

14

NEAR LIBERAL, KANSAS
FEBRUARY 13TH

The Stryker bumped and rattled as it turned down one of the many roads leading around the countryside. They were on a circuitous route to the Campbell farm. Jake had shown Sergeant Turner the location on his map and the grizzled NCO input the coordinates into their Blue Force Tracker system. Once they were input, he turned the column of vehicles in the opposite direction. There were far too many infected around to go directly to the farm, so they would try to trick and confuse them by taking every back road marked on the map.

After some discussion with the platoon sergeant, he'd agreed to have everyone turn off their BFTs until they could sort out what was happening down at Fort Bliss and with the foreign troops on American soil. That had been over an hour ago and they were navigating off a paper map that the lead truck had picked up during one of their fuel stops the previous day.

Jake looked at the strange survivors seated across from him. The American had his head resting on the wall and his mouth open. The man had materialized out of the snow only a few minutes after a pistol fired twenty or thirty shots inside the terminal. He was shirtless and shoeless, heavily muscled, and wore thin hospital pants. He had a reddish beard that looked odd on his Asian features.

Guy was some sort of government contractor or something. He didn't really go into details, but he was confused about where he was and even what month it was. He'd said something about being in Brazil on a mission and then suddenly ended up here. Pretty wild story. He seemed legitimately shocked to learn that the infected ruled the United States now. Everything that Jake had heard before he went AWOL made it sound like it was that way worldwide.

The one shining light out of the entire ordeal was that Grady had one of the Iranians in tow when he showed up and told him that Colonel Albrecht had taken his own life after emptying two 15-round magazines into the infected. Everything else about this mission was a complete clusterfuck.

So much for Sua Sponte, he groaned—which reminded him about the other major problem he had. There were about thirty soldiers riding around in a column of Strykers. And apparently, those soldiers had come north to arrest him. What did that mean when they got to the farm?

The whine of the diesel engine changed pitch once more, indicating that they were slowing down. The vehicle turned sharply and went up a slight rise, and then he heard the sound of the big wheels going over a cattle guard set in the driveway. They'd arrived.

He reached out and tapped Grady. "Time to wake up, man. We're here."

The contractor came alert instantly, wiping at the corners of his mouth. He reached over and nudged the Iranian. "Taavi, we're here, bro." The Iranian blinked away the sleep in his eyes.

"You know this guy?" Jake asked as the engine shut down and the ramp began to lower.

"Not really. When I woke up, I was strapped to a table. The crazies were all over the place. He helped me out, took off the restraints."

Jake shrugged, still not sure what to make of the other man. "Keep an eye on him. The Iranians are behind all of this. We need to figure out what they're doing here."

"No worries, little buddy. I've got this."

Jake gritted his teeth at the comment and walked down the ramp. He had a lot of shit to deal with and getting into an argument with the stranger wasn't high on his to-do list. It was close to four a.m. so everyone in the farmhouse was probably asleep when they pulled up. He needed to get inside and let them know to be cool and *not* get into a firefight with Turner's men.

"Hey, sir. We need to talk," Sergeant Turner said as he emerged from the vehicle.

Jake held up a hand. "Hold on, I need to make sure my people don't start shooting at you guys first."

He didn't wait for the NCO's answer. Instead, he went quickly toward the farmhouse porch. "Hold on right there," a female voice called out firmly, but quietly, stopping him several feet from the house.

"Katie?"

"Jake? You're back!"

He craned his neck upward. The young woman was in the lookout stand that Vern had built beside the chimney in the early days of the outbreak. "Yeah. Did Sidney and Sally make it back?"

"They got in right before dusk. There was a whole bunch of infected on the highway, riled up by... Well, by all those trucks you just showed up with probably. Grandpa isn't going to be happy about you bringing them here."

"We tried—"

"What in the Good Lord's name is going on?" Vern grumbled, opening the front door.

"Good morning, Mr. Campbell."

"Jake," the old man acknowledged. "What's all this?"

"These are soldiers from Fort Bliss. They're here to see what all those planes are doing flying around."

"Fort Bliss? I thought you said your base down there was overrun."

"It almost was," Turner said from behind him. "But we were able to put down the riot and secure the gates." The NCO walked up and extended a hand. "Sergeant First Class Turner, I'm in charge of this unit."

Vern eyed the man suspiciously before shaking his hand. "Sergeant First Class, huh? Where are your officers or a sergeant major or something?"

"Mostly dead. There's a few in the hospital who were too injured to go on this mission. I'm the highest ranking person left in my unit."

Vern looked beyond the two men to the vehicles. "How many men you got?"

"Forty-one, plus the two men who were with Lieutenant Murphy when we found them."

He nodded and turned his focus back on Turner. "Now, what are y'all doing here again? Jake said something about investigating planes, but those only showed up yesterday. I reckon it'll take a lot longer to drive from El Paso than it did before the Lord's curse came."

"We've been on the road for several days, sir."

"Look, it's four in the morning. I ain't got time for made up Army boloney. What are you really doing here in Kansas, Sergeant?"

"They came looking for me," Jake said.

Vern looked at him. "Is that right?"

"Yes, sir," Sergeant Turner agreed. "Our mission was to apprehend Lieutenant Murphy and bring him back to Fort Bliss for trial. But that changed—"

"Trial for what?" Vern asked, his eyes narrowing.

"We learned that the charges against him were completely fabricated," Turner said. Behind them, soldiers had begun to drift up, forming a semi-circle around the conversation.

"It's complicated."

"Un-complicate it then," Vern demanded. "What did Jake do that warrants sending forty men halfway across the Southwest, through dangerous territory? He's been living under my roof with my granddaughters and I want answers. Now."

"We were led to believe that he caused the food riots in Camp Three," Sergeant Turner replied. "We know now that the commander actually forced the situation, doing it to cut the refugee population in half so we could feed the survivors."

"So he didn't do it?"

"No, sir," Turner said. "We raided a house and Colonel Albrecht got infected. Then—"

"What in tarnation are you talking about?" Vern asked. "Let's go inside. It's cold out here and I need coffee to follow your convoluted story." He turned and walked back into the house.

The small group of men followed him inside to the kitchen. Carmen stood at the top of the stairs, her arms wrapped around her children. She waved, but did not come down. All the soldiers in the yard must have scared her. Jake waved back, smiling to put her at ease, before going into the kitchen.

"How many refugees were, what'd you say? Cut in half? And who's this colonel fella? I thought you were in charge," he heard Vern ask as he walked into the middle of the conversation.

"It's still undetermined how many died, but there were at least two hundred thousand who were killed in the crossfire between Army units and the armed rebels."

Jake blanched. He knew that once the powder keg in Camp Three exploded that a lot of people would be hurt or injured, but he had no idea that it was so many. "Bhagat got what he wanted then," he said bitterly.

"Yeah, apparently, sir."

"And Jake here caused that rebellion?" Vern asked, attacking the question from a different angle as he was prone to do when he wanted to verify facts.

"No, sir," Turner said. "We believe that the general is working with the Iranians and the North Koreans. They're operating under the guise of the United Nations to invade the US."

"Son of a bitch!" someone behind him said. Jake turned to see Grady Harper, the contractor, standing at the front of the crowd wrapped in a poncho liner. "Fucking Norks, man."

"Excuse you, Mister Whoever You Are." Vern shot Grady a withering look. "I may let a few curse words slip by every now and again, but not that one. Not in *my* home." The old man looked back at Jake. "Who's that?"

"His name is Grady. He was at the airport in town," Jake answered. "I just met him so I don't have his full story yet, but apparently he was there, at the beginning of all this, before the outbreak."

"My team was operating in—" Grady paused. "Ah, fuck it— Whoops, sorry. I meant to say *forget* it, there's no more need for secrecy. We were in North Korea, investigating video footage of the crazies, stuff from a lab before it got out. Then we were diverted to Brazil to confirm or deny if what was going on there was the same thing we saw in Korea."

"And was it?" Vern asked, all eyes on the contractor.

"Yeah. It was the exact same stuff. Then my team was attacked. I got knocked out and taken prisoner or something. I still don't know about that part. Everything's fuzzy up here." He tapped the side of his head.

"Okay. I think you've got a lot of information about how all of this started," Vern offered. "But first, the sergeant here was telling us about some turncoat general and how Jake is involved in all of that. You may have some fuzzy memories, Mr. Grady, but I'm trying to figure out if the man who's been living under my roof and spending time with my granddaughters is somehow responsible for the death of—what did you say? Was it two hundred thousand people?"

"Yes, sir," Sergeant Turner replied. "That what I said. You can rest assured that the lieutenant didn't cause those riots. The situation in the refugee camps was terrible—*is* terrible. We try to provide some sort of law and order, but there are rapes and murders daily, sometimes several a day. Food is always scarce and there are gangs that steal food and belongings from others with little or no repercussions. We made the decision early on to allow the refugees to keep their guns because the way the infection spreads. If there was an outbreak, armed citizens could help to respond. Well, that came back to bite us in the ass when all those people banded together and tried to demand more food and supplies, all stuff that we didn't even have."

Jake nodded. "So I got in trouble and they sent me to the refugee camp for thirty days as punishment," he said. "They wanted me to make a stink and let people know that I was a soldier. Sidney had come from the camps. She told me to lay low, pretend to be just another survivor who'd just arrived. While I was in the camp, I learned that there was a group already planning a revolt. I convinced Caitlyn Wyatt to leave Fort Bliss with me before things got worse."

Vern's lips thinned. "So you went AWOL."

"I went AWOL," Jake admitted. It was like a weight was removed from his shoulders by finally revealing the truth of why he left. "I'm sorry, Mr. Campbell. I didn't mean to lie to you, I just—"

"Can it, Jake. I figured out that you went AWOL in just a couple of days. There was no reason for you to travel all the way up here. I knew you was trying to get away from something."

"You're not mad?" Jake asked.

"Disappointed, sure, but like I said, I already knew the truth so it isn't a big shock to me." He looked up from where Jake sat. "Okay, so we have a foreign army on US soil, a general who might be working with the foreigners, and a whole bunch of US Army soldiers on my land. What are we going to do?"

"Sir, if I may," Grady said, raising his hand.

"Go ahead, son."

Before the contractor could speak, gunfire erupted outside. "What in tarnation?" Vern grumbled, rising from the wooden kitchen chair that he'd seated himself at while water for his coffee boiled in the teapot.

Jake glanced through the window and saw tracer fire arcing out across the night from positions around the vehicles toward the road. "No, no, no..." he grumbled. "Tell your men to stop shooting, Sergeant! All it's gonna do is bring more of them here."

Turner rushed out of the house and Jake heard him bellowing orders to the soldiers outside. "You brought them here, Jake," Vern accused. "You make this right."

He nodded and ran out. There were probably twenty or so infected running awkwardly toward the farm from the south. Jake thought the convoy had come from the north, so the infected must have heard the sounds of the Strykers and come running from wherever they'd been.

"Sergeant Turner, I need your men to fix bayonets if they haven't already. Those things bleed and die the same way they did down in El Paso—except the cold up here makes them slower."

"Yes...sir," Sergeant Turner said before yelling for the squad leaders to have their soldiers attach their ancient M9 bayonets. "And stop firing your goddamned weapons!"

The infected were closing on the farm quickly. The cattle guard slowed their advance as several of the creatures with smaller feet fell when they slipped between the steel rails, snapping ankles and legs in their frenzy to reach the non-infected. They were quickly trampled to death as the others stumbled, kicked, and crawled across them to reach the other side of the driveway.

Jake watched as the dismounted soldiers, most of whom he assumed were infantrymen, pulled the 7-inch long blade from their issued sheath and affixed them to the lugs on the end of their rifles. The squad leaders lined up their men across the width of the driveway between the fences, while the motors of the Strykers' CROWS platforms whirred, the barrels of their .50 caliber machine guns slewing side to side in overwatch.

And then it was shear carnage as the infected reached the line. Men stabbed and slashed, jabbed and parried. The blades split the skin of the creatures like a hot knife through butter and the tide quickly began to turn as the infected died. Seeing the soldiers working in concert together and utilizing bayonet techniques that most of them probably hadn't attempted since basic training was glorious. It made Jake's heart swell with pride in the fact that they were completely destroying the infected without using firepower.

It was over in minutes. The infected, too dumb to defend themselves, lay in piles along the front of the line of soldiers. "There will be time for celebration later, ladies," Sergeant Turner said. "Make sure you finish the job so one of these bastards doesn't get back up when your back is turned," he continued, reminding them to ensure the infected were all dead by either slitting their throats, or destroying their brains. "And clean up the ones down by the road that didn't make it past that cattle guard."

Sergeant Turner began sending scout teams down the road in either direction to provide advanced warning and he had the remaining soldiers carry the bodies across the road to dump over the fence. Jake didn't bother to tell him about the back forty, the place where Vern had the bodies of the infected placed in piles inside his property's fence line.

Jake felt the heat from inside the house on his backside and he turned to see Sidney walking out. She stopped beside him and jutted her chin toward the Strykers and the flurry of activity from the soldiers in the driveway. "They came to take you back to El Paso."

Jake knew it was more of a statement than a question, but he chose to treat it that way. "Yeah. I'm not going though."

"What do you mean?"

"I have responsibilities here," he replied. "You guys are my family now and I'm not going to let the Army take that away from me."

He felt the intensity of her stare on the side of his face, so he turned. "What?"

"You mean Carmen and the kids?" she asked.

"Yes, Carmen. Katie and Sally, Old Vern, and you and Lincoln. Heck, even the new kid, Mark, is part of our group now. Every one of you is important to me and we need to stick together if we're going to survive this."

She ducked her chin. "You know, I was really pissed off at you for sending us back to the farm yesterday."

"Yeah, I figured."

"Turns out, we made a huge difference. We saw those Army trucks pass by on the highway. Not even three or four minutes later a bunch of infected followed along down the road. If we hadn't been there to put them out of their misery the group that wandered up here this morning might have been more than double the size."

Jake smiled, impressed with how far Sidney—and the two Campbell women—had come in their training and now, in their combat experience. "Good job, Sidney!" he beamed proudly. "See, I knew you were gonna do awesome."

His smile was infectious and she grinned back at him, locking eyes. "Thanks, kid. We had a good teacher." Jake stared back at her, once again feeling the electricity between them and the incredible attraction that he had toward her. She was *not* his type. If anything, she was the exact opposite of his type. She was rail-thin, covered in tattoos, had short hair, cursed like a sailor, and was fiercely independent, almost to a fault. Carmen, on the other hand, had the curves he liked, one small, discreet tattoo, a motherly nature, and she relied on him to protect her. True, her Puerto Rican temper was the stuff of legends, but when she calmed down she was *very* forgiving.

Goddammit. Say something! he berated himself, beginning to feel stupid for just staring at the woman. "Sidney, I—"

The crunching of several pairs of boots on the gravel made her smile falter and the moment passed. She looked toward the sounds and he followed suit reluctantly. It was Sergeant Turner and three others, all staff sergeants. "Sir, we need to talk."

15

FORT BLISS MAIN CANTONEMENT AREA
FEBRUARY 14TH

"What do you mean, 'They've gone offline'?" Major General Neel Bhagat asked, pounding his open hand on the table in front of him.

"It's what the S-6 told me this morning, sir," the general's aide, Lieutenant MacArthur replied. The commander was receiving his morning briefing from the Division Operations Officer and asked a seemingly offhanded comment about the platoon he sent north to bring in Lieutenant Murphy. "Get the Six in here right now. I want an update on that traitor."

Bhagat ground his teeth at the term "traitor" as the operations officer discussed the division's actions from the previous evening. He'd labeled Murphy as such, but in reality, it was him. *He* was the traitor to his nation. Maybe not in the classical sense, but the secrets he kept would certainly have him behind bars if it ever went to a military tribunal, which he was working hard to ensure that it wouldn't.

A lifetime of being treated as a second class citizen was the fuel that had sparked a friendship with a brilliant young biomedical engineer student named Aarav Sanjay. The two of them crossed paths when Neel was just a lieutenant stationed at Fort Benning, Georgia. Both being of Indian decent, they'd hit it off extremely well and formed a small cricket league in the backwards South that had continued up until the infection spread.

Over the years, their friendship had strengthened as Bhagat was promoted, more for the Army's equal opportunity program than for his stellar performance over deserving peers. The policy, meant to highlight the Army's strength through diversity, only made him angrier at how people of color were treated in America. He should have retired as a lieutenant colonel, not given a brigade command and then advanced to the general officer ranks.

He discussed his feelings openly with Aarav, both having similar life experiences. Whereas Neel knew that he was promoted beyond his abilities because of the color of his skin, Sanjay was held back because of his. Sure, he found semi-fame as a reoccurring guest on GNN anytime they needed a scientist to comment on biomedical matters, but it was not enough to quell the desire to truly make an impact and change the systematic suppression of minorities, here in the States and worldwide.

Aarav was literally brilliant and had begun to seek alternative means to further his research since he was limited in the US by policies, regulations, and of course, by religion. He was able to make contacts with some extremely influential people and began working with them. Bhagat never fully knew what his friend was working on, but he suspected that at some point Aarav was radicalized. Not in the religious sense, but in the sense that he no longer had any qualms with human experimentation. The perceived political pressure of being a close, personal friend of someone like that had been enough to cause Neel to sever ties with one of his closest friends since he'd become an adult.

That had been almost four years ago.

Neel was truly surprised when Sanjay arrived at Fort Bliss that fateful day in early April last year. He'd been evacuated to the desert safe haven from the CDC in Atlanta where he'd been working on a cure. That day was when Neel Bhagat's world fell out from underneath him.

In a private office call, he learned of Sanjay's dealings with an organization made up of Iranian and North Korean terrorists. His former friend told him that he'd initially worked with them because they gave him access to experiment without limitations, asking him for relatively benign results at first that became increasingly more directive, demanding certain outcomes. The terrorists had kidnapped Sanjay's family, which was a terrible revelation in itself, but what the scientist told him next still haunted him to this day. Aarav Sanjay created the disease that ravaged most of the world.

Sanjay was confident that if he could continue his work, he could find a cure or a vaccine, so against his better judgement, Neel had given him the use of an entire floor of the Beaumont Medical Center on post. Then the man was killed in some bizarre gunfight and he'd thought it nothing more than a tragic coincidence until he received the report from the platoon leader who'd responded to the hospital and helped to clean up the mess. That was the first time his path crossed with Lieutenant Jacob Murphy.

Sanjay had been experimenting on patients. The logs that Murphy's men collected and turned over to Bhagat personally showed that the doctor hadn't been trying to find a cure, he'd been actively trying to infect people who were immune, to make the vector stronger. He'd been duped completely by the man he once called his friend. Even so, Neel covered up his work, sealing off the medical center with all of its secrets inside.

Then, months later, as life in the besieged base settled into routine, Murphy had been the one to test the concept of raiding food warehouses within helicopter distance. Bhagat had even given the little shit a division coin.

Murphy appeared on his radar for a third time right about when the general received rock-solid intelligence of foreign invaders operating out west and sketchy reports of more in the Florida area. He was stymied as to what he could do. On the one hand, he commanded the largest remaining military force as far as he knew. On the other, they were trapped behind the walls of Fort Bliss hundreds of miles from anywhere even remotely strategically important for an invading military force. Telling his soldiers that the infected they fought against on a daily basis were not the real threat would have been pointless, so he sat on the information. In the meantime, the president had ordered him to reduce the refugee population to give them a few more months of food until the government could come up with options to fight the invaders. Neel saw an opportunity to start the uprising by punishing Murphy for dereliction of duty. It was a simple matter to blame the uprisings on the lieutenant's big mouth. It would have killed two birds with one stone, eliminating the lieutenant who knew about the hospital logs and reducing the number of mouths to feed.

But that had backfired. Now, Bhagat had a personal vendetta against the kid because he'd outsmarted him and escaped. To add insult to injury, there were freaking foreign troops operating freely on US soil and he could do nothing about it cooped up behind these walls.

He sneered, and then realized the room had gone silent. "Is everything alright, sir?" the operations officer asked.

"It's fine," he muttered. "Go ahead."

"Yes, sir. The third brigade…"

It was all the same to Bhagat. A unit killed a shitload of infected on the perimeter. The infected continually walked into the engagement area like they were completely oblivious of their impending demise. Then, their bodies were burned to ash by the engineers. *Whoop dee fucking doo*, he thought. It was the Vietnam body count all over again. He wanted answers about Kansas.

A harried-looking Hispanic officer burst into the room after a quick knock. It was the Division Signal Officer. "Ah, sir. I'm sorry I'm late," Major Calamante said.

"It's okay, Juan. You weren't invited." He waited until the major sat down before asking him about the operation in Kansas. "Lieutenant MacArthur said that you told him Colonel Albrecht's platoon in Kansas is off the radar. I want an update."

"Well, ah, sir…" Major Calamante began. Bhagat hated the whiney little son of a bitch, but with zero potential for replacement, he was stuck with him. He had an annoying way of pausing while he spoke that drove the general crazy. He was probably part of the so-called "No Captain Left Behind" program that promoted captains to major at a rate of 99 percent, regardless of ability, a few years back. All it did was dilute the talent pool, but the previous Global War on Terror had necessitated the promotions. "We tracked them via BFT to the last known location of Lieutenant Murphy's Stryker. Umm, they were onsite for about six hours. We, ah, we did not receive any communications from them."

"Wait," Bhagat growled. "When was this?"

"Yesterday morning, sir."

"Why wasn't I informed that they'd reached the objective?"

"Sir, I didn't know. This is the first I'm hearing about the deep fight," Colonel Tovey, the operations officer, replied.

Imbecile, Bhagat thought. While he felt that he'd been promoted beyond his abilities to the general officer rank, he sure as shit knew he could have done a better job than most of his current staff officers. He turned back to the signal officer, "Did you try to call them?"

"Yes, sir. Umm, my NCOIC did attempt to reach them, but didn't have any luck."

"Are they out of range?" Neel asked. "I thought satellite comms negated that."

"Ah... It's supposed to, sir. Umm, there must have been an issue with their radios, or umm, they could be jammed."

"Or they turned them off," the operations officer grumbled.

Neel shot him a withering look. "Continue."

"Ahh, okay. They left the farm after mid-day, then, umm, went northeast toward Kansas."

"All of them or just a few vehicles?"

"All five of the Strykers that are still operational went together." The signal officer paused, waiting for the general's follow-up question. When it didn't come, he said, "Umm, they headed toward a small regional airport in Liberal, Kansas, but stopped about half a mile away."

"*Liberal*? What kind of stupid name for a town is that?" The operations officer forced a laugh.

Major Calamante cleared his throat, pushing ahead to finish his update. "They were positioned outside the airport for around four hours. Then they went back to the highway and then drove in circles all over the side streets, often doubling back for no apparent reason—"

"Either navigating around blocked routes or they were trying to lose a mob of infected," Bhagat stated. It probably appeared confusing to the signal officer, but their actions were easy to envision for him, a lifelong Infantry officer.

A lightbulb illuminated behind the major's eyes. "Ahh. That makes sense, sir. Umm, after they *evaded* pursuit for about twenty or thirty minutes, their BFTs went offline and, umm, we haven't been able to reestablish comms with them."

"So, they're missing, just like Lieutenant Murphy?"

"Ah, yes, sir."

"Goddammit," Bhagat said, smacking the table with an open palm. "Is it a problem with our tracking system? Or—" He stopped, the idea settling into his stomach. "If a vehicle is destroyed, does the BFT continue to transmit?"

"Ah, well, umm, it depends, sir," Major Calamante replied. "If there is power to the system, it would, umm, transmit for a few hours. Umm, but if everything was completely destroyed in a catastrophic event, then, umm, it's possible that it would shut down."

Bhagat glanced at the operations officer. "Those UN jets could have accidentally engaged them."

"Accidentally, sir?" Colonel Tovey asked.

"*Accidentally*," Neel stated emphatically. "The president has authorized the UN to operate on US soil, so we will continue to allow them freedom of movement." He paused. "Not that we can do anything about it if they stay away from our immediate area."

"Umm, yes, sir," the major interjected. "If all five of them were hit with one large bomb that catastrophically destroyed their power source, then umm, yes. It could destroy all the BFTs."

"When will there be a satellite overhead to look at where they stopped transmitting?" Bhagat asked, pushing the problem of the UN troops to the side until he had time to figure out what to do about them.

"Ah… There should be one overhead in, ah, within the next two days. I don't have the scheduled flight path with me, sir."

For the thousandth time, Bhagat cursed that they didn't have tasking authority to reallocate the remaining satellites. The Air Force up at Cheyenne Mountain still ran the show with satellite employment and they made sure to keep a close watch on the intact Air Force bases, the Army had to analyze whatever feeds came from them.

He pressed his thin lips together. "Get me the info as soon as we're done here." Turning to the operations officer, he said, "I need some operating space outside the walls. The flow of infected has slowed significantly over the winter, so I want patrols going out into the city and the desert beyond. We need to begin expanding our perimeter."

Colonel Tovey blanched. "Sir, is that the best move, given the situation?"

"Do you mean the infected situation or the UN troops?"

"Both, sir," he replied.

"It's a *smart* move, Dave," Bhagat stated. "That uprising gave us a little breathing room with our capacity, but there are ten different FEMA camps set up in and around the city—probably with truckloads of food and supplies still sitting there. The reduction of infected in the area should allow us some breathing room. But more importantly, our intel about the UN troops is spotty, almost non-existent."

He paused and cleared his throat. "We know that the bulk of the forces are made up of North Korean troops, but there are reports that the Iranians have also volunteered to supply troops to the UN effort."

"Goddammit," someone at the end of the table muttered. He thought it was his intelligence officer.

"Problem, Mike?" Bhagat asked the Division Intelligence Officer, Major Michael Craig.

"Sir, that information was classified as TS and you're the only one who's been read on to the operations."

"Then read everyone on," the general ordered. "It's time we started trying to be proactive around here instead of being stuck in the defensive. Dave briefs me every day that the infected are thinning out due to the distances they have to travel across the desert to get to us, and now we have information that a third country—one that has wanted all of us dead for a few decades, by the way—has joined the UN relief effort. It's time the IC stops all this compartmentalized read-on bullshit and we begin making preparations to save all of our asses," he said, using the acronym for the collective Intelligence Community.

Someone cleared their throat and Bhagat turned to see his aide swallow noticeably. "Sir…"

"What is it, Freddy?"

"Colonel Albrecht called on the sat phone the day they were at the objective."

"He did?"

"Yes, sir. I'm sorry, I should have said something before."

"What did he say?"

"That they were at the objective and preparing to move up to the house. They saw several fast-movers overhead—non-US jets. I… I told him about the North Korean and Iranian UN troops, sir."

"Mother fucker!" the intelligence officer cursed. "Why don't we just tell the goddamned refugees while we're at it?"

"Can it, Mike," Bhagat barked, telling the intelligence officer to be quiet. "You weren't authorized to disclose that information, Lieutenant MacArthur."

"I'm sorry, sir. It just slipped out. You were on the phone with the president and Colonel Albrecht called with a real-time threat. That's why I told him to lay low and avoid the jets."

"Did you tell him to disconnect his Blue Force Trackers so the enemy couldn't track him through SIGINT?" Mike Craig asked.

"No, of course not, sir" Freddy Mac said. "I only told them about the threat and that they needed to keep a low profile until Division could sort things out about the UN troops. Then, I forgot about the call since so much else had happened," he added.

Yeah, right, Bhagat thought. His aide hadn't forgotten about the call, he'd been thinking about it the entire time. It just so happened that now was the perfect time to come clean and say it slipped his mind.

"Alright," Neel said. "Do you have any *more* information that you might have forgotten, Lieutenant MacArthur?"

"No, sir," the young officer replied, staring intently at the table in front of him.

"Okay. So what is our next step?" the general asked. "We are going to begin pushing the perimeter a little each day to give us some breathing room and maybe earn us some much-needed supplies, and we're going to engage the IC to see what we can find out about the North Koreans and the Iranians," he said, pointing toward the intelligence officer. "And, we're going to keep searching for Lieutenant Murphy. What am I missing?"

"Um, sir, one more thing."

He looked up at the signal officer. "Yes?"

"Sir, the, um, the *enemy* may be actively jamming our signals—that may be why we couldn't get radio comms with Colonel Albrecht's team."

"So what are we going to do about it?"

"Well, ah, I could send out the Division EW teams, sir. They could attempt to counter the enemy jamming, but I'm not sure what it will do if the BFTs were turned off by the colonel and his men or if they were destroyed."

"Do it. Send your men wherever they need to go and let's reestablish comms with that element."

"Okay, sir."

"Good. What else?"

He waited for his pared down staff to answer. When no one did, he pushed back from the table and stood. "Okay, everyone has their marching orders. Let's get to work."

16

NEAR LIBERAL, KANSAS
FEBRUARY 17TH

Sidney cupped her breast and shook it slightly as the crying baby refused to suckle. "Come on, Lincoln. Eat," she pleaded. He refused her milk and she was worried about him.

A soft knock on her door made her look up. "Who is it?" she asked, elevating her voice to be heard over the baby's cries and the low growl emanating from Rick James' throat.

"Carmen. Can I come in?"

"Yeah, of course. Come in," she called over her son's cries.

"Still not taking to the breast?" Carmen asked. She wore a robe, secured at the waist with a long belt that boasted a holstered pistol on her hip.

Sidney shook her head. "No. Ever since he took a bottle that first time, it's like he's done with the boob."

Carmen chuckled softly and closed the door. "My son was the same way. He never took to breastfeeding and would only drink from a bottle." She gestured toward the small stack of formula in the corner. "Good thing Jake was able to get all that formula, huh?"

Sidney grunted. "He'd still be stuck in there if it weren't for me and Katie."

"And don't you ever let him forget it," Carmen said. "He gets all high and mighty sometimes. It must be that West Point education. It's good to bring him back down to earth every once in a while."

"So…" Sidney let the word hang in the air. It'd been three days since Jake returned from town with a whole bunch of Strykers and a bunch of soldiers. In that time, the soldiers had all voted—*voted!*—to go AWOL after learning they were potentially being used as pawns in a foreign takeover. Whether the general down in Fort Bliss was actually involved or not was up for debate since all they had was a dead man's assertions that he'd kept information about the foreigners secret from the rest of the Army.

The soldiers had decided to remain a military unit, loyal to the United States, but not the corrupt leaders that had gotten them into the predicament. They'd disconnected the tracking systems from the vehicles, which meant they had to rely on old-fashioned maps to go wherever they were headed, which also meant there were a lot of map reading classes in the evening around the farmhouse as the older soldiers taught the younger generation how to navigate without GPS.

Something else odd had happened, the bearded guy, Grady, had somehow become heavily involved in the platoon's leadership. He'd been a Special Forces operator a long time ago and was working as a CIA contractor when everything went down. Apparently, he was pretty high up in the organization and had seen a lot of crazy stuff. His self-confessed lack of memories for the past year was a red flag for Sidney and she avoided him whenever she could. He claimed that he had snatches of memories and visions of doctors doing things to him, but he had no clue where the time had gone.

Yeah right. The dude was hiding something. She was sure of it.

Grady's companion, or prisoner—or whatever Taavi was—seemed content to remain with the soldiers. He didn't speak any English whatsoever, so who knew what was going through the guy's mind. He'd probably cut everyone's throat the moment he got the opportunity.

"So," Carmen said. "I think he's going to go with them."

"Really?" Sidney asked in disbelief. "He was talking about—Hold on. Can you hold Lincoln while I make him a bottle?"

Carmen smiled and pulled a bottle from the pocket of her robe. "I heard him fussing, so I figured that even if he took the breast, he'd need a top off."

"You are Super Mom," Sidney grinned. "How do you do it?" She lifted her bra up into place, ensuring the thick pad was over her nipple before she dropped her shirt and reached for the bottle.

"It was a lot of trial and error," Carmen admitted. "I still screw up every day though. My kids are just old enough that my mistakes usually aren't that big of a deal."

Once Lincoln was feeding, Sidney returned to their earlier conversation. "So, back to what I was saying. A couple of days ago Jake was saying he wouldn't leave with the soldiers if they tried to take him back. But now he's going with them on some stupid mission?"

Carmen nodded. "Yeah. Grady has convinced him that if they can make it back to DC, or New York if DC is overrun like you say it is, then they might be able to find a cure for this thing."

Another soft knock at the door made her look up in annoyance. "Who is it?"

It was Jake this time. "Sorry to bother you. I just heard the little guy crying."

"Yeah. Come on in," Sidney said. He opened the door and stepped inside the room, closing the door behind himself. He nodded toward Carmen nervously.

Sidney stood and gestured to the chair. "You wanna hold him and feed him?"

"I, ah… No, not really."

"Don't be such a pussy," Carmen said. "Hold the baby."

Jake relented and sat in the chair Sidney had occupied. She knelt over him, taking in his musky odor as she handed him the baby. She crinkled her nose. "You need a shower."

"I washed my hands," he replied. "Haven't had time to get cleaned up yet."

Sidney handed him the bottle. "Just hold it there, he'll suck on it."

"Do I burp him or whatever?"

"In a little bit." She sat on the bed and glanced at Carmen leaning against the wall. She wore a slight smile as she watched Jake feeding the baby. "Carmen just told me that you've decided to leave with Grady."

"I kind of figured that's what you two were talking about when Miguel said Carmen was in here."

"So, was all that stuff the other night about us being a family just bullshit?" Sidney asked, addressing the elephant in the room.

"What? No!"

"Keep your voice down," Sidney hissed, pointing at Lincoln. He was already beginning to drift off, content to let the warm formula dribble down his cheek and pool along his neckline.

"No," Jake repeated, quietly this time. "It wasn't bullshit. But that Iranian dude, and possibly Grady as well, has been inoculated against the infection. They—"

"How does he know that?"

"Let's just say that Grady's a different kind of cat. I'm not sure if he's all there anymore. They experimented on him like crazy."

"They who?"

"He doesn't know. He remembers that they were foreign with dark hair, but that's about it."

"Okay, so what do you mean that he's not all there?" Sidney asked, concerned that the man had been hanging around the farm.

"He's convinced that he's immune, first of all. He has several oval scars on his forearms and one peeking out from his beard that he says were absolutely not there before his team went to Brazil."

Sidney nodded her head. "We knew that there were some people who were immune. We found that out while we were still at Fort Bliss. Even if he is immune, what does that have to do with going to New York?"

"Funny, it turns out that being immune doesn't do much good if you get ripped to shreds by the infected. Ask all the Iranian soldiers back at the airport."

"Makes sense. If a bunch of them get riled up and attack movement, then keep attacking when their infection doesn't spread, then you'll end up getting killed. But why does he think those soldiers were immune?"

Jake nodded his head in agreement. "Taavi showed him through gestures and drawing pictures and shit that he's gotten vaccinated against the virus."

"That must have been an excruciating three hour conversation," Sidney deadpanned, remembering her time in the Peace Corps when she was deployed to both Senegal and to Bangladesh and didn't speak the language in either country.

"So you know what that crazy fucker did last night when most of us were asleep?"

"Who? Grady or Taavi?"

"Yeah, your story is very confusing, *mi amor*," Carmen said.

"Grady," Jake answered. "He's immune—that's how he ended up getting captured when his team was all killed. He said his captors did all sorts of experiments on him and his memory is coming back in pieces and parts. One of the things he remembers is them having infected come into his cell. He couldn't remember why, but had an idea and went out last night into town. Then the crazy fucker made a bunch of noise to call the infected to him. Now, do you see why I say that he's kind of fucked in the head?"

Sidney leaned forward. She'd seen Grady throughout the day and he seemed unhurt. "What happened?"

"The infected came running to where he was—a couple hundred of them according to him. But they stopped about five feet from him and wouldn't get any closer. They shifted away and wouldn't let him get closer to *them*. When he was satisfied with his little experiment, he started walking and they parted away from him. He just walked back here and they didn't follow him. Ain't that some shit?"

Sidney scoffed. "And you believed him? Maybe you're the one who's crazy."

Jake shrugged. "I mean, it makes sense, in a fucked up way, doesn't it? How are the Iranians or the North Koreans, or whoever, supposed to take and keep the US if they have to fight the infected just like we do? Why not come up with some type of, I don't know, repellent or some shit, that will give them a way to have freedom of movement without worry of constant attack?"

"Like a mosquito repellant?" Carmen asked. "That's just stupid, *mijo*."

"Kind of, but not the same," he answered, ignoring the jab. "They injected him with all sorts of shit. He has an entire *year* missing. What if they came up with something that works better than a vaccine? He thinks that's what they did to him and they were trying to test it in the field, with the American infected when the soldiers were attacked. I didn't believe him, so I made him show me."

"And?" Sidney asked.

"It worked. We went out to the highway this morning. He walked out into the middle of a small group of them moving up the road and they avoided him. Came directly at me."

"Okay, so it works, but why are you guys going to New York?" Sidney pressed. "Why not go to Fort Bliss where the CDC relocated to? I know they were taking people who they thought were immune over to the hospital and testing their blood and stuff."

Jake shook his head. "We don't know the status of General Bhagat. He's keeping the fact that foreign militaries are operating on US soil a secret from everyone there. What else is the guy hiding?"

Sidney shrugged and decided to play devil's advocate. "Or, he could just be trying to influence what he can and knows that telling his soldiers about the invaders won't do anything but make them more worried since they're stuck on that base defending against all the infected."

"You and I both know that at this point the infected down there can be handled by a couple of companies of soldiers as long as they have ammo. I think there may be more of them up here, surviving off the old corn harvest, than there are down in the desert around El Paso now."

"Maybe. But I find it hard to believe that a guy in his position is behind a plan to overthrow the United States," Sidney countered.

"He sure as hell had no problems letting a few hundred thousand people kill themselves, and then blaming me for it," Jake grunted, rocking slightly as Lincoln stirred from his outburst.

"I'm not defending him," Sidney replied. "But I'm also not walking in his shoes. He has millions of people to care for and not enough resources to do it. If cutting out some of those mouths to feed could prolong the life of the rest?" Her voice inflection turned the statement into a question. They'd never have the answer for it, though.

"Regardless," Jake said, "Grady is planning to go to DC to his company's offices to try to raise some of his old contacts. If that doesn't work, we'll go into New York."

"Is everyone going?" Carmen asked.

Jake nodded. "Most of them. We have three soldiers who want to stay here and help Vern if he'll have them."

"Let me guess," Sidney scoffed. "Two of them are those guys who've been following Katie and Sally around like little puppy dogs."

"Yeah, plus one of the medics, Specialist Weir. He had a close call when they were at the Cullen farm and says he's done traveling the country."

"Are they just gonna sit around and do nothing?" Sidney asked.

"No. They're gonna do whatever Vern needs them to do. But they're also gonna help pull security around the farm while I'm gone."

"*Ahem*," Carmen said, making an effort to clear her throat and get their attention. "Why are *you* going, Jake? Why can't the others go and we stay here, like we have been?"

Jake nodded. "I was waiting for you to ask that."

"Well?" she pressed.

"I need to go. I can't... It seems stupid to you guys, I'm sure," Jake said. "I know that I have a good thing going here, and I'm still planning to leave. I realized something the other night when I was headed toward the airport. I haven't done all that I can in our fight. I want to find a cure for this so your kids—so Lincoln—can grow up and not face death at every turn. This is an opportunity to do that."

"Okay, I understand that part of it," Carmen said. "Why you? Why are you leaving us?"

"These are *my* soldiers," Jake said. "Well, about a third of them at least. I abandoned them once, and it was the hardest decision of my life. I'm not going to do that to them again."

"So, you're abandoning your new family because you're guilty?" Carmen asked.

Sidney saw the flash of anger in her friend's eyes and she was leaning forward with her hands clenched at her sides. She'd held it in until she got the reason for Jake's decision to leave, but the fiery Puerto Rican was about to lose her shit. "Carmen, please," she said. "The baby's sleeping."

Carmen nodded and crossed her arms across her chest. "Well?" she demanded quietly, aware of the baby's slumber.

"It's my duty, Carmen. I *have* to go."

"No you don't, *pendejo*. You *want* to go. You've abandoned me before. You left me in that camp for months. Now, when we come here, you keep going into town for diapers and formula for the baby." She glanced up at Sidney. "It's not your fault, *mamma*, you are amazing and so strong for bringing a baby into this world. But I can't deal with a man who wants to leave me at every opportunity he gets."

"Carmen, that's not what I'm doing. This is my duty."

She chopped her hand across the air to silence him. "That's it. I'm done. I can't do this anymore." Carmen stopped and turned into the hallway.

"Carmen, wait," Jake called softly.

She turned back. "Don't bother coming to *my* room tonight, Jake. I'm done with the bullshit, okay?"

"Carmen?" She was gone. He stared at the empty doorway for a moment before sighing. "Well, that didn't go like I thought," he muttered, looking down at Lincoln.

"What did you expect, Jake? Did you think she would cheer for you to go off and fight the war while she got left alone here, where, oh by the way, it's not safe from the infected—and maybe from the Iranians or whatever now too?"

He nodded sullenly. "I just think I've gotta do this. I can't explain it."

Sidney smiled. "I think I understand. It's a calling."

"Something like that," he muttered.

She leaned over and patted his knee. "Just come back to us, okay? We're all trying to make the best of things here. Those soldiers who are staying should help to keep the infected away, but we like *you*. Carmen needs you. She may not say it, but having you here for her and the kids is extremely important."

"*Hmpf*," he grunted. "She sure has a funny way of showing it."

"You've got a lot to learn about women, Jake."

"You don't know anything about my past or what I know about women," he replied, indignantly.

"I don't need to know the specifics." She grinned mischievously, letting her feelings surface for a brief moment as she arched an eyebrow. "Maybe one day you can show me what you know." She liked Jake, but immediately felt guilty for betraying Carmen's trust. She had to put a stop to where her body was urging her to go.

"I—"

"Here, give me Lincoln and go to bed," Sidney ordered. "You need your sleep before you leave."

She leaned over and lifted the baby gently from him, once again taking in the strong odor of a hard day's work that emanated from Jake. It was no longer an unpleasant smell to her like it would have been a year ago. Now it felt…right.

She laid the baby on the bed. When she turned back, she was surprised to find Jake standing close behind her. "Sidney, what do you want from me?"

Sidney pushed lightly against his chest, backing him up into the rocking chair. "I want you to go on your mission to save the world. Then come back to us here in Kansas."

"No, I mean—"

She sighed. "I know what you mean, Jake. It's complicated right now, okay? You have Carmen, and—"

"Not anymore, apparently."

"She just needs time," Sidney countered. "You have Carmen, and her kids look up to you. I'm still dealing with some feelings from Lincoln's father's death." She took a tentative step forward and placed her hands on his hips. "Maybe things will be different when you get back. Maybe not. I don't know, but for right now, we can only be friends."

He frowned and then she noticed the twitch at the corners of his mouth. "No," she said. "And not friends with benefits. Just friends. Okay?"

He nodded and she pushed against his hipbones. "Now, go on. Get to bed—or wherever you're gonna sleep tonight. You've got a long trip ahead of you and it isn't going to be easy avoiding the infected on the ground and the jets overhead."

"Are you gonna see us off in the morning?"

"It depends on what time, and what the little guy is doing," she replied truthfully.

"Alright. Well, if I don't see you tomorrow morning…"

"Goodnight, Jake. I'll see you later." Another soft push, this time to his back, and she followed him to the door. She shut it behind him and wondered what the heck she'd gotten herself into.

If Carmen wanted to re-stake any type of claim on Jake when he returned, then she was the first one out of the mix. She certainly didn't need to be involved in some crazy post-apocalyptic love triangle. That wasn't fair to any of them, but most importantly, it wasn't fair for Carmen's kids. She wasn't that type of person and she'd be furious if Lincoln's emotions were jerked around like that.

That final thought solidified it for her. She would let Jake be and not pursue him if he actually did return from New York. Of course, the odds of him traveling across country, then back, were slim to none.

"Oh, Jake," she whispered at the door. "Why are you such a fool?"

17

NEAR LIBERAL, KANSAS
FEBRUARY 20TH

"Oh, come on, Sidney," Vern grumbled. "We're doing just fine. You don't need to do this."

She shook her head emphatically. "We got lucky yesterday, Vern. And you know it. All it would have taken was for Katie to have not looked out the window when she did and..." Sidney let the statement remain unfinished.

Everyone had been exhausted after a long day of repairing the barbed wire that the Strykers had broken when they pulled out of the farm a few days ago. What Vern had thought would be an easy job turned into a nightmare of physical labor as three of the four strands had slipped off their posts for hundreds of feet. In the past, the old farmer would have used his tractor to stretch the wire and secure it to the posts, but there was no more unleaded gasoline for the tractor. So, the men had to pull the wire taut by hand while Sally and Sidney reused the bent and sometimes broken fasteners to lash the wire to the posts. It was tough work and they decided to trade security for an extra set of hands, pulling the lookout down from the roof to help.

As they were finishing their work near dusk, a group of seventeen infected stumbled up the farm's driveway. To a man—and woman—everyone had been focused on repairing the fence line and none of them saw the infected. The creatures hadn't seen the repair crew and didn't scream to announce their presence as they closed in on the unsuspecting party.

In the farmhouse, Katie and Carmen were making dinner for the tired crew. Katie happened to look through the kitchen window and saw the infected coming toward them. She'd grabbed her rifle and ran out onto the front porch, firing as she went. It got the attention of the infected, so they turned toward her. The soldiers barely averted a disaster as they sprinted from the fence detail and intercepted the creatures before they reached the house.

And baby Lincoln.

"But she *did* look out the window," Vern replied. "We made a mistake. Should have never pulled Caleb out of the crow's nest. Won't happen again."

"Caleb," she scoffed. "The only reason that kid stayed behind was so he could try to get in your granddaughters' pants."

"Woo wee," Vern whistled. "Who pissed in your Cheerios this morning, missy? I'm supposed to be the grumpy old man on the farm. It's my job to defend those girls' honor. Not yours."

She frowned. He was right. Sidney had never been the cheery, laugh at everything ditz that a lot of her friends growing up were, but she was *generally* optimistic. Since the fall of the old world, she'd become increasingly less so. "You're right, you are a grumpy old man," she said, repeating the words he'd just spoken. "I think… I think I'm freaked out about the baby. Lincoln could have been killed yesterday — not that you guys aren't important, but well, you know."

He nodded solemnly. "Yes, ma'am. I know exactly what you mean. You're that boy's mother and he means more to you than life itself. You'd give your own life to save him — and the Good Lord wouldn't fault you one bit for it neither."

Vern sighed and slapped his hands down onto the legs of his dirty overalls. "But, like I said, we made a mistake. *I* made a mistake. I chose to disregard our security in exchange for time. I learned that lesson almost fifty years ago in Vietnam when eight of my buddies were killed while they were filling sandbags, and here I went and forgot all about that. It won't happen again, Miss Sidney."

"I appreciate that, Vern. I really do. But I don't think the security plan that you worked out with Jake is for the best anymore, and yesterday proves it. Those Iranian airplanes and the Army Strykers running all over the place have got the infected in the area all worked up. Leaving the main road open in the hopes that a government vehicle will come along to save the day isn't cutting it anymore. The infected can bum-rush the wire and be on us in a couple of minutes."

"So you want to close the road?" Vern asked.

"Yeah. I want to put out some of that concertina wire that Jake left. Maybe a few hundred feet down on each way where the lookout can see the infected before they're right on top of us. I mean, we know that your regular barbed wire fence is somewhat of a deterrent when they're just wandering around. We've watched them bounce off of it and head off in a different direction; they'll probably do the same with the wire."

Vern held up two fingers. "I've got two problems with your idea. One, it's concertina wire, not barbed wire. That stuff is designed to make an enemy get all tangled up, so they probably won't just bounce off like they do on the fences."

"It's designed to get tangled in *clothes*," she amended his statement. "Most of the clothing has rotted away from them at this point."

"Okay," he conceded. "Maybe we could at least shoot them while they're at the concertina like we do the ones that do end up getting tangled in the barbed wire."

"Jake always said that being able to have standoff distance was the best defense against the infected."

"What are y'all talking about?" a young male voice asked through a stifled yawn.

"Good morning, Mark," Sidney greeted the boy.

"We're just talking about beefing up our security a little bit," Vern answered his question.

"I heard you say something about standoff distance—may I?" he asked, pointing to the coffee pot.

"Of course, son," Vern said, pulling the toothpick that he'd been chewing on from his mouth. He pointed at the coffee pot with it before cramming the little piece of wood back between his teeth. "You don't have to ask."

"That's not how I was raised, sir," Mark said. "Thank you." He poured himself a cup of black coffee and sat at the table across from Sidney.

"You want any milk?" she asked, wrinkling her nose at the dark liquid.

"No, thank you. This is how my mom drank it and I just developed a taste for it." He took a sip and smiled dreamily. "Hot, brewed coffee is so much better than the cold instant stuff I used to make at the grocery store."

Sidney smiled at the way he relished the simplicity of a warm cup of coffee. She hoped that Lincoln would turn out to be like Mark. He was a resilient boy, who'd lived alone with the horrors of the infected for almost a year. He knew a thing or two about surviving. "You were gonna say something about the standoff distance idea?"

"*Hmm?*" He opened his eyes slowly. "Oh yeah. I made a ring of shopping carts to act as a barrier at the grocery store. It gave me room to rush out, kill any of the freaks—uh, I mean any infected. Jake said the design was a good use of standoff distance."

Sidney nodded politely. He wasn't as helpful as she'd hoped. "That's what I want to do here too," she said. "I want to close off the road to give us that distance to figure out what to do before they're right on top of us and we're forced to make a bad decision."

Mark sipped the coffee again. "I don't know why that road is open," he said. "Seems like it's just inviting a disaster. My mom always used to say that when there was an obvious fix to a problem, but you went ahead and left the problem alone. Most times a little problem just got bigger and bigger until it exploded."

Sidney glanced at Vern and raised an eyebrow. Maybe the kid was going to be helpful after all.

"Okay, okay," Vern agreed. "You're right." He rubbed his pants legs again. "Besides those Cullen brothers and the Army trucks that Jake brought back with him, I haven't seen anyone on that road in nine or ten months. Just been holding out hope like the stubborn old man I am."

"Stubborn *and* grumpy old man," Sidney teased, eliciting a chuckle from Mark. "You had two points earlier. The first one was about the infected getting tangled in the wire so we'd have to deal with every one of them instead of only a few like we do with the fences. What was your other concern?"

"Darn it, Sidney. What *if* someone comes along down that road? What if the Army shows up or if there was someone running for their life from a mob of those things. That concertina will wrap around a car's axle and put a stop to it permanently."

"What if it stops the Iranians?" Mark offered.

Sidney grinned again. The kid *was* helping her argument. Giving them some time to hide from the Iranians was a huge reason to close off the road, even if she hadn't thought about it in those terms. "We'll put up signs warning people to stop—in *English*."

"And Spanish," Mark cut in. "Used to be lots of laborers here before the collapse."

"And Spanish," she agreed. "I doubt the average Iranian could read either of them. Taavi sure didn't seem capable of it."

"Mark my words, there's something off about that guy," Vern grumbled. "I think he's a lot smarter than he's letting on."

"Well, he's gone for now, but you're actually reinforcing my point. If Taavi were to tell his fellow Iranians where we are, that wire could give us enough time to get everyone down into the cellar and close it up." Vern had a trap door disguised as regular wood flooring underneath the kitchen table below her feet. The secret entrance led to a cellar under his house that he'd spent years digging out carefully by hand in the hard Kansas dirt.

"I guess that would be a good thing."

"Okay, it's settled. I'll take the wire to the road and set it up with the help of those three soldiers. They should know how to do it."

Vern laughed. "With as much fuss as those three put up for helping with the barbed wire, good luck. They sure don't make infantrymen like they used to."

"They're not infantry," Mark stated.

"What?" both Sidney and Vern asked at the same time.

"Yeah. I was talking to them the other day when Jake left. I'd thought about joining the Army after high school, so we were just hanging out. They taught me how to play Spades. Anyways, I mentioned that I wanted to go infantry and they were like, 'No, man, you gotta get the Army to teach you a skill so you can get a good job after you get out.' Of course, everyone laughed because there aren't any jobs anymore."

Sidney rolled her wrist. "Skip all of that until you get to the part where Jake didn't leave us with soldiers who actually know how to fight."

"Well, Caleb Stout is personnel, does like pay and paperwork. Rob is a medic. And Brown is a supply clerk. They all know how to fight, they had to go through Basic Training, but that's not what their regular job is in the Army."

"Son of a—"

"Watch your mouth, girl," Vern cautioned.

"Bitch," Sidney continued. She may have been a guest in Vern's home, but there were some times when a curse word was absolutely appropriate and now was one of those times. "Do they even know how to use the scoped rifle up there in the crow's nest?"

Vern grunted around the toothpick. "*Hmpf.* I hadn't thought to ask about that. I figured soldiers riding around the country in combat vehicles would be infantrymen or tankers. Never thought we'd send out support personnel to do the fighting."

"I know why the Army did that too," Mark said.

"Goodness, son. How much information did you pump them boys for?"

Mark shrugged. "There's no TV, no video games, no radio, only a few books… There wasn't anything else to do except talk." He took a long sip of coffee, tipping the mug up, emptying it. "Their unit—I can't remember which one they said—got wiped out in a riot when a bunch of refugees went crazy."

"That's probably the uprisings that Sergeant Turner told us about when they first got here," Sidney said.

"Yeah, so everyone who was alive and healthy enough to fight got sent up here to arrest Jake for starting the riot."

"And then they all decided to cut their losses after Jake told them the truth about what was happening outside that base."

Sidney nodded in agreement with Vern. "Seems like we got the short end of the stick here."

"Did Jake know they weren't infantrymen?" Vern asked her.

"He said that Specialist Weir was a medic, but never mentioned anything about the other two."

Vern frowned. "Well, nothing we can do about it now. My granddaughters aren't infantrymen, but they've learned and proven that they can be useful in a fight. We'll just have to hope that these boys can do the same."

Sidney groaned audibly as she pushed herself to her feet. Her body was still not at a hundred percent after her pregnancy. "You're right, Vern," she said. "Time for those three to get some OJT."

"On the job training?" Mark asked.

"That's right," Sidney agreed. "We used to train all of our Peace Corps volunteers after they arrived in country. We called it OJT and they had to pick things up fast or risk getting left behind."

"What are you going to train them in?" Mark asked, seemingly interested.

"Not me," she laughed, having decided the best way to tackle their newfound problem with a legitimate—and funny—solution. "Vern was an NCO in the Army. *He* can train them to be infantrymen and how to defend our perimeter."

"Now wait a darn minute—"

"Meanwhile," Sidney said, cutting him off. "You and I will go put that wire in place."

"Sidney—" Vern grumbled.

"Vern," she replied impishly. "I'll need two pairs of gloves, your wheel barrow, and some stakes to secure the ends."

"And the stop signs," Mark added.

"Yes, of course. And some spray paint or regular paint." She pretended to bounce on her feet and clapped lightly, mindful of Lincoln sleeping upstairs. "This will be fun!"

Vern threw the toothpick from his mouth toward the trashcan and missed. "This is the last cotton-pickin' thing I want to be doing."

Sidney leaned down and gave him a peck on the cheek, making the old man blush. "Oh, relax. You'll do great!"

18

CAPE GIRARDEAU, MISSOURI
FEBRUARY 20TH

Taavi yawned expansively as he stood shivering in the hatch at the back of the Stryker vehicle. He'd grown bored of staring at the wall inside the vehicle, so he'd manipulated the latch until it clicked back and he was able to heave the hatch open. The countryside looked much the same as it had when they'd stopped several hours ago, and the same as the day before, and before that as well. Brown, drab grass grew alongside a paved road lined with skeletal trees.

He knew it was winter here, they had the same seasons in his country, but he'd always imagined America to be lush, green, and fertile year round. He shivered once more, pulling the blanket he'd been given on their first night closer. His lengthy assignment in the jungle highlands had softened his ability to adapt rapidly to the environment as he'd done as a child in Iran.

They'd been traveling for days. Honestly, he'd lost count of how long they'd been on the road. In fact, the passing of time had become a blur for him after that dog, the Facilitator, had murdered his family when the labs and the facility that he'd worked at for so long was overrun by the Cursed. He'd been in and out of bouts of depression, thinking about what they'd done to his beautiful children and what those animals were doing to his wife.

It made his stomach flip as he stared at the fields beyond the road. Every so often, one of the Cursed would appear and begin to run after the convoy. *Pfft, convoy!* he laughed. This little procession of vehicles would not be able to withstand the Cursed, just as his men in Brazil had failed, and the poorly armed scientists and pilots had failed at the airport after they'd landed and discovered that the Air Force had ironically just established that location the previous day as a refueling site for their jets.

The Cursed were unstoppable.

He saw that now. They'd been foolish to believe that they could control them once their scourge was unleashed upon the world. Allah had guided the scientists' hands to create the perfect killing machine. For the first time in his life, he hesitated upon praising Him. Few were immune, and those who were rarely lived long in the infested areas. Was this disease the next great extinction cycle? The difference was that Allah had used his followers to develop it instead of doing it himself.

Of course, you idiot! he berated himself. Before the arrival of the Cursed, the Earth's population was upwards of eight billion people. Within a few years, the vast majority of the infected will have starved to death, leaving only the strongest among them, and God's chosen people—plus those backwater rubes, the Koreans. He'd never agreed with the plan to wipe out the non-believers and believers alike. He thought there were other, more traditional ways to bring about the global peace promised by the Prophet Mohammed. But, the mass murder of billions must have been Allah's will, otherwise, why would He have allowed it to happen?

Shaikh gripped the rough metal of the Stryker's hatch as they hit a small bump and over the headset he wore, he heard Grady Harper say, *"Sorry back there, Taavi.*" The soldier did not know that he could speak English, that he'd been educated in the UK prior to returning to Iran to enter the Army's officer corps. He'd kept all of it secret, pretending to be just a dumb foot soldier, and yet, the men and women had treated him fairly. Sure, every once in a while, someone said something insulting to his homeland, but it was never directed at *him*. The soldiers seemed to be genuinely concerned for his well-being. They'd accepted him into their ranks after he showed them that he was willing to jump in and help with tasks for preparing each night's bivouac site.

He considered telling them the truth of his origins often, then disregarded the idea each time his gaze met Harper's. The man had endured an entire year of testing at the facility, so Shaikh knew that his mind was likely addled, but every so often there was a spark of recognition in those eyes. Shaikh hadn't visited the labs or the experiment rooms very often, choosing to send his lackeys instead. He *had* walked through the cells on a daily basis, though. He was sure that Harper had seen him often, even if he was recovering from whatever new hell the scientists had visited on him.

The radio crackled to life once more as the lieutenant, Jake, called out to all of the vehicles. *"Alright. The map says there's another bridge up ahead."*

Shaikh looked into the distance. He could see the bridge, although it wasn't the first time they'd tried to cross the massive river and been denied due to a collapsed bridge. Jake said the US Air Force had bombed the bigger bridges in the cities to try and stop the spread of the disease. Little did they know that the council had planted agents at multiple key locations across the country, including New York where they were headed, so destroying the bridges did no good. Upon learning that the city was safe, he wondered what happened to that agent and how New York was spared. He would never learn the answer to the mystery, of course, but it was an interesting mystery.

In addition to the thoughts of where the New York carrier was lost, Shaikh wondered what the true nature of that lab was. He'd been told they were working on a vaccine to ensure that Allah's chosen people did not contract the disease—which meant Iranians because other Muslim nations had fallen to the Cursed, and somehow, their Korean counterparts.

The scientists were obviously working with people who were immune as seeking them out and bringing them to "safety" had been one of his force's key roles in addition to facility security. But what he'd seen the sole surviving patient do was remarkable. He'd watched how the Cursed had avoided contact with the man, even though he was strapped to a gurney and would have been easy prey. His own sense of self-preservation had been the sole reason he freed Harper.

And now, here he was, gallivanting around America with an armed group of soldiers who thought he was a simpleton, on the way to New York with Harper. They weren't even sure what they were going to do once they got there, just that there had been universities with doctors and scientists in the city before it was isolated. The Americans were hoping that was still the case.

Regardless, he didn't trust the look in that old man's eyes back at the farm, so he'd thrown in with this lot. They seemed good enough—for heathens— and were intent on seeking out a cure, which is what he thought the scientists at the facility were doing anyways. So until they did something that violated God's will, he would stay with them and help in whatever way he could, unless, of course, a way opened before him to return to Iran so he could kill the Facilitator.

He watched the bridge nearing and then it disappeared behind trees and buildings as they came up to a town. Shaikh knew from experience that the outskirts of most of the American towns that they'd driven through were riddled with the vacant shells of restaurants and shopping centers, all utilitarian in nature. It was usually once they made it to the downtown areas where the homes and businesses began to resemble what he'd grown to think of as iconic American living. The town they headed toward now, Cape-something, was much the same.

There'd been considerably less of the Cursed in the area than there had been at other points of their trip, but their luck changed when they exited the main highway that they'd followed south and turned east onto another road. The infected choked the highway, with more streaming in from the sides.

The call over the radio came to "button down the hatches" which Taavi had learned meant to close the hatch and lock it. He reached across the hull and grabbed the first of the doors. As he began to lift the heavy metal up, the vehicle shuddered, throwing him forward as it lost considerable speed. The hatch slipped from his grasp, and his fingernails caught against the edge as an unknown number of kilos slammed the door back into place.

Taavi cried out in pain. His hand felt like it was on fire. All around him, the screams of the Cursed were answered by the deep staccato of the Strykers' heavy machine guns.

"Get that hatch closed, Taavi!" Harper yelled over the radio. He was up front in the gunner's seat operating the machine gun.

Shaikh ignored the fire in his hand. He had to get the door closed or the Cursed could tear him from the vehicle and swarm the inside. Biting his lip to take his mind from the pain, he attempted to lift the hatch once more, but it wouldn't budge. He strained against it, but the damn thing wouldn't move. *What is happening?* he wondered.

He tried again, the hatch remained unmoving. Had he broken it somehow? The machine gun on his truck stopped firing as the big vehicle continued to drive forward. The Cursed streamed from the side of the roadway toward the Stryker. He scrambled for the pistol at his waist, abandoning his efforts to close the damned hatch.

The pistol pulled free of its holster. Armies all over the world used the standard 9-millimeter gun that he'd been given for protection, so he was familiar with it. His training took over. He'd sent thousands of pistol rounds downrange during his time in the Army. This was just like any other day at the range.

Except he only had two spare magazines, forty-five rounds in total.

He aimed at the nearest of the animals rushing toward the truck. It was less than ten meters away, and there were a hundred more beyond that one. He fired once, hitting the Cursed center mass and chastised himself as the thing kept coming. They were akin to a criminal high on *shishe*, a methamphetamine that had recently become popular in his country. Anything less than a killing blow would be ignored until their body shut down. He had to aim for their head.

Shaikh fired again, watching in satisfaction as the head snapped back and the creature tumbled forward, its momentum carrying it to within a meter of the truck. He aimed at another when he was slapped roughly on the calf.

"Move!" a muffled voice shouted, barely audible over the headset he wore.

He looked down into Harper's bearded face. He understood the man, but he didn't have time to comply. The Cursed were closing in. As he fired, he wondered why the operator had abandoned his machine gun to come to the back of the vehicle. Another of the diseased dogs fell by his hand.

Harper slid up beside him, uncomfortably close in the small hatch. "I said, move!"

Taavi looked at him and saw the bigger man reaching for the hatch. "It is broken," Taavi said in English. Now was not the time for childish games.

Harper looked at him sternly for a split second as he fired another round, followed quickly by another as his first shot missed the one he'd been aiming at entirely. Pistols were a poor weapon choice for stressful situations, as the slightest lack of concentration would ensure that the shooter would miss his target. If he survived, he'd need to get a rifle.

Harper turned back and grasped the hatch. He pushed a lever inset on the panel that Shaikh hadn't noticed in his frantic struggle and the hatch lifted away from the hull. It must have locked in place when he dropped it.

"Down!" Harper ordered, lifting the door. Shaikh fired one more round, further into the crowd, before flicking the pistol's safety on and ducking inside the vehicle's interior. It was more of a frustration shot than anything else, one meant to hit anything in the crowd. He'd let the one advantage that he'd held during this trip slip away during the heat of the moment.

First one hatch fell into place, then the second rapidly after that. Shaikh sat heavily against the hull, examining his left hand in the dim light. The life-or-death adrenaline rush was already wearing off and the pain flared once he saw the damage. Three of his fingernails were ripped away. Two of them still held on by a thin connection of tissue. It was extremely painful, but he'd be fine. It was much better than having his hand smashed under the weight of that door.

Harper sat down across from him and plugged his CVC helmet into a dangling coil of communication wire behind him. He turned back to Shaikh, staring hard at him. "So you can speak English, huh, motherfucker?" the man asked, his voice thick with menace.

Shaikh was not accustomed to feeling fear from any man. Even the Facilitator, a man who did unspeakable things to people on seemingly a daily basis, did not strike fear into him the way that Harper did in that moment. His gray eyes bore into Taavi's soul.

Despite the threat implied in Harper's tone and the stare, Shaikh did not back down. He had too much pride for that. His hand tightened around the pistol's grip and he hardened his resolve, staring back at the operator. Pushing the transmit button as he'd seen the others do, he said, "Yes. I understand English perfectly."

Harper sighed and leaned back. "Son of a bitch. I knew it. You always seemed too helpful for someone who was completely clueless." He scratched at his beard. "The dumb foreigner thing is an act too, huh?"

Taavi nodded. "I went to university in the United Kingdom before returning to Iran to serve in my country's army."

"Officer, huh?" Harper asked. "I thought so. I don't know what those symbols are on your uniform, but I can smell an officer."

Shaikh pointed to the epaulets on his shoulder. "I am a major in the Iranian Army."

"What were you doing at that airport?"

Taavi's heartbeat quickened. In many snatches of overheard conversation, he'd heard Harper say that he didn't remember any of the specifics of the last year, so there was a chance that he wouldn't know about the role the security chief had played during his imprisonment. "I was there with a small ground force. We were trying to establish a refueling point for the jets so they could land, rearm and refuel, then continue their attacks on the Cursed."

It was close enough to the truth to be believable. The airport *was* being prepped for that exact purpose by the Air Force team they'd stumbled across when the C-130 landed. Every other person who'd been there was dead now, so he could stick to that story without fear of being discovered.

"The Cursed? You mean these looney fuckers that the Army guys call the infected?"

"It is the same," Shaikh agreed.

"Okay. So the part about Iran being here as part of the UN mission is true?"

Shaikh shrugged honestly. "I do not know, Harper. I was sent here from my country, from my home, to fight against the abominations. If we are part of the United Nations, then that information did not reach my unit. I did not even know that we were in America until we landed and I saw the maps in the terminal."

Harper grunted. "Shitty way to fight a war, man." He glanced at the empty gunner's station. "I've trusted you so far. You're not my enemy in all this, those damn things out there are." He threw a thumb over his shoulder toward the Cursed outside. "You gonna shoot me in the back if I go back to that machine gun?"

He adopted the most offended look he could muster. "No, of course not. We have a common enemy. To kill you while they are a threat to me would be one of the dumbest things I could do right now."

Harper frowned before he ducked his chin once, hard. He put his hands on his knees and stood. "Good enough," he said before unhooking his helmet from the dangling communication wire.

Taavi watched him shuffle up to the gunner's station, then sit back down. Within seconds, the machine gun atop the Stryker began to fire once more.

He sighed as he relaxed his grip on the pistol. He dropped the magazine and replaced it with a full one, then slipped the weapon back into its holster. The lieutenant in charge didn't seem to be particularly smart, but he knew that Harper was. He'd have to shore up his alibi before the next time they stopped. It would have to be a blend of the truth and half-truths. Sticking as close to the truth as possible was the easiest way to keep his story straight. And he *needed* to keep his story straight so he could one day return to his homeland and find a way to kill the Facilitator for what he'd done to Taavi's beautiful family.

He let that anger and hatred wash over him. He *must* be successful at deceiving the Americans if he ever wanted an opportunity to avenge his family.

19

NEAR LIBERAL, KANSAS
FEBRUARY 20TH

Sidney heaved a sigh of exhaustion as she set the spring-loaded post pounder down in the grass. Her front deltoids burned in agony from the exertion of lifting the post pounder up to head height, then slamming it down onto the top of a metal fence post over and over until each post was about two feet in the ground. The heavy tool had been loud, the sounds of her pounding on the posts echoing across the plains. The only thing she could hope for was that the wind played havoc with the infected's senses the same way it did hers.

Mark rubbed at one shoulder through his coat, and a thin line of sweat ran from under his beanie hat along his cheek. "That was tough work," he said, grimacing.

"Yeah," Sidney agreed. "I'm gonna be feeling it for days."

"Katie told me that her grandfather put in all of the farm's fences by hand." He gestured weakly at the fence post pounder. "With that."

She shook her head. "Damn. I can't imagine fencing in a whole field with this thing. We did…" She counted the fence posts they'd placed. "Sixteen? And I'm exhausted. I wish we had a hot tub."

His eyebrows shot upward and Sidney rolled her eyes at his youthful innocence. *Not much longer*.

"You hear that?" Mark asked.

She cocked her head, straining to hear over the dull buzz in her ears. They hadn't seen any infected while they put in the fence posts, which was a testament to the winter taking its toll on their population. But, the sound of the repeated pounding all but guaranteed that they were on their way. The damn things were predictable that way.

"No," she replied. "I can't hear anything."

"I heard a scream," he whispered. "We need to get off the road."

She wrapped a V-shaped metal clip through the concertina wire and around the fence post she'd just finished putting in. "Okay, we're just about finished," Sidney replied. "Grab a couple of these clips and finish up on the other side."

They worked quickly, their exhaustion momentarily forgotten as they used pliers to twist the clips into place around the posts. The clips would keep the wire secured and stop it from coiling back up. As they worked, they continuously cast furtive glances down the road beyond their small obstacle. Inside her mind, an alarm was blaring for Sidney to drop what she was doing and run. The boy's ears were much better than hers, but if he'd heard a scream, then the infected had to be nearby.

Sidney's fingers were numb from the cold as she repeated the process several times. Beside her, Mark did the same. She saw him wipe his nose with the sleeve of his jacket, leaving a glistening trail. That's all they needed was to get sick.

"Okay, let's go," Sidney directed, grabbing Vern's tools when they'd finished the job. They headed up the road toward the house and then she heard it.

Screams.

It sounded like a lot of them. Mark began to run and she matched his stride, the fence post pounder banging awkwardly and painfully against her thigh. Inside the metal pipe, the spring-loaded weight slid back and forth noisily. "Dammit," she muttered and stopped to set the big tool down. Vern would understand. She could come back later and get it.

Without the added weight of the fence post pounder, Sidney sprinted the last fifty feet of the road's asphalt and then turned onto the gravel driveway leading home. Ahead, she saw a figure in the crow's nest beside the chimney gesturing for them to keep running.

The voices of death drifted on the wind as she leapt from the gravel onto the porch. There was no time to turn and see how many of them there were. No time to determine if her work from the day creating the obstacle was a waste. Blending in and remaining out of sight was their best chance for survival with the infected. Without visual confirmation of their hunt, they would grow bored and seek other prey.

Sidney was through the door a split second after Mark and then locked it behind them. Vern sat at the kitchen table as if he'd never left. She knew that wasn't the case. The old man had probably been working in the barn or out securing the fence line on the rest of the farm.

He looked up, alarm clearly written on his face as Sidney lowered the metal bar into the brackets that

Vern had secured on either side of the door. "Trouble?"

Sidney nodded, taking gulps of air. "Infected," Mark said, having recovered more quickly from their sprint than she had.

Vern stood and lifted the chair as he pushed it back to keep the legs from scraping. He picked up his old hunting rifle. "How much time do we have?"

"I don't know," Sidney replied. "We heard them. Didn't see 'em. The soldier in the crow's nest was waiving us in like crazy, so they must be close."

The old man frowned. "Caleb's up there. I'll go to the window upstairs and see what I can see."

Sidney watched him go, then went to the sink and poured a glass of water. She gulped it down before refilling it. If the infected somehow made it up to the house, they would be able to see anyone through the window above the sink and she wouldn't be able to get another glass until they were gone.

"I'm gonna go check on Lincoln," Sidney said to Mark. "Go make sure those other two soldiers are awake—but be quiet about it."

She crept up the stairs, wincing as the old boards creaked under her weight. The sound wasn't loud enough to make it outside of the house, but it still made her cringe. As she neared the top of the stairs, she heard Mark's whispered voice drift through the house, telling the other two men to wake up. Sidney had already had it with those three. They refused to do any work except for guard duty in the crow's nest. It had taken Vern threatening them with eviction to make them repair that fence. Jake had said they'd be helpful, but they were only a burden as far as she was concerned.

Until now. She didn't know how many of the infected her hammering was bringing toward the farm, but the three extra guns would be a huge help, especially since they'd brought the suppressed rifles, something the original group at the farm only had three of themselves after Jake took his personal weapon with him.

She tapped the wooden door to her bedroom and then opened it. Carmen lay on her side with the baby nestled up beside her on the bed. She lifted her head gently. "What's wrong?"

Worry must have been written clearly across her face. "Infected," Sidney replied. "Don't know how many."

Carmen rolled onto her back, continuing until she was sitting up. She stood and walked around the bed to where her pistol sat on the table beside an empty bottle.

"How is he?" Sidney asked as crouched beside the window and pulled the shade once to make it roll up about a foot so she could see the road below.

They were too far away to discern individuals, but she saw heads bobbing on the road beyond where she'd put in the fence. The mass of former humanity looked to be about a half a mile or so from reaching her new obstacle. That many of them would just bowl through the wire, it was meant to stop ten or fifteen, not a horde.

"He's good. Took a whole eight ounces," Carmen said. "He started laughing like crazy when we played peekaboo."

Sidney turned to her and smiled. The absurdity of talking about mundane day-to-day life while their imminent death was approaching wasn't lost on her. She'd often rolled her eyes during movies when people would have completely normal conversations in the middle of gun battles and high stress situations, but she understood it now. It was the mind's way of keeping the body from going into shock.

"How's it look?" Vern's gruff voice came from the doorway.

"Not good," Sidney answered. "I can't tell for sure, but looks like a few hundred of them about a mile away."

Vern frowned. "I told you that fence was a bad idea."

"It wasn't a bad idea," she hissed, trying to keep her voice low enough to allow Lincoln to sleep. That's all they needed was for him to wake up and begin wailing. "That road is a liability. Leaving it wide open was just inviting disaster."

"Making all that darned noise putting in those fence posts was what brought all them things here."

Sidney gritted her teeth and counted to ten inside her head as Vern said something else that she didn't allow herself to hear. He was their host, without him, the five of them would be out on the street. She'd just been trying to contribute to the group's safety so she wouldn't feel so bad eating all of their food.

"I'm sorry, Vern," she allowed herself to say. "I thought it was the best thing for us. You were right." That last part made her scream inside because the old man was most definitely *not* right about the road.

Vern's features softened. He was nothing if not predictable. The old man would fight you tooth and nail about something, but the moment you agreed with him, everything became right in the world.

"Well, there's nothing to be done about it now. We'll take care of this mess and those fences will work just like you planned once this big group is gone." He shuffled into the room and pointed at the baby. "But I think little Lincoln there is gonna need to be moved back to Carmen's room. We're gonna need those windows."

Sidney nodded. Her bedroom was at the front of the house overlooking the driveway and the road— not the best place for the baby if they had to defend against an attack, like now. She leaned her rifle against the wall next to the spear she'd made from a closet rod and kitchen knife. She hoped she *never* had to use that thing. If she did, they were as good as dead.

She dropped her coat on the chair, went to the bathroom and washed her hands. Then she picked up the baby from the bed. He stirred slightly as his head lifted from the bed, but stayed asleep. She held him to her chest, carrying him to Carmen's room.

Carmen's other children, Patricia and Miguel, were in the room playing with the few toys that Jake had brought back from the grocery store. The nurse grinned. "He's such a good boy."

Sidney agreed with her. "He is. Thank you for helping me with him so much."

Carmen shrugged. "I'm not much use with guns and stuff, so I'm just glad I can help wherever I can."

"Hey!" a harsh female whisper came from down the stairs followed by muffled conversation.

"What's that?" Carmen asked.

Sidney shook her head and handed the baby to Carmen, who accepted him naturally. She was much more gentle and experienced with him than his own mother was.

As Sidney padded down the stairs, the sound of arguing got louder. The voice of Katie was easily discernable, but the she couldn't quite make out what the males said.

"...after I let you fuck me, you're gonna just take off and leave?" Katie asked.

The wall between them muffled the response. Sidney didn't like the implications of the small snatch of conversation that she'd caught. She hurried the last few steps and turned into the kitchen.

Directly into the barrel of a suppressed M-4 rifle. "That's far enough, Sidney," Caleb said.

"Caleb?" Sidney asked, throwing up her hands. "Who's up in the crow's nest?"

"Fuck the crow's nest," Demetrius Brown said. "This place is about to get overrun. We ain't staying around here with you fools to die defending a damn house that you can find anywhere."

"You can't find a farm like this *anywhere*," Katie hissed. "We have running water, electricity, food. We're set up great here. We just need to—"

"Can it, bitch. We're leaving."

"You're not taking our stuff," Sidney asserted impotently. She'd left her rifle in the bedroom upstairs. She couldn't stop them if they wanted to take everything that the Campbells owned.

"We'll take what we want," Brown replied.

"We've been planning to leave for a few days," Weir, the medic stated. "We got the truck filled with supplies."

"My truck?" Vern asked, coming down the stairs.

"*Our* truck," Brown corrected him.

"Now you wait a doggone minute," Vern protested. "I put you up under my roof, fed you—fought alongside of you...and this is how you repay me? It's been a mighty long time since I was in the Army, but I know they didn't teach you to act this way."

"You're right, Mr. Campbell," the medic replied. "It's been a *long* time since you were in the Army. We don't appreciate you trying to act like some sort of drill sergeant or something." He held up his hands, letting his rifle hang from the sling. "We don't want any trouble. We just want to go somewhere where all of these infected aren't, maybe Canada where it stays cold."

Weir turned toward Katie. "You're welcome to come with us, babe. It'll be a tight fit in the cab of the truck, but we'll make do."

"Are you kidding me?" Katie seethed. "I'm not abandoning my grandfather—my home—for some guy that I barely know."

"I think he knows *everything* about you," Brown sneered.

"What's that supposed to mean?" Vern asked, looking from the soldiers to his granddaughter.

"Grandpa..." Katie whispered, her eyes fixed on the floor.

"The infected are at the new fence!" Sally called from upstairs where she'd presumably been watching from a window.

"That's it," Weir said. "We're out of here."

He shouldered past Vern and Sidney. "Rob..."

The soldier turned back. "You coming or not, Katie?"

"Don't do this," the youngest Campbell begged.

"Are you coming, or not?" Weir repeated.

Katie shook her head, the blonde locks flying wildly in her assertion that she wouldn't leave her family. "No."

"That's it then, Weir," Caleb grunted. "That dumb bitch is the only reason we stayed this long. You done got what you wanted. Let's go." He dropped the barrel of his rifle and stepped around Sidney, who slowly lowered her hands.

Her shoulders were on fire. She hadn't been aware of how tense her muscles had become as she stood there with her arms raised.

"Still ain't gonna allow you to take my truck," Vern asserted. "A man's gotta stand up for what—"

Brown butt-stroked Vern in the side of the head from behind. The old man grunted as his knees buckled underneath him. Katie cried out and Sidney barely reacted in time to catch him before he fell further. The dead weight carried her forward and she tripped over Vern, falling to the side. Her back impacted against the corner of the kitchen table. A jolt of pain traveled the length of her body.

"Be grateful we didn't just smoke all y'all," Brown said as he stalked through the door without bothering to shut it behind himself.

By the time Sidney was able to sit up, Katie was beside Vern. "Ugh," she groaned, attempting to reach the center of her back where she'd hit the table.

The sound of tires on gravel echoed through the house, spurring Sidney into action. She pushed herself up painfully and walked to the door. The old Ford pickup's red tailgate was all she saw as she looked through the door. She considered taking aim with one of the rifles and putting a bullet in the head of whoever was driving, but she abandoned that fantasy as quickly as she dreamed it up. It would have been a tough shot for an experienced marksman, and she'd only learned to shoot a gun about two or three months ago.

"Goddammit!" Sidney cursed as she closed the door and put the metal bar into place.

"You...shouldn't take...the Lord's name in vain," Vern said haltingly from the floor, where his head rested in Katie's lap.

"Grandpa!" Katie exclaimed.

"That's me," he grunted as he tried to sit up.

"No, just—"

"We ain't got the time to sit around, girl," he said, gripping Katie's leg to pull himself up. "*Whoa*," he exclaimed, holding the side of his head. "Those boys sure had me fooled."

294 THE ROAD TO HELL

"Me too," Katie muttered.

Vern rolled over onto his hands and knees so he could get up. "We've got some things we need to discuss later, young lady."

"Yes, sir," Katie replied.

Sidney rolled her shoulders, wincing at the pain, but immediately regretting it. Vern had just been *beaten* with the buttstock of a rifle and he was still moving around. *Suck it up, buttercup,* she heard Jake's voice in her mind. A quick accusation toward him for saddling them with the three soldiers flashed through her mind and she stifled it just as quickly as it'd appeared. Jake hadn't known the men would act this way. He wasn't to blame for what they'd done.

"Hey!" Sally yelled, all attempts to remain silent abandoned. "Who's in Grandpa's truck?"

Sidney looked up the stairs. Sally stood on the landing, the other suppressed M-4 rifle on her hip. "You don't want to know," she mumbled.

"What?"

"Demetrius, Caleb, and Rob took off," Mark called up to her. "Beat up Mr. Campbell and took the truck."

"What!" Sally exclaimed. "Grandpa, are you alright?"

"Yeah," Vern replied. "We need to get to our positions. If those three open the fence, we gotta start shooting right away. Thin the herd."

It was a sad procession to the farmhouse's second level as Sally joined Katie near the middle of the stairs to help their grandfather the rest of the way. Sidney stumped along after them, attempting to stretch out the rapidly forming knot in her upper back. Mark brought up the rear, holding Vern's hunting rifle and the suppressed rifle that had at one time belonged to one of the farmhands who'd died before Sidney and Jake showed up.

Sidney and Mark went into her room, where she scooped up the M-4 before crouching at her window. Vern and the girls went into his room. That left no one besides Carmen to watch the back side of the house, and she only had the pistol. If any of the infected had made their way south through the fields, they were the least priority compared to the mob making its way down the road.

She eased the window upward, the old home's counter-balanced windows creaking as they made their way along the track. Shooting out the glass would have been simply stupid, especially in the winter. Similar sounds echoed down the hallway, telling her that the Campbells had opened their windows as well.

Sidney saw the red truck edge toward the mob of infected that were milling around the fence that blocked the way toward town. She brought her rifle up. Through the small scope, she saw that the fence she'd spent all morning erecting had done its job. The infected were unsure of where the sounds they'd followed had come from, so they were unwilling to get tangled up.

Until they saw the Ford.

The sight of the rusted, old truck riled them up and they began throwing themselves at the fence. The truck's bright red brake lights illuminated the early evening dusk. Then the white reverse lights appeared and the truck began fishtailing backward until the driver pulled the steering wheel hard, sending the back tires into the ditch alongside the road. The engine roared loudly as he put it into gear and pulled the truck out, heading in the opposite direction of the horde toward the first row of fencing that she'd installed that morning.

The truck rumbled up the road, speeding by the driveway. Sidney turned back to the mob. The first of them had successfully trampled over their brethren caught in the concertina wire.

"They're through the wire!" she called out.

"Just let 'em pass," Vern replied. "Maybe they'll chase after those morons and not even turn up the drive."

Sidney resisted the urge to begin shooting. Vern was right. The infected hunted by sight and sound. Right now, they were chasing a loud, giant red target. She pivoted on the windowsill again, peering through the scope at where the truck had stopped in front of the wire opposite of the mob. The Ford's bright headlights illuminated it clearly. At this distance, the concertina looked like thin, white strands of spider silk, but her ripped and tattered jacket was proof that the stuff was razor sharp and deadly.

The soldiers were going to have to cut the wire to get past it. Two of them jumped from the passenger side of the truck and began using small handheld wire cutters, probably from the multi-tools that seemed to be a universal attachment on every soldier's belt. It would take them a long time to cut through the thick wire with just those small pliers.

The driver of the truck backed up, picking up speed in reverse. The bumper slammed into the first of the infected, bending it in half as the creature's head impacted against the tailgate. It fell under the truck as the driver kept going, taking out several of the infected before he'd lost too much momentum and had to drive forward. He was attempting to give the other two as much time to complete the task as possible by taking out the infected with the truck.

The ear shattering sound of jet engines broke Sidney's attention. Overhead, a plane roared by, seemingly close enough to touch. The pilot opened fire with his machine gun, rounds impacting all around the infected. She let out an involuntary *whoop* of jubilation. The Air Force was here!

The jet banked around and followed the road, lining up his shots perfectly on the infected. The poor creatures whirled this way and that, unable to determine where the sound came from. The pilot shot skyward once more, then executed a barrel roll to bring him in line with the infected once more. He fired a longer, sustained volley, ripping the last knot of infected to shreds before firing at the Ford and into the men cutting the wire. Their bodies danced a disgusting ballet as the bullets tore through them.

Sidney watched in horror as the truck began to burn. It rolled slowly to a stop within twenty feet of the wire. In the light of the dancing flames, she saw the bodies of the two soldiers splayed across the concertina wire. Neither of them moved.

The jet circled low, fired another quick volley and then roared off toward town.

"Darn it," Vern said over the screech of Lincoln's frightened wails. "I loved that truck."

Sidney grinned at the old man's perseverance. The Air Force had clearly made a mistake by shooting at the truck when they were killing the infected... Right? Surely they hadn't shot at humans on purpose.

Right?

20

NEAR LIBERAL, KANSAS
FEBRUARY 20TH

It took them ten minutes to mop up the infected on the road. Vern refused to let anyone leave the house to see if the soldiers needed aid until he was sure that all the creatures out there were dead.

"That's all we need is for one of y'all to get bitten," he'd said. He was trying to look out for everyone that he could and it was smart to be cautious in their new world. One slip up and you were as good as dead.

Carmen was practically frantic by the time she handed the baby off to Sidney so she could go see whether the men could be saved. Sidney sat in her room holding Lincoln and watched as the older woman made her way down the driveway with Sally and Mark providing security for her.

Vern watched from the window in his room as well. Between the two of them, they were capable of taking out any threat that remained. She'd lose a couple of seconds to respond to an immediate threat because she would have to put the baby down, but luckily, the infected were basic in their actions and could be taken care of easily if it was only one or two of them.

Katie stumbled into the room, obviously troubled over what they'd just witnessed. Sidney figured that she and Rob Weir had been hooking up by the way they acted around each other, but the whispered piece of conversation that she'd overheard before the soldiers stole the truck confirmed her suspicions. Vern suspected the truth, but he would be livid if he ever found out for sure. Now that the kid was dead, though, Sidney wondered if he'd continue to press for the truth. Probably not.

"How are you doing?" Sidney asked.

"I'm... I'm a little fucked up right now," Katie replied, mouthing the words 'fucked up' quietly so her grandfather wouldn't hear her from the next room. "I barely knew them, but they were people, you know? It doesn't bother me to kill the infected, but I just watched three guys get blown up right in front of me—one of them I'd been with a couple of times." She frowned and sat down on Sidney's bed. "It's just weird."

"I'm sorry, honey," she said, shifting the baby into the crook of her arm so she could reach out to put a hand on the younger girl's knee. "We live in a fucked up world. Nobody thought those boys would take off—well, *I* didn't think so at least. Never saw it coming."

"You know, for a split second, just the tiniest of a moment," Katie held up her thumb and forefinger, "I thought about going with them when they asked." Tears rolled down her cheek and her frown deepened. "If I had…"

"Don't think about what ifs," Sidney interjected into the space left by the girl's trailing off. "It'll drive you crazy. Trust me."

"Yeah, but—"

"Don't do it," Sidney asserted. "There's nothing you can do about it. The only thing you can do is be thankful that you're still alive, and you can mourn the loss of a friend, even if they turned to ungrateful shits during their last moments on Earth. We'll bury them and I'm sure Vern will say a few words over their graves. He's a very forgiving man."

"Yeah. I'd like that."

"It's the right thing to do. Until today, they were our friends. They helped out around the farm and," Sidney squeezed the girl's knee, "Rob helped out *inside* the farm a little bit."

"A *real* little bit," Katie said, smiling around the tears.

"Oh. He had a little dick?" Sidney whispered, grinning.

"Like smaller than the length of a dollar bill." The smile widened. "The first time, I thought he wasn't like fully hard or something."

"Man, I hate that."

"I wasn't expecting it. As big of an ego as he had, I thought he would have had something to back it up. Nope."

It was Sidney's turn to frown wistfully as she thought about Lincoln's father. "It's been my experience—and I've had a lot of it, let me tell you— that the big, boastful guys who talk about the size of their junk are the ones with the littlest dicks. They're compensating for it."

"How many?" Katie asked, leaning forward.

Sidney shrugged. "I don't know. Let's just say that I'm a free spirit. It's just sex, y'know? It feels good, why deny yourself a little bit of pleasure in between periods of mind-numbing hours of work."

"Yeah, that's true."

Movement outside the window brought her attention back to the task at hand and she turned her head. The trio had returned, coming up the driveway toward the house. They each wore a large camouflage backpack across their shoulders, while Sally and Mark carried an additional suppressed M-4 rifle.

"Looks like your sister's coming back," Sidney stated. She scanned the road for movement, any sign that one of the infected still lived. There was none. "Let's go down and see what they can tell us."

Katie shook her head. "No. You go. I'm going to go up into the crow's nest to keep watch. We've worked too hard on this farm to let something like this mess us over."

She stood up and started to turn, hesitating for a moment. "Thank you, Sidney. I know that we're all in a shitty situation here, but I'm thankful that we have you and Carmen now. Grandpa just doesn't understand some of the emotional needs that we have."

Sidney got to her feet, grunting as her abs and leg muscles strained while she tried to keep the baby balanced perfectly in her arm so he wouldn't wake up. "Katie, I'm glad we're here too. I'm not a big believer in God and all that like Vern is, but I do think we were brought here for a reason." She stepped forward and placed her free arm around the younger girl's back, bringing her into an awkward half hug that Lincoln's sleeping form necessitated. "We'll be okay."

The embrace lasted a few seconds longer than Sidney meant for it to, but she could feel that the girl needed it, so she just let it happen. She tried to pass along some of her own learned and newly discovered strength to Katie through their contact.

Finally, Katie pulled back and said simply, "Thanks," before she walked through the door. Sidney grabbed her rifle and followed. In the hallway, Katie and Vern exchanged a few words before the girl went to the pull-down stairs to the attic so she could go out to the crow's nest.

Vern watched her go. When she was out of sight, his eyes found Sidney's. "Thank you."

She ducked her head before stepping onto the stairs lightly. By the time she'd made it to the bottom, the front door was opening and Sally came through. The others followed her and placed their spoils in the hallway.

"That was a quick trip," Sidney remarked as the Campbell girl went into the kitchen to wash her hands.

"There was nothing Carmen could do."

"They were probably dead instantly," Carmen agreed. "That jet shot them with exploding rounds or something." She held up bloodstained hands in the rough shape of a circle as big as a basketball. "The exit wounds were like this. Even if they'd survived, there isn't anything I could do to save them from that."

Vern nodded. "Wounds from aircraft fire are particularly nasty. Saw the after effects of US close air support all the time in 'Nam."

"Why would the Air Force fire on the truck?" Sally asked, returning from the kitchen holding a hand towel. "The infected can't drive, they know that. Anyone in a moving vehicle is obviously not an infected."

"I don't think that jet was ours," Vern stated, letting the words hang in the air as he set about making a new pot of coffee. "I think everyone's gonna need some of this."

After a few seconds of waiting, Sidney couldn't stand it anymore. "What do you mean, Vern? You think there are more Iranians around here?"

He looked out the window for a moment before sighing and turning back. "Yeah, I do. That Taavi feller may not have said much while he was here, but what Grady said about the airport in town makes me think they're gonna try again."

The old man picked up his empty coffee mug and leaned against the counter. "There are only two ways they can take over this country. They either push inward from the coasts, killing the infected as they go, or they land planes at airports to create all sorts of little bases that they can patrol out into the surrounding countryside, expanding their area of influence a little farther each day. We did the same damn thing in Vietnam—excuse my language. Lord, I'm sorry for that outburst."

Sidney rolled her eyes. It was just the word 'damn'. "What do you mean?" she asked.

"We had patrol bases, fire bases, camps, and airfields all over South Vietnam so we could affect the greatest area. We did the same thing in Afghanistan and in the Iraq war too. I think *that's* what they're doing. They already had one big cargo plane at the airport and they landed two jets there. I think they're gonna keep trying to establish a base. That jet was probably just flying around looking for targets before they land troops."

"And it doesn't matter to them if they kill civilians or infected," Sally surmised.

Vern cocked his finger and "fired" it at her. "Bingo, sweetie."

Lincoln stirred, first yawning and then whimpering in hunger. "So what do we do about it?" Sidney asked as she stepped over to the sink to fill a bottle.

"First, we all drink some coffee because it's gonna be a long night," Vern replied. "Then we begin preparing a secondary position, someplace we can fall back to if this one is compromised. We need to have supplies stashed in the new location as well as backpacks with supplies for a few days here at the house so we can be ready to go at a moment's notice."

Sidney grinned at the old man's use of some of the larger words. She could tell they were ones he'd learned in the Army decades ago, but had never forgotten. "So a bug-out bag and all that stuff, right?"

Vern shrugged. "I think so. Maybe? You kids make up all sorts of words for things these days. It's something that I've been thinking about for a while. Just never had a pressing need to act on it before."

"So you want to abandon the farm, Grandpa?" Sally asked.

Vern grunted. "If we have to, sweetheart. Being alive is more important than where you put your head down each night."

Sidney nodded. She understood his sentiment. "Okay, so where do you suggest—" She stopped mid-sentence and pointed out the kitchen window. "*That* looks like another cargo plane."

Everyone crowded around her to see out of the small window above the sink. Off on the horizon, in the direction of Liberal, a large plane flew slow and low. It looked like it was going to land at the airport.

"Yeah," Vern said. "That's what I was afraid of. They learned a little bit from the first time they tried to land at the airport. Planes make a ton of noise, and draw a whole bunch of infected to wherever they are. That jet was cleaning up the area so the big cargo planes can land and the foreigners can start building their walls."

Sally frowned. "Is this how things are gonna be from now on? I mean, *we're* the good guys, right? How are we the ones who are scurrying around, hiding from foreign invaders? Where are all of our allies?"

Sidney pulled the bottle from Lincoln's mouth and pointed it at Sally. "We view ourselves as the good guys, but most of the world doesn't. They were happy to take our money, but wouldn't have shed a tear at our demise." The baby began to cry and she sighed, pushing the nipple gently between his lips.

"Well, those days are behind us anyways," Vern said. "I doubt there's any country left that's capable of doing much besides keep their head afloat under a sea of infected."

Even though Sidney had put the bottle back in his mouth, Lincoln still cried about the loss of his bottle. She wobbled it back and forth to let the baby know it was back in his mouth. His lips closed around the silicone and quiet descended on the kitchen once more. "So what do you need us to do, Vern?"

21

NEAR LIBERAL, KANSAS
FEBRUARY 24TH

Miguel's teeth chattered so loudly that Carmen was afraid the soldiers on the path would hear them. She pulled the children close to her for warmth. They'd been hunted from the moment they woke up that morning and the chase had seemingly come to an end. The men outside would kill them—or worse—and move on without a care in the world.

Tears flowed down her cheeks. How had she allowed herself to get separated from everyone else? They'd been running to the hideout that Vern and the others spent the last few days preparing when she fell at the back gate, twisting her ankle violently. It may even be broken. Sidney tried to help her, but she became too much of a burden, slowing them down far too much, so they decided to leave her in a heavy thicket just inside the small copse of trees beyond the farm's fences with the promise that they'd return for her as soon as the trucks carrying the soldiers had left the farm. Little Miguel and Patricia refused to leave their Mama, regardless of what she told them to do.

That had been more than an hour ago.

Carmen cursed herself. She should have worked through the pain in her ankle and forced herself to travel the two or three miles to the small, abandoned house they'd established as their first fallback position. But she couldn't do it. The pain was too intense. Only her strong will and sense of self-preservation stopped her from crying out in pain any time she moved.

Definitely broken, she thought, touching the outside of her boot tenderly. She knew if she took it off, the swelling would be too much to put it back on. For now, the only thing she could do was keep her children quiet until the soldiers went away and Sidney could come back to her.

But she knew that wasn't going to happen. They all knew that wasn't going to happen. It'd been abundantly clear from the moment they started planning that once the soldiers found the farm, they wouldn't leave it alone. Vern could disable the power by flipping the breakers at the solar panels, but there was simply no hiding the cattle and the chickens—or Sidney's stupid cat that had run away from her when she tried to put it in the carrier. The invaders would know instantly that the farm had recently been occupied and they'd search until they found the occupants.

Vern's idea to set up the different safe houses and rendezvous points was just to make them feel better about the inevitable. Now that the soldiers had come, the farm was lost and they had to leave the area.

"M-M-M-Mama," Miguel stuttered through the full body shakes. "S-s-s-so c-cold."

She stroked his head through the beanie hat he wore, trying to soothe him. "It'll all be over soon," she assured him. The thick rubber grip of the Gerber knife in the small of her back reassured her. She knew what she needed to do.

During this entire ordeal, she'd only killed one person: the employee she'd seduced to allow her and the children inside the warehouse. He'd gone to investigate noises on the loading dock a couple of weeks after they arrived and was bitten. She'd killed him with a screwdriver through his eye. Because Ben had been her protector, she didn't see a need to have a weapon before he died. After that, she'd opened one of the packages in the camping section and taken the orange-handled knife as a last resort weapon. She'd never needed to use it, until now.

Carmen had seen internet videos of Islamic extremists and knew what those animals were capable of. She wouldn't allow her children to be taken as sex slaves by the foreigners or skinned alive for sport. God have mercy on her soul, she would spare them that horror.

The crunch of boots on the pathway's crystalized snow made her stiffen. She forced herself to look through the twisted jumble of leafless brambles to the path where six men made their way toward her hiding place from the direction of the farmhouse. In the distance, she could hear the low rumble of a diesel engine as whatever transport truck they'd brought with them followed along unseen where it could watch over the patrol.

Cold, rigid muscles protested as she reached around to pull the knife from her back pocket. The entire thing came out, nylon case and all. It took her a moment to fumble with the Velcro fasteners that kept the sheath closed around the knife blade.

Scrrtch!

The sound of the Velcro echoed across the morning stillness, telling every one of the cursed soldiers exactly where they lay hidden. As one, the men's postures changed. They hunched down, their leisurely stroll through the woods had turned into a predatory prowl. They were the hunters. Carmen Agusto and her children were the prey.

"Not today, you bastards," she screeched, pulling Miguel's head toward her to expose his neck as the Gerber descended downward to take her son's life.

"Y'all set?" Vern asked the small group of women and the teenager, Mark, as he pulled the small pair of folding binoculars away from his eyes.

One by one, the four heads nodded. The old man didn't like what was about to happen. Their actions would set loose an unstoppable tidal wave—one that they may survive initially, but it would inevitably be the death of them all.

That's just how these things went. His granddaughter's assertions that they were the good guys and should be on the moral high ground were the ramblings of a liberal arts major. His son had wasted good money sending those girls to that stupid university that filled their heads with all sorts of non-practical nonsense. Being the good guys only went so far when it came to the real world.

Yes, they'd all end up dead, but hopefully the Good Lord would weigh their actions along with the sum of their daily lives and grant them passage through the Pearly Gates.

"Good," Vern mumbled, lifting the binoculars up once again. The soldiers below were overly confident that all they had to deal with were the infected. They strolled casually, none of them even wearing the blue helmets that they had looped over the canteens on their hips or any type of ballistic vest. "I count six of 'em, all on foot," he continued. "They don't have any backup that I can see—wait. No, they have a truck of some kind. There's a machine gun up top."

He dropped the binoculars. "That's it. The mission is off. We don't need to throw our lives away uselessly."

"And what about Carmen?" Sidney snapped. "And those two precious babies?"

Vern grunted and pointed at the bundle beside her. "What about *your* baby? We do this and they open up with that machine gun, we're toast."

Sidney stared at him, chewing her bottom lip gently. "Let me see those binoculars."

He lifted the strap from around his neck and passed them to her. She adjusted the focus for a moment after she put the rubber cups against her eyes, then panned down to where Carmen and the children lay behind the thicket. They were incredibly exposed from the back side. Vern hoped they were more concealed from the front.

After watching the injured woman for several seconds, Sidney slid the binoculars along the path back toward the farmhouse. She stared, unmoving for a long while. Without removing the binos from her eyes, she said, "I'll take the shot."

"What?" Vern asked, genuinely surprised.

"There are six men on foot," she stated, loud enough for the others to hear, "and two men in the truck—one on the machine gun and the driver. My weapon is zeroed out to...well, I don't know. Jake never got that far in our sessions, but I know I can hit a man-sized target on the far side of your first field. That's about where the truck is now."

"Hitting a stationary target and hitting a man, killing him in cold blood, while he's riding in a moving vehicle, are two completely different things. We weren't expecting them to bring the truck. We should pack it up and save it for another day."

"No," Sally said.

"Yeah, Grandpa. No way," Katie echoed. "We're gonna save Carmen."

"Or die trying," Mark finished the group's input.

"Are you people off your rockers?" Vern huffed. "This isn't some game. Those soldiers down there aren't some group of dumb-dumb infected that will wander into your line of fire. They *will* shoot back, and they'll be tryin' to kill y'all."

Sidney frowned. "Vern, I hope that you're just worried for your grandchildren's safety and not thinking straight because of it. Otherwise, you've got a lot of soul-searching to do, old man."

"I— What do you know about— I—" he sputtered. The girl calling him out was right. He *was* worried for the girls and that was clouding his judgement. They *were* the good guys—or at least they were supposed to be. Leaving Carmen to the hands of those monsters was by far the most un-Christian thought he'd done in decades, maybe even his whole life. All that talk about judgements being passed, if he abandoned that family down there, then he *knew* what Saint Peter would say: Turn away from the straight and narrow, keep on the wide path toward the fires of Hell.

"Oh, doggone it. You're right," he sighed. "Okay, you take the gunner, I'll take the driver."

"No," Sidney replied again. "You're rifle isn't suppressed. It'll alert the others too soon. You take out one of the soldiers on foot. Sally will take the driver."

He nodded. It was sound tactical advice. "Fine." He raised his voice slightly. "After these two kill the truck team, we'll start shooting. I've got the lead man. Katie, you shoot the one in the back. Mark, you get the next man. That'll leave three more, so once your target is down, shift your fire toward the ones in the middle. Don't get distracted with what each other is doing, just hit your target first."

"Got it," Mark said, wiping sweat from his forehead, despite the chill.

They let the soldiers approach Carmen's hide location. When they were about twenty feet from her, their posture suddenly changed and the man that Vern had his rifle trained upon dropped into a high crouch, alert for movement. They knew Carmen was there.

"It's time, Sidney," he stated. "Show us what you can do."

He heeded his own advice and did not look toward the truck. Instead, he kept his scope on the chest of the point man, the one who was now only a few feet from Carmen. Beside him, the woman's rifle emitted a dull *thunk* as that suppressor did its job to block most of the sound. Another shot further down their small scrimmage line told Vern that Sally had fired at the driver.

He heard a mumbled curse from Sidney, but forced himself to ignore it. Exhaling slowly, he squeezed the trigger.

The report from the 30.06 was deafening in the quiet morning, jarring him as it bucked against his shoulder. The baby began crying almost immediately. Vern knew the rifle was loud, but he'd forgotten how loud it was after not using it for so long. At first they'd relied on John's silenced .308 before he died, but Vern had never gotten the hang of the weapon. Then, after Jake and the other two soldiers arrived, their suppressed M-4s became the daily carry weapon of choice. The smaller caliber rifles had almost no kick when they fired, allowing even the most inexperienced shooter to keep them trained on their target after firing.

Between the intolerable screams from the baby and the shock of the rifle's recoil, it took Vern a moment to reacquire the man he'd shot. He lay on the ground, squirming with a hole in his stomach. The old man decided that he would have to adjust his aim point to account for the bullet drop over the distance.

Rounds began to whiz past them as the remaining soldiers fired at them. The sheer number of bullets meant that Sidney had missed the machine gunner. Most of the rounds impacted against the trees above them since they were dug in behind a fallen log roughly the same height as the standing soldiers. Vern forced himself to remain calm as the chattering of the automatic weapon reached him across the distance, bringing long-suppressed memories with it of a time when he was eighteen and ankle deep in the perpetual mud of a Vietnamese jungle.

"Get thee behind me, Satan!" he said as he swiveled his rifle to one of the soldiers on the trail. The man was attempting to crawl away to cover. Vern knew that if even a single one of the enemy survived, then his family—and his new, extended family—was as good as dead.

His rifle barked again. This time, the sound and kick weren't a surprise and he was able to keep the target in his sight picture. The crawling man shuddered as the round tore into his back. Vern didn't take the time to ensure the man was no longer a threat; instead, he began searching for another target. He found a man on the far side of the tree line who fired indiscriminately in Vern's general direction, but wasn't even trying aim. Vern dropped him with a single round through the face.

Then it was all over and everything fell silent once more. The gentle purr of the truck's engine as it rested against the trunk of a tree was the only sound Vern could hear. He hadn't realized that sometime during the fight, the machine gun had stopped spitting bullets at 950-rounds a minute in his direction.

"Let's go down there and get them," Sidney said as she started to stand up with the baby carrier in one hand and her rifle in the other.

"Hold on," Vern directed. "Let me make sure there ain't no nasty surprises waitin' for us down there." He brought the binoculars to his eyes, scanning the trail below. Five of the bodies lay still, the snow underneath them smeared with blood. The sixth soldier—the one he'd shot in the back—had crawled into the far tree line, the rust-colored smear told him that he'd gotten the man good. But an injured man was *not* a dead man. They'd need to be cautious until they could verify his whereabouts.

A thick trail of blood ran down the truck's windshield from the soldier who manned the machine gun. He was slumped over, a hole in his chest and another through the top of his head where Sidney must have tagged him a second time to be sure that he was dead. Two holes near the bottom of the windshield showed where Sally had hit the driver.

"Okay," Vern grunted, pushing himself to his feet. "There's one unaccounted for. He crawled off into the woods with a trail of blood behind him as wide as a cow's backside. We need to be careful until we're sure he's dead."

The girls didn't wait to hear the last part. They were already calling out softly to Carmen as they ran toward her hiding spot. Vern turned to Mark. "Can you provide overwatch from back here, son? I don't want us gettin' caught with our pants down."

"Yes, sir," the teenager said, sliding back down behind the log.

Vern touched the bill of his hat with two fingers in response and stepped off toward the trail. The small copse of trees wasn't big in comparison to other forests that he'd been in, but it was massive for the southern Kansas landscape. It took him several minutes to pick his way over the fallen timber and around piles of underbrush that the county had labeled as "nature conservation areas" and hadn't allowed anyone to clear the stuff away.

By the time he reached the group of women, he saw that Carmen was crying, sobbing really. She hugged her boy's body to her, rocking back and forth as Katie held the girl. Vern thought the boy might have been hit in the crossfire until Miguel turned his head and smiled at everyone in embarrassment.

"I almost…" Carmen sputtered.

"But you *didn't*," Sidney cooed, wiping away a few dead leaves stuck in the older woman's hair. "That's all that matters."

Vern was confused until he saw the bright orange handle of a knife on the ground, the blade partially hidden by the leaf clutter that seemed to defy the snow around them. It didn't take him long to put two-and-two together, Lord knows he'd seen it enough times back in Vietnam to sear the memory onto his brain. The girl was planning to kill her children instead of allowing them to be taken prisoner. She had far more resolve than he'd given her credit for.

The baby continued to cry from the carrier on Sidney's back and it was grating on Vern's nerves. The sound was like a dinner bell for the infected, and they'd already rung it enough during the firefight. "Miss Sidney, please get him to quit making such a fuss or what we did here this morning was for naught."

He didn't wait to hear her response; it probably wouldn't have been pleasant anyways. Instead, he continued past them to the blood trail. The man's rifle lay in the crunchy, frozen snow near the center of the path. Vern followed the smear of bloody, packed snow until he heard the wheezing gasps of breath and an odd gurgle that took him a moment to place. Then he remembered the sound. It was the sound a man made when they'd been shot through the lung; the proverbial sucking chest wound.

Vern Campbell had spent a lifetime trying to forget the sounds, the sights, and the...the feelings of combat. He'd thought those demons were put to rest a long time ago, but they'd resurfaced. Killing the infected had not evoked the emotions that the past thirty or forty minutes had. He'd violated the Sixth Commandment, and he felt *good* about it.

Logically, he knew that the soldiers would have killed him and the others, so the Lord would forgive him, but he *enjoyed* killing those men. He'd exalted in his skill as a warrior, to be able to meet the enemy and survive. He'd been scared of how it made him feel when he was in the jungles and rice paddies of Vietnam, and he was scared of how it made him feel now.

Vern stepped into the woods along the path and saw the man he'd shot, the one who was making all the ruckus. He lay on his stomach, legs scrabbling uselessly in the snow. The gurgling sound told Vern that he was slowly drowning in his own blood as it filled his lungs. It was a terrible way to die, and he ought to know, he'd seen several men go through the pain and the terror of knowing they would die while they waited for the helicopter to come. Even with friends and medics around them, those men had been terrified and alone.

He couldn't imagine how this man must feel, thousands of miles from home and completely alone.

"I'm sorry, son," Vern said as he knelt beside the man. He started to roll him over onto his side to relieve the pressure and the pain, but stopped. The gooks would sometimes pull the pin on a grenade if they knew they were goners so they could at least take out a Yankee in death. Was this man the same way as them—were all of these men the same way, spiteful, even in death?

He went around to the other side of the prostrate soldier and rolled the body toward him, to keep the man's torso in front of his own in case there was a grenade. He held the man up for several seconds, gritting his teeth against the possibility of an explosion only a few inches away. When nothing happened, Vern straightened up and positioned the body so the man was on his side. The blood would drain out of his lungs this way. It wouldn't stop him from dying, but it would at least ease the pain and help his transition.

"There you go," Vern said aloud, then said a quick prayer that the man's soul would go to whatever version of Heaven that he believed in. He stood, looking down at the man, who kept repeating something in a foreign language. "I don't know what else to do for you, son."

It was true. He wasn't a doctor or a medic. He remembered something about covering the wound with a plastic bag and taping on three sides to allow the air and blood in the lungs to escape and not let more in when it sucked back against the hole, but they had zero supplies with them. They'd been forced to run from their home and the small packs each of them had were just a change of clothes and some food in case they got delayed making it to the fallback position. That would need to change. They'd need to include a medical kit and beef up the other supplies in the bags once they went back.

For now, the only thing Vern could do was stare at the man as he died. He'd watched men die only twice before—he'd seen plenty that were already dead or died later on, but only those two had died of wounds in front of him. It was saddening to think about the potential that those people had and that they never got to experience the rest of their lives because they'd died in some far off land, doing the bidding of their nation. Is that how these men, these invaders of his country felt? Were they just doing a job and trying to make it back home to their girl, like he and so many young Americans before him had been?

"Aww, heck, mister," Vern grumbled. "You're making me question what's happening here. I never would've thought that I'd be like those NVA lunatics, fighting for my life over a small patch of ground that I call my own. But you people have made that happen." The man's eyes pleaded with him to *do* something, but Vern couldn't do anything except talk to him. He wanted to shout at the man, but it wouldn't do any good, the foreigner didn't understand English, so he kept his voice even and steady. "We were just fine on our own over here and you people attacked us, created those darn infected, and then invaded after they'd wiped out most of your resistance. *Hmpf.* I guess that's what we are now: the Resistance." He thought about it for a moment. "Yeah. I like that. That's what we are, we're the Resistance."

The man had stopped babbling and his eyes were lidded and vacant. Vern knew the man was gone. "So long, fella."

He went back out to the path and eyed the bodies. They all looked dead, but he couldn't be sure, so he went to each one, checking for a pulse. When he was satisfied, he waved his hand over his head, then swept his arm from Mark's direction to where he was to bring the boy in.

"Okay, we gotta be smart here, ladies," Vern said to the women as he came back up to them. "There's—Oh, good Lord! I'm sorry, Miss Sidney." She had her breast out, feeding the baby in an attempt to keep him quiet.

"It's alright, Vern," she replied. "I'm not embarrassed. It isn't anything you haven't seen before. This was just the easiest way to shut him up."

Vern grunted, pointedly keeping his eyes on his granddaughters. "We made a lot of noise. Any infected within five miles is gonna be headed this way. We need to search these bodies, take anything we may need and get to safety."

The girls were still comforting Carmen. "We think Carmen's ankle is broken," Sidney stated. "She isn't going to be walking very far."

Vern looked around for a moment, thinking they could fashion some type of stretcher for her out of tree limbs. Then his eyes settled on the big truck pushed up against the trunk of a tree. "Well, we already made enough noise that a little more won't matter that much," he said, pointing toward the truck.

"Good idea," Sidney answered. "Are we going to the first fallback location or are we going back to the farm?"

He thought about it and then asked, "What do you think? I'm leaning toward abandoning the farm all together. We could move the cattle up slowly, a couple each day, and then—"

"Then what?" Sidney interrupted. "It would buy us a couple of days, but it's only delaying the inevitable."

He sighed. He'd been thinking the same thing. "So what do you propose?"

"We take the fight to them."

"Eh? What's that?" He'd heard her perfectly clear; he just wasn't sure of what she meant.

"If we abandon the farm, they'll just find us again in a few days. We're in *Kansas*, it's not like we could hide out in the mountains. It's a miracle that this little copse of trees is even here."

"Arbor Day project by the high school about twenty-five years ago," Vern muttered, remembering his son's participation in the venture and how much time they'd spent constructing those underground water traps to keep the saplings alive long enough to make it on their own.

"Whatever," she dismissed his interruption. "If we let them have free run of the area, they're going to find us. I'm sick of running and hiding. I say we start setting some traps and kicking these bastards out of our country."

He tried not to laugh at the absurdity of a woman with her breast out, feeding a baby, telling him they were going to fight an insurgency, but the look in her eyes when he met them told him that she was dead serious. "What kind of traps?"

Her eyes sparkled as she grinned. "I don't know. *You're* the soldier with all the experience fighting against the revolutionaries. You tell me."

The wheels in his head began to turn. He believed her to be right about the Iranians, or Koreans, or whomever. They would eventually find them, regardless of where they tried to hide. There hadn't been very many of the big cargo planes, three in total since they'd begun keeping an eye on the airport, so there couldn't have been very many soldiers yet. If they could destroy the enemy's foothold in the region before they built their walls and established themselves, then maybe they could carve out a small area where their little *resistance* movement could grow.

It'd be a lot of dangerous work, with little to no guarantee of success. *The Devil will find work for idle hands*, he reminded himself of a phrase his preacher used to say all the time when he was a child. If they didn't do *something*, then the invaders would surely bring them in.

Plus, they had the element of surprise. The enemy would only be preparing to repel the mindless masses at first, they wouldn't have any idea that anyone was actively trying to infiltrate their defenses until it was too late.

"I've got some ideas," Vern finally said. "But they don't involve no traps and sittin' around waitin' for the enemy to come to us."

22

PERTH AMBOY, NEW JERSEY
FEBRUARY 28TH

"I need a refill, sir!" Corporal Jones shouted at Jake through the helmet comm to be heard over the sound of his machine gun. The lieutenant was only about twelve inches away from the gunner's station, but he might as well have been on the other side of a raging river for all the noise the guns around them made.

Jake gritted his teeth against the stupidity of the CROWS platform. It was a .50 caliber machine gun mounted externally, controlled from inside the vehicle through cameras, sensors, servos, and other types of electronics. But to reload the damn thing, *somebody* had to open the hatch and expose themselves to enemy fire—or in this case, to the infected.

"Mother fucker," Jake muttered. It was his responsibility to change the ammo. There were two soldiers in the back of his truck, both of whom could technically climb through the air guard hatch in the back and crawl along the top of the vehicle, but that would be stupid. His hatch was directly beside the CROWS and he was the commander of the mission— even if he'd gone AWOL and was now unofficially back in the fold. "How many more rounds do you have?"

"Only about ten."

Even feathering the trigger, the best Jones could hope to get was five or six aimed shots, then he'd be empty. Ten rounds would have been devastating against the human enemies the weapon system was designed to combat, but against the infected, all it did was call more of them to the area.

As if they needed that to happen.

They'd changed their destination early in the trip after a near-disastrous run-in with an infected mob near Louisville, Kentucky. The city wasn't even that big, but the infected were out in force and surrounded the small convoy. Only the giant engines of the Strykers and their massive tires had kept the convoy from being hopelessly trapped. Even with those, it was touch and go for a few minutes when one of them became high-centered on a mound of bodies.

Once they were out of that mess, they headed directly for New York City instead of trying to make it to Washington, DC first. There were very few infected and plenty of evidence of human survivors when they made their way into the mountains of West Virginia. Jake had considered trying to find them, but ultimately decided against it, rationalizing that if the survivors wanted to be found, they'd have made themselves known.

The mission had taken a turn for the worse when they reached the nearly continuous urban sprawl of eastern New Jersey. The snow and ice covered highways were often choked with abandoned or wrecked vehicles that had to be bypassed or sometimes moved out of the way, usually under the threat of nearby infected. They tried to go to the bridge onto Staten Island, but of course the New York governor had called for the destruction of the bridges into the city almost as soon as the outbreaks began.

They'd tried to find some type of docks with actual boats in the nearby Harbortown Port, but it had yielded little results. The area was a construction wasteland—great for fields of fire in most places, but not what they needed as far as providing transport across the Staten Island Sound. The infected had swarmed them from the surrounding city, blocking their return to the highway and forcing them southward to try to find a different way across the Sound.

Jake knew that *somewhere* along that godforsaken shoreline would be a marina or docks with a boat large enough for all of the soldiers to fit. His intuition had paid off when they rumbled up on the Harborside Marina a few miles south of where they'd initially tried to cross. Sergeant Turner immediately directed the Strykers to form a barrier in front of the marina's entrance while a couple of soldiers went down to the bobbing boats to see if any were useable.

Parked nose to tail as a makeshift wall, the big trucks lost their advantage of mobility. Instead, they were like a line of bunkers, impenetrable by the infected. The occupants could have stayed inside them for as long as they had food and water—in theory. Jake knew the men and women in the platoon were already going stir crazy since they'd been sleeping inside the vehicles for so long and were only allowed out of them for refueling missions. If things didn't change soon, he'd end up with a mass desertion on his hands—fitting, in a way, considering that he'd gone AWOL himself.

In desperation, Jake had authorized the platoon to turn on their Blue Force Trackers. That way, if there were any Army units keeping watch from New York City, they would see the trucks pop up on their screen. They were well away from Bhagat's sphere of influence so staying dark didn't matter anymore.

"That's it, sir," Jones grumbled into the mic as the gun above them went silent. "We're black on ammo."

Jake thumbed the comm over to the platoon frequency. "This is Red One in Truck Three." He'd taken to calling himself by his old call sign once again. "We're black on ammo. I need verification that no infected are crawling on the hull so I can pop the hatch to reload."

He waited while soldiers in the adjacent vehicles checked the outside of his Stryker through their periscopes to ensure there wasn't a nasty surprise waiting on him when he went outside. After a moment, the radio crackled to life. "*Hey, L.T. This is Grady.*"

"Um, what is it, Harper?" He hated the way the operator pronounced the abbreviation as 'El Tee' like he was some sort of goddamned Vietnam War soldier from a movie.

"I'm immune to these fuckers. Why don't I just hop out and change your ammo for you?"

"Negative, Harper!" Jake said too loudly into the mic. "You may be immune, but you sure as hell aren't bulletproof. Those things would rip you to shreds and then this mission would have been a waste of time."

"Fuck that," the CIA man laughed. *"I'm not afraid of a few thousand creepy-crawlies. Truck Three, right?"*

"Goddammit, Harper! I said negative. Do not leave your vehicle."

The headset was silent for a moment and he pushed his head up against the circular hatch to look out through the M-45 Periscope array. He saw the hatch of the trail vehicle pop up. Then, a heavily accented voice came over the radio.

"Ah, sir? This is Shaikh. Grady just left the vehicle."

They'd all been shocked when they learned the Iranian could speak fluent English, making them wonder what information he'd gleaned from them when they thought he was just a foreigner who didn't speak the language. The man professed to have no knowledge of his nation's overall goal in the United States except to help the UN exterminate the infected—what he called the Cursed. He'd stated often enough that he was happy going wherever they could kill the most of them since he'd still be performing the mission that he was ordered to do, even if every other member of his unit was dead. The jury was out on whether Jake believed him or not, but for now, every gun counted.

"Mother fucker," Jake cursed before hitting the transmit button. "Thank you, Shaikh. Keep up the pressure on the infected."

He tapped his gunner's pant leg. "I'm going up," he said when Jones looked over at him.

"That crazy fucker is gonna change the ammo, sir," Jones replied. "No reason you should go out there too."

Jake shook his head violently. "I'm going."

He disconnected his CVC helmet from the curled length of communications cord and grabbed his M-4 before depressing the lever to unlock the TC hatch. He pushed against it and surged rapidly upward, bringing his rifle up to scan the immediate area for the infected. So far, they were still held at bay at around a hundred and fifty meters by the withering fire from the six trucks—five, considering his was out of ammo.

Boots thumped onto the vehicle behind him and he turned quickly. "Whoa, Jake!" Grady laughed, holding up his hands in mock surrender. "I said I was coming over to change out your ammo, buddy."

Jake placed his hands on the hull and jumped. He caught his weight with his arms and then shimmied his butt onto the roof. "And I said to stay in your fucking truck, Harper. If you get yourself killed, then we abandoned the Campbells back in Oklahoma for no damn reason."

Grady knelt beside the CROWS and opened the tray on the .50 caliber, then swept away a few errant links. "Look, *sir*, I'm as much a part of this platoon as you are. I'm immune to those fuckers, so I'm trying to do my part to keep us *all* alive. You get me?"

Jake seethed inside. The man was infuriating like only special operations guys could be. They were often extremely confident, refusing to listen when people told them that they weren't Superman, and as a result they came off as condescending, even when they didn't mean to be.

"Listen, dammit," Jake said. "I need you to stay safe. You may be the best—and only—chance for America's survival. Can you please—"

Grady brought his rifle up and fired two rapid shots just to the side of Jake's chest. The lieutenant jerked, thinking the operator was shooting at him. "What the fuck, man?"

Grady laughed like he was two steps away from being committed to a mental institution, and pointed behind Jake with one hand while continuing the reload procedure with the other. He turned to see a pair of infected lying motionless twenty feet from the Stryker.

"No can do, bro," the operator said. "Even before everything went to shit, I was only good at one thing, and in my line of work, I made sure that I had every opportunity to practice my skills." He finished loading the .50 and racked the charging handle before patting the barrel of the gun. "You can't dangle a blooded lamb in front of a lion and expect him to do nothing."

"What?" Jake asked, glancing at Grady before turning his gaze toward the marina. *Where are those fucking soldiers with the boats?*

"I'm not gonna sit tight, all safe and sound, buttoned up inside my vehicle while guys are fighting for our survival. It's not who I am." To emphasize his point, he brought up his rifle and fired several rounds into the massing mob of infected.

"I'm in charge here, Harper," Jake stated. "Without good order and discipline—"

"Save it, L.T. I don't give a shit about your good order and discipline. That's why I got out and became a contractor. I can contribute to this fight, and you can bet your ass that I'm gonna keep doing so."

A head popped up between Jake's legs. It was Jones. "Sir, the .50's loaded. I need to get back in the fight."

Jake grunted and brought up his hand, pointing at the far off Truck Six. "You get your ass back to your truck, Harper. My men know how to utilize *all* of the equipment that they have to stay in the fight as long as possible. You can die for all I care. I really don't give a shit anymore. But don't you dare endanger any one of them, or I'll shoot you myself."

Grady grinned widely. "Aww yeah! Now you're starting to sound like an officer that I'd actually take orders from instead of some pussy Academy fuckwad."

"Fuck you, Harper. The sooner we can get you onto a boat and into the city, the better."

"Then we finally see eye-to-eye, *boss*."

The operator stood, fired a few more rounds, and then hopped over to Truck Four's hull. Jake watched him jog across the roof, mindful to stay behind the truck's CROWS as it rained fire down on the infected toward the west. When he leapt over to Truck Five, Jake dropped down and closed the hatch.

"Light 'em up, gunner," he said with a raised thumb.

The machine gun began to rock overhead and Jake turned his attention back to the water. The men he'd sent were still not visible through the periscopes. He grabbed the handset for the radio that was set to the dismounts' frequency. "Boat Team, this is Red One, what's your status, over?"

There was silence and then, "Sir, this is Sergeant Turner. We raided the manager's office and got a whole mess of keys. So far, we've got two boats running that can hold about thirty guys, max. Give me a few more minutes to find another boat with fuel. Over."

"Roger," Jake replied. "We need to have room for rucks and ammo. There's no telling what we'll find in the city. Over."

"Acknowledged, sir."

Jake nodded absentmindedly, knowing that the man on the other end of the radio couldn't see him. "Red One, out."

New York City had been isolated for almost a year. There was likely mass starvation and lawlessness, probably worse than anything that he'd seen back at Fort Bliss. Hell, going into the city *might* be more risky than being outside with the infected.

He turned back around and peered through the periscopes at the thousands of infected streaming toward the sound of gunfire from the surrounding city. They ran as best as their malnourished bodies could handle into the steel wall that the Stryker gunners laid between them and the rest of the platoon.

Jake hoped the boat team would get enough transports for everyone before the Strykers ran out of ammo. If they didn't, the best case was that everyone would be trapped inside the impenetrable vehicles until the infected grew bored and wandered off in search of new and interesting prey. Worst case, the pressure of all those bodies against the sides of the vehicles would push them into the water where everyone would drown.

"Come on, Sergeant Turner," he mumbled quietly. "Get those boats up and running or else we're gonna be in some serious shit."

He glanced back at the harbor and his eyes drifted toward the city, imposing and daunting, beyond the narrow Sound. "Get those boats up so *then* we can really get into some serious shit," he amended.

23

FORT BLISS MAIN CANTONEMENT AREA
MARCH 1ST

Major General Bhagat skimmed the morning report. He'd had two electronic warfare teams go missing from their hide sites overnight, each about a hundred miles or so from the base. They could have gone off the net for any number of reasons, from the mundane excuse that the batteries for their comms equipment had died, to being overrun by the infected still wandering around the desert somehow, all the way to the very real possibility that they'd gotten rolled up by an Iranian or North Korean patrol.

There'd been no overt signs that the UN troops were operating in the desert. They were keeping well away from the base. But Bhagat had been able to get updated satellite feeds showing a camp near Carlsbad, New Mexico. It was set up near the intersecting lines of two hundred and sixty mile bubbles around both Fort Bliss and Holloman Air Force Base. His intel officer said the distance from each was significant in that they were beyond any standard type of flight distance from either base, hence, undetectable if the inhabitants weren't specifically looking for them.

Fort Bliss had been unable to talk reliably with the Air Force jockeys at Holloman for several weeks. Bhagat had increasingly begun to believe the Division Signal Officer when he said their radios were being jammed, so he'd sent out three teams to try to reach Holloman, along with two electronic warfare counter-jamming teams. They'd lost contact with the last of the recon teams yesterday.

"And now the EW teams," Neel mumbled under his breath. He took a sip of black coffee and grimaced. He preferred cream or milk in his coffee, but the base was out of both, so he had to make do with black coffee. It was a very small sacrifice to make considering what people outside the walls must have endured over the last year.

He skimmed the one-pager until he got to the paragraph one up from the bottom. He set his coffee down when he read it. The BFTs on Lieutenant Murphy's stolen Stryker and on five of the six Strykers that Jim Albrecht had taken northward to find the little traitor had been turned on. Except the location pings from the vehicles that the signal personnel scanned for hourly didn't make any sense. All six of the vehicles were in New Jersey.

"Freddy, get in here," the general bellowed through his open door.

"Moving, sir," came the aide's response. Within seconds, the tall, lanky lieutenant's head popped into the doorway. "Yes, sir?"

"Get me the Three, the Six...and the Two. I don't care what they're doing, get them up here now."

"Yes, sir."

While Lieutenant MacArthur set about calling the three staff officers he'd requested, Neel reread the paragraph about the Strykers.

> Update to 1LT Murphy arrest: At 0734 MST, 6 BFT systems were powered on almost simultaneously in Perth Amboy, New Jersey. The city is adjacent to Staten Island, New York. The Stryker IFV that 1LT Murphy

stole in October is among the vehicles, including 5 of 6 Strykers that COL Albrecht took to Oklahoma to apprehend the lieutenant. Previously, last BFT ping was on 12FEB near a small local airport in Liberal, Kansas. Unknown whereabouts of 6th Stryker. All attempts to communicate via BFT have been ignored.

"What in the hell is Jim doing up near New York?" Bhagat grumbled aloud, sipping his coffee as he read the paragraph a third time.

"Ah, sir?" Lieutenant MacArthur reappeared at his door. "The Two and the Six are on their way up. I spoke to the G-3 Sergeant Major, and he said the Three is showering after this morning's PT."

Neel looked up from the paper with murder in his eyes. "Then go down and get him."

"Yes, sir."

Was Jim Albrecht still in command of the unit? The fact that one of his brigade commanders had gone AWOL was concerning. Jim had been a trusted agent, responsible for directly overseeing the combat operations of 3,900 men and women until the revolt reduced his command down to a few dozen— something even the infected hadn't managed to do.

He'd shown unwillingness to go after Lieutenant Murphy, but Bhagat was able to convince him that he needed to go after the traitor. There was a lot of information missing from the story that he needed answers for.

A knock at his door indicated the arrival of one of the staff officers. He looked up to see the Division Signal Officer. "Ah, sir... Lieutenant MacArthur said you, uh, wanted to see me?" Major Calamante said in his characteristic halting pattern of speech.

"Yeah. Come on in and have a seat, Juan. The others will be here in a few minutes."

He waited until the intelligence officer came in before he moved to the conference table. "The Three is on his way, but I'm not gonna hold you two up." He dropped the morning update sheet onto the table and sat down. Jabbing his finger onto the paragraph at the bottom of the page, the general said, "What are my Strykers doing in New Jersey?"

Bhagat watched their reactions. The intelligence officer's face showed genuine surprise, meaning he didn't know about the latest change in events. The signal officer, on the other hand, blanched. The man was likely realizing that he should have come upstairs to brief the general immediately, as directed several weeks ago, instead of putting it in a report.

"Well, ah, sir," Calamante began.

"Cut the crap, Juan," Bhagat said, cutting him short. "I want answers. Don't give me some made up garbage."

"Yeah, um... Well, sir, we monitor the net for the BFT signals around the clock, even though it's pretty manpower intensive."

"I don't care that one of your signaleers didn't get a few extra hours of sleep," Bhagat said. "We're not doing any type of large scale combat operations that require staying in contact during movement. We just send guys up to the wall and shoot the fish in the barrel below. Don't make excuses."

"Ah, yes, sir. Sorry. Um, so we monitor for the BFT signals of the, um, six Strykers that Colonel Albrecht took and the Stryker that Lieutenant Murphy stole. Um, we think, based on signals intelligence that one of First Brigade's Strykers was left in a little town in New Mexico—the name escapes me right now."

"Santa Rosa," the intelligence officer piped up.

"Um, yeah, that's right," Calamante agreed. "We never spoke to them, but we know that they entered that town with six trucks and left with five."

Bhagat rolled his wrist. "I know all this already."

The major nodded. "Yes, sir. So they, ah, they went dark after they went by that airport in Kansas."

The general looked to the Two. "Any satellite intel about what's going on at that airport?"

"Yes, sir. It appears to be a refuel point for the transnational UN flights. The runway is just large enough for C-130 cargo planes and fighter jets to land and take off. In fact, there were a C-130 and two MiG-29 jets sitting near the terminal when the satellite passed overhead. We've observed several of these types of operations at smaller, isolated airfields across the Midwest. It makes sense that they're avoiding larger airports in heavily populated areas in favor of these airfields to reduce the chances of being discovered and overran by the infected."

Bhagat nodded. The signal officer may have been an idiot, but his intel officer was good at his job. "Good assessment, Major Blackledge." He turned back to the Six. "So, they went offline in Kansas. How far is that airport from the farmhouse that Colonel Albrecht targeted?"

"It's about thirteen miles, sir," the intelligence officer answered.

"So it's possible that they got rolled up by the UN troops at the airport?"

Major Blackledge shrugged. "That depends on whether we are considering the UN forces as hostile."

The major seemed to pick his words carefully as he continued. "There have been indications that the Iranians and North Koreans that make up the bulk of the new UN force may not have the United States' best interests at heart. Yes, they brought in stabilization teams almost immediately to work at our nuclear power plants, shutting them down or keeping them running as needed, but…those actions would be prudent for any force looking to occupy a location long-term."

Another quick knock at the door preceded the Three. "Dave," General Bhagat said in greeting.

"Sorry I'm late, sir. I didn't know—"

"It's okay. This is a last-minute meeting," Neel said. "Did you see this morning's update?"

Colonel Tovey sat down to the general's right. The smell of fresh soap drifted off the operations officer, not the unpleasant, unwashed smell of one of the other two officers who'd entered. Bhagat wasn't sure which one it was. "Not yet, sir," Tovey said. "I approved the operational highlights, but haven't gotten a chance to review the other staff sections' input."

Bhagat slid the paper over and pointed to the paragraph. After a few seconds of Tovey's lips moving as he read silently, he looked up. "What the hell does that mean, sir?"

"That's why I brought you three in here," the general replied. "Why are my Strykers in New Jersey, of all places? What is that? Two thousand miles?"

"Probably, sir. If not more."

"We've had one telephone call from Jim Albrecht since this whole thing started," Bhagat said, glancing at his aide who'd sat at a chair along the wall. "He was told about the UN presence and within ten or twelve hours of that phone call, all of their BFTs went offline. Why is that?"

"I could only venture a guess, sir."

"Then guess, Dave," Neel directed the operations officer. "What chain of events led one of my brigade commanders to go off the rails and abandon his family here in Fort Bliss?"

"My guess," Colonel Tovey began, "is that he's dead and the lieutenant that they went to apprehend has taken over the group."

"That's a pretty far-fetched guess, Dave," the general replied, staring at his operations officer as if he'd never seen the man before. "I didn't mean make up a wild claim like that, but let's go with it. Why do you think Lieutenant Murphy is in charge of them instead of dead?"

He pointed toward the daily update page. "We know that Murphy's Stryker is with them, so they're together somehow. He could be dead and they commandeered his vehicle once they found him, but that still doesn't explain why they'd go to New Jersey."

"Ah, sir? If I may?" the intelligence officer said.

"Go ahead, Todd," Neel answered.

"We just know that they were in New Jersey when this signal began broadcasting. That's pretty strange behavior to drive completely across the country without having them on and then flip the switch when they were near New York. I think they're trying to signal someone in the city."

"Go on."

"Do you have a map, sir?"

Bhagat looked over at his aide. "Freddy, can you pull up a map of—" He looked back to Major Blackledge.

"The United States, sir. Specifically New Jersey."

Neel nodded at the lieutenant as he moved over to the general's computer and began manipulating the mouse. The internet had been spotty, at best, but it should be sufficient for the intelligence officer's needs.

"Okay, so while he's doing that, continue," the general ordered.

"So we know that New York City is still intact. The governor dropped all the bridges and blocked the tunnels, supposedly the subway tunnels as well—anything that connected the islands to the mainland—as a way to try and stop the spread into the city."

"Last we heard, sir," Dave cut in, "the city was still intact with no infected."

"The IC's assessment is that New York City is still intact," the intelligence officer confirmed.

"Can you imagine the hell that it must be?" Bhagat mumbled. "There are twenty million people there, we had a little under four million and were prepared with food supplies. New York City had nothing."

"Here you go, sir," Freddy MacArthur said from the computer as he hit the button to project the screen's images onto the television mounted to the side of the conference table.

The map of New Jersey came up. "Can you scroll toward Staten Island?" Major Blackledge asked.

"I... Ah, I'm not sure which..."

"Here, let me," Major Calamante said. "I'm from the Bronx." He went to the computer and re-centered the map over Staten Island.

"Zoom out just a bit," the intelligence officer directed. When the screen showed the bump out of New Jersey toward New York, Blackledge said, "Stop."

Major Blackledge stood and went around the table, pointing at the screen. "See, they were right here on this highway when the signals went live, right, Juan?"

"Um, yeah. I believe so."

"How long were they there before they went south?"

The signal officer referred to his notebook. "I don't know, around five minutes. Then they went south into this area." He ran his cursor in a circle over an area that had a marker centered over it indicating it was a point of interest.

"What is that?" General Bhagat asked.

"Um…" Major Calamante looked at the map. "It says 'Harbortown Ports', but I know for a fact that nothing's there." He switched to satellite imagery. "See, it's just a massive construction project."

"Okay, so where'd they go after that?" Todd asked.

"They went south for about mile and they've been there ever since."

"About a mile?" Todd stated, looking at the map. "Like around the Perth Amboy Harborside Marina?"

Juan nodded. "Yeah, that's about right."

The intelligence officer looked over at the general. "I think they were trying to make it into New York City, sir. They were on the highway, came up to the destroyed bridge going over to Staten Island and began broadcasting their BFT for any friendlies in the city to hear. Given how quickly they left, they were probably pursued by the infected. They went south to find a boat over to the city, found the harbor and made their stand there."

Neel scratched at his chin. "Sounds entirely plausible. Do we know if anyone replied to their BFT signals?"

"Negative, sir," Juan replied.

"Hmm…" Bhagat thought about the implications of the platoon going to the city. "Were they seeking safe haven there, or what?"

"We don't know, sir," the signal officer said. "All we know is that they began broadcasting."

"We could have offered them safety here," Todd stated. "What if they weren't seeking safety, but something else altogether? What if they were trying to get in contact with someone in the city, someone who might be able to help, like a scientist or something?"

"We have scientists here," Neel said.

"Not really, sir. Most of the research personnel we had here were killed with that outbreak last March. What if they were trying to get somebody who was immune to a scientist in the city to begin working on a cure?"

"That's not possible," Bhagat scoffed. The statement dragged the memory of his old friend's betrayal from the dungeon he'd locked it in. Aarav Sanjay hadn't been working on a cure as he'd professed. "There's no curing those things out there." He jabbed a finger in the general direction of the walls. "But, of more pressing concern is what's happening to our scouts that we send out."

Colonel Tovey sighed. "I don't know, sir. You saw on our daily update that the teams we've sent out to try to scout on that base have all gone offline— probably killed. We don't know if that's from the infected or if that's from something else."

Bhagat nodded. He'd thought the same thing before he called this impromptu meeting. He gestured at the intelligence officer. "Before you came in, Dave, Todd had just asked the most pertinent question of the morning. Are we going to begin considering the 'UN troops' enemies?" He made quotation marks with his fingers in the air as he said the words. "I know what the president has said, but the president is also in a bunker somewhere and hasn't poked his head up out of the sand in almost a year."

"It's a sticky situation, sir. I don't think the Iranians and the North Koreans are here to help keep us safe," Colonel Tovey stated. In his periphery, he saw the signal officer slink back to the table from the desktop computer. "I think it's the opposite. I think they caused this and they're here to wipe out the rest of our resistance so they can take our land."

Neel grimaced. "I'm beginning to think the same thing, Dave. I don't like it. There're too many problems with them being here. The first of which is that they conveniently had a security forces package ready to go in the middle of a worldwide pandemic. The next is that their population wasn't decimated like ours was. The whole thing stinks. Now I've got missing troopers near a UN base that just happens to be on the edge of where we could reach it with a combat force and near the round trip flight limit of manned aircraft out of Holloman."

"I agree, sir," Dave said. "But what can we do about it? The Iranians and the Norks seem to be a few steps ahead of us all the time, plus they have the blessing of the POTUS. So unless we're talking about disobeying his orders…"

Dave trailed off. Neel knew what he was doing. The operations officer had left it open for his commander to commit treason, but hadn't actually suggested it himself. *If we go down that road, how are we any different than that traitor, Murphy?*

He didn't have an answer for that yet. One thing was certain; he needed to confer about the situation with a few trusted people. "Major Calamante, I need you to figure out a way to set up a VTC with Colonel McTaggert, the base commander over at Holloman Air Force Base. I don't want to hear about us being jammed, just make it happen."

"Roger, sir."

"Check that, make it a SVTC, secure point-to-point. Send along the info that it's to be him only, nobody else." The signal officer nodded at his request to take the unclassified VTC to the secret level.

"Timeframe, sir?"

"Any time. There are no meetings that we have around here that are more important than the conversation I'm going to have with him, so whatever fits his schedule."

"Roger," the man answered, scribbling notes into his book. He was already planning on the logistics of the operation. *Maybe he isn't a terrible staff officer*, Bhagat thought.

"Alright. I've got to prepare some notes for the SVTC. In the meantime, I want everyone here to keep an ear out for Lieutenant Murphy and try to figure out what they're actually doing up there in New Jersey."

The three officers nodded in unison and Bhagat pushed his chair back from the table. They each sprang to their feet and rendered hand salutes. He returned them and looked out the window at the dreary gray sky.

"Might be a storm coming," he said. "A giant, fucking mess of a storm."

24

LOWER NEW YORK BAY, NEW YORK CITY, NEW YORK
MARCH 1ST

"Well, I'll be, L.T. You did it!" Grady chuckled, slapping Jake Murphy on the back. "You believe this shit, Taavi? Here I thought we were gonna have to walk all the way to the lab. But fuck me if we aren't on a nice little pleasure cruise."

The operator looked over to his companion, Major Shaikh. The man's dark skin was pale and he appeared as if he were only a moment away from vomiting up the MRE he'd eaten earlier. "I guess you ain't really been on a boat too often since you grew up in the desert, have you?"

The Iranian shook his head and then ran over to the side of the boat, leaning over. Grady watched his back arch as he emptied the contents of his stomach. "Damn, Taavi. We aren't even really in open water. This is just a glorified bay."

He laughed, relishing in the open air after over two weeks cramped inside that tin can Stryker vehicle. The salt spray off the ocean stung his eyes when he looked toward the front of the boat, but he didn't care. They'd overcome nearly impossible odds to make it this far and now they were on to the next leg of their journey, only two soldiers fewer than what they'd left Kansas with.

That small thought sobered Grady's mood. They'd lost two men when they abandoned the Strykers to go to the boats. He didn't know the specifics of it, but somehow, both of them had become separated during the footrace to the water's edge. By the time the boats shoved off, the docks and shoreline had been jam-packed with the infected. The creatures snarled their hatred of the humans that had eluded their grasp. All of the soldiers knew the two men were goners, but the lieutenant had anchored the boats twenty feet offshore for over an hour, giving the men every opportunity to appear. They never did.

Grady spat a lump of phlegm into the ocean. Off to their left, maybe four hundred feet or so, was Staten Island. It looked as if the island was packed shoreline to shoreline with homes and businesses, presumably all occupied prior to the outbreak. Now? None of them knew. He'd glimpsed occasional people along the water's edge, but none of them paid the small three-boat flotilla any mind. Fishing boats seemed to be in abundance on the water, so they were used to them speeding by. There were hundreds of boats going back and forth across their path, obviously trying to keep the remaining population alive. The other boaters were a hard-looking bunch, bundled against the icy weather, the sea spray, and likely concealing weapons. They did not appear friendly in the least—a fact not lost on Grady.

The world he'd awoken to—or more appropriately, the world that he'd been *released* into—was completely different than anything he'd experienced, and he'd been in some major shitholes in his lifetime. He'd been on presidential guard duties in Africa that had almost ended in disaster, taken part in the bombing of the Chinese embassy in Belgrade, been the point man for the US response to the whispered rumors of biological experiments on humans, and a whole host of other missions that were an organized mess inside his skull. Nothing had prepared him for the wanton disregard for life that he'd experienced since awakening in that Oklahoma airport. He used to think that people in Sub-Saharan Africa thought life was worthless until now. Now, they slaughtered the infected by the thousands without anyone blinking an eye.

And those men and women in the fishing boats looked back at them the way the soldiers in the platoon looked at the infected. Another person's life was truly meaningless to them.

His mood soured further and he adjusted the M-4's two-point sling on his shoulder, loosening the nylon that wrapped around his back and connected with the rifle near his hip. Best to keep it close with a round chambered, especially once they made landfall.

As they sped past an inlet that looked to have a small harbor in it, Grady reassessed the buildings on the shoreline. They'd traveled beyond the closely packed single family homes and now several unkempt beaches were off to their left. There were still plenty of homes and businesses, but they were set farther back, away from what had once been miles of sandy beaches for native New Yorkers and tourists alike. The shores were littered with trash, beached boats, and even a large container ship had wrecked by a large hotel, its contents half on and half off of the ship as it had rolled to one side on the rocky bottom.

He felt a tap on his shoulder and turned to see Taavi with a thumb sticking up in the air. "Good to go?" he asked.

"I am feeling better. Your food is shit."

"Thanks," Grady chuckled. His gaze lingered on the Iranian for a moment too long. What was his end game? He'd professed to having no love for his fellow Muslims, but the operator had seen too many insider attacks in his day. Whatever they said, he could never truly trust them. When pressed, the major admitted to wanting to go back home to Iran to oversee the burial of his wife and children. Beyond that, the man wouldn't say any more.

"This place sure went to hell, didn't it?" Lieutenant Murphy asked, jutting his chin toward the shoreline.

"I never made it to Staten Island," Grady admitted. "But I spent quite a long time in the city, including a week of counter surveillance training and stealth shadowing operations in a dense urban environment. I wasn't overly impressed with the parts of the city that our instructors had us train in, though."

"That container ship over there is like something right out of a post-apocalyptic movie or something."

Grady laughed. "Hell, sir. *Life* is like a post-apocalyptic movie these days."

The lieutenant pointed to his gunner, Corporal Jones, who stood behind the steering wheel of the boat. "Jones is from New Jersey. Grew up on the water and came to New York City a lot as a kid. He says there's a big harbor about halfway up Manhattan in Hell's Kitchen that'll be our best point of insertion. After that, we'll have to go overland through the city to Columbia University, where the internet rumors say the CDC is working on a cure."

Grady had come along on the mission, practically planned most of it, so he knew about the labs in the university's biology department, but he'd done some research of his own on one of the Campbell girls' cell phones using the intermittent internet connection. He was willing to bet that the CDC information was a ruse in case anyone in the city decided to hit the place. His money was that they'd show up at Columbia's main campus and be shit out of luck. The real work was going to be happening up in the biochemistry and molecular biophysics labs at

Columbia's Irving Medical Center about three miles north of the main campus. But they had to go to each of them to be sure.

"These people look very friendly to you, Harper?" the lieutenant asked, again gesturing toward the capsized ship with his chin. Grady knew it was to avoid making an overt pointing motion in the direction of the scavengers going through the containers in case they were trigger happy, but he had to laugh because it looked incredibly stupid. *Must've been one of those dumb shit things they taught these kids at West Point*, he thought.

"I don't know, L.T. The ones that I've seen clearly didn't seem too bad. More like they want to know if we've come to save them from this hellhole and if not, just what the fuck we're doing here. Food's gotta be scarce, forty more mouths to feed isn't gonna sit well with anyone."

Jake nodded. "Yeah, I guess you're right."

Once they passed the container ship, a macabre scene greeted them on the shoreline. A long row of crosses dotted the sand. A person was nailed to each of them. The shouts of alarm from the other soldiers in the boat made Grady raise his arms. "Calm down, everyone. Those people may have been infected or murderers, or rapists. We have no idea what's going on here."

Jake tapped Jones on the shoulder. "And we're not about to find out, Harper. Speed up, Jones. We need to put this place behind us."

The corporal nodded and pushed the throttle down a little lower. The boat actually leveled out the faster they went, allowing the soldier to sit in the chair instead of stand behind the wheel. Grady turned to make sure the other two boats followed suit, which they did. Then he brought up his rifle, peering through the scope at the crosses.

There must have been thirty or forty of them. The few that he scoped held dead men and women. None of them had a severe amount of blood on them or the telltale red stain on their chests where they'd thrown up that nasty shit, so he believed they'd been human, not infected. He had no way of knowing whether they'd been dead when they were put there or if they died on the crosses, but he imagined that if they were there as a punishment and a warning to others not to do the same things, then they were probably nailed there when they were alive.

"Hell of a way to get your point across," he muttered, dropping his rifle.

"What's that?" Jake asked.

"Nothing, L.T.," he replied. "I'm just thinking out loud about what we've gotten ourselves into."

The lieutenant looked him in the eyes. "We're doing the right thing here, Harper. We can't fight against these things forever. Sooner or later, we're gonna run out of ammo or food, then people have to leave their shelters. I don't think there's a way to cure the infected. A vaccine to keep the disease from spreading is about the only way I can see humanity surviving this."

Grady set his jaw. The way the kid talked about a vaccine was akin to when religious zealots talked about their deity. It wasn't healthy. Jake had taken Grady's idea to find a lab to figure out what the hell those scientists had done to him and created an entire world-saving scenario in his mind.

"I'm not sure if those doctors up here will be able to find a way to reproduce what was done to me—if there's anyone even at the campus anymore."

Jake ducked his chin, ceding the point. "We have to try though. Otherwise, what's the point of staying alive if you know you're guaranteed to become an insane killing machine eventually?"

Grady grinned. "Uncle Sam turned me into an insane killing machine a long time ago, L.T. A damn fine sexy one, too."

Jake rolled his eyes. "God, have you been drinking?"

They passed under a bridge and a plume of water appeared next to the boat, then another, followed by several more. Grady looked up at the bridge where people were throwing large cinder blocks and bricks from above. "Mother fucker!" he screamed as he brought his rifle up.

"No!" Jake shouted. "We don't know what they're doing."

Grady broke his cheek-to-stock and looked at the lieutenant. "They're trying to hit our boat, that's what they're fucking doing."

"But we don't know *why*. They may just be—"

The second boat took a cinder block right to the bow where a soldier lay. The heavy block punched through the flimsy fiberglass and threw the soldier overboard. The driver slowed and the boat began to take on water immediately.

"No. No. No," Grady mumbled. Stopping was exactly what the marauders on the bridge wanted. From two hundred feet above, people began to jump and he thought they would surely die from the fall until he saw that they had ropes attached to their chest and midsection. He brought up his rifle. Each of the four men who'd jumped carried large spears that looked like pitchforks and canvas bags hung low from their belts.

"They thought we were fishermen and they're trying to steal our catch," he stated aloud as the men were lowered quickly by others standing at the railings. "Well, fuck them."

By the time he'd shot the third man, the people holding the ropes above abandoned the fourth would-be thief. He fell the remaining hundred and fifty feet, screaming. The whole thing took less than ten seconds. "Gettin' slow in my old age," Grady grumbled.

Jake stared wide-eyed at him for a moment, then shouted, "Bring the boat around. Let's help them." He looked up at the bridge, adding, "Everyone else, shoot anyone who even peeks over the edge of that bridge."

They circled back to the second boat. The third was already beside it. "How bad is it?" Jake asked.

Grady appraised the damage in between scanning for targets above. There was a two-foot wide hole through the bow. He couldn't see from his vantage point how extensive the damage was, but the boat was definitely taking on water. The front was sitting lower in the water than the stern.

Sergeant Turner, who'd been driving the boat, pointed toward the far shoreline. "We're gonna be lucky if we make it to shore before we sink."

"Okay. Let's head for shore and hope you make it," Jake said. "*Not* Staten Island, that other side. I don't want to have to cross that bridge if we don't have to."

Grady grunted in approval. Beaching the boats and staying together, even if it meant they had to go overland through the city, was the right call. They couldn't afford to abandon fifteen men.

Turner's boat began limping toward the shore while the third boat stayed back to pull the soldier from the water before following behind the second and then alongside the damaged craft. Grady's boat pulled smoothly into line on the opposite side of Turner's.

"Where are we headed, Jones?" Grady asked.

"I think that's the Verrazano-Narrows," the gunner replied, pointing at the massive grey bridge they'd passed underneath. "Which means we're headed into Brooklyn."

"How far is that from Columbia University?"

"A *long* way, man. I don't even have a guess off the top of my head. It's at least fifteen miles. Some pretty shitty neighborhoods in between here and there if I remember right, but I'm not an expert on the city."

Grady glanced over his shoulder back at Staten Island where the crosses were still visible on the beach, and then at the bridge where they'd been attacked from above. They hadn't even stepped foot into the city yet and he knew it would be the toughest mission of his life. Fifteen miles on foot through neighborhoods that were bad *before* the end of the world seemed like some pretty shitty odds that they wouldn't make it to the university where the labs were supposed to be.

As they neared the shoreline, he saw that a paved path ran along the water's edge, bounded by a waist-high guardrail for as far as he could see. Jake steered the little flotilla toward the gentlest slope where they could beach their boats and hopefully avoid getting completely soaked when they jumped out.

The boats crunched as they hit the rocky shallows. "This is where we get off, boys. Make sure you lock up." A few half-hearted chuckles responded to Grady's dumb joke. He lifted his pack onto his back and splashed into the water beside the boat. The water poured in over the tops of his boots, soaking his feet and sending an electric shock up his spine.

He maneuvered his way up the bank to the guardrail and then rolled over it until his boots were on the bike path's solid pavement. Kneeling, he scanned the highway beyond for threats as the rest of the platoon made their way off the boats and up to the road where he was. Several soldiers followed his example, kneeling to keep an eye out for anything that was out of place.

Taavi sat down beside him, not bothering to keep watch. "Happy to be back on land, buddy?" Grady asked.

"You have no idea," the Iranian said. He pulled up the cuff of his jacket to expose the small compass on his watch. He moved his arm around for a moment until the little ball inside spun freely and he examined it closely. When he was satisfied, Taavi faced eastward and got onto his knees to pray.

When everyone was together, Jake pointed in their original direction of travel along the water. "Jones says if we keep going this way, we can take the path all the way around until we come to the first set of docks that we'd looked at for landing before we found the harbor way up in Manhattan.

"As far as we know, there aren't any infected in the city," Jake continued. "So don't assume that everyone we come across is a threat."

"But don't let yourselves get suckered into an ambush," Grady cautioned. The soldiers nodded in agreement.

Jake gave him a hard look before continuing. "We are US Army soldiers. We will not shoot citizens who don't pose a direct threat. Understood?" Several people grumbled in acknowledgement. "But, like *Mister* Harper said, don't let anyone get the drop on you. Alright, we've got a long way to go through some pretty rough neighborhoods. I want to make it at least halfway before we have to find a spot to hole up for the night. Let's get moving."

"You heard the lieutenant, men," Sergeant Turner hissed. He'd seemingly mastered the art of adding a menacing tone of authority to his voice while keeping the sound low enough that it wouldn't travel far. "We're walking from here on out. Keep your heads on a swivel and don't bunch up in case we stumble into some type of goddamned ambush."

"Come on, Taavi," Grady said, stepping off behind Jake. "We've got miles to go before we sleep." While he tried to be upbeat with his quote from the famous poem, he was confident that he'd just taken his first step on the road to hell.

EPILOGUE

LIBERAL, KANSAS
MARCH 1ST

Basir dove behind the truck into the snow piled up alongside the road as bullets pinged off the big vehicle's hood. Glass from the windows rained down on him. He was confused and scared. They were supposed to take over this country with ease. The population had been wiped out and the Cursed were starving to death, if not already dead.

"Don't just lay there, you idiot," Sergeant Dehkordi barked. "Return fire. Kill the infidels."

Basir looked to his squad leader to see if *he* was exposing himself to return fire. Of course he wasn't. The man cowered behind the tire at the rear of the vehicle. "Why are you not shooting?" he asked the older man.

"Do as I say, Private," Dehkordi ordered.

Basir shook his head. He didn't want to die in the middle of the United States, his corpse frozen for all time in the icy wastes. *How could anyone live here? Why would anyone live here?* he amended. He needed more information. Maybe it was all just a misunderstanding.

"Who is shooting at us, Sergeant?"

"Does it matter? Now get up and start firing!"

"What if it's somebody from the battalion and they are mistakenly firing upon us?" That was a very real possibility. The Cursed made everyone jumpy. They'd killed hundreds of them over the past two weeks, but there were still many thousands more just in the local area. The commander had several teams like this one patrolling the countryside to eliminate the Cursed in the vicinity of the airfield.

He risked a glance underneath the truck to where his squad mates, Piruz and Marzban, lay bleeding in the road. Piruz was certainly dead; the thick mass the color of putty protruding from the back of his head was what was left of his brain. Marzban was probably dead as well. He'd been hit several times and was unmoving. The white of his coveralls had multiple deep red stains across his chest and abdomen.

His friends were not hit by errant fire from Iranian scouts. They were under attack from Americans. Those very same people they'd come here to help were attacking them. The thought infuriated him.

"Allāhu Akbar!" Basir shouted as he surged upward. He fired several rounds from his AK over the hood of the truck in the direction that he thought the ambush had originated.

Suddenly, his vision blurred as he spun around, facing the opposite way than he'd been facing. His knees buckled and he fell to the snow once more. A dull throb in his shoulder made him wonder if he'd dislocated it when he fell. He didn't understand how that had even happened. Had he slipped?

No. That was unlikely, he'd— Pain rocked his body as the quick burst of adrenaline wore off. Basir looked to his shoulder; a flap of ragged flesh was all that remained of his deltoid muscle. Hot blood poured from the wound, melting the snow and turning it red.

A buzzing in his ears threatened to overtake his ability to hear Sergeant Dehkordi's insistent shouting. "Private Khadem! Are you injured?"

Basir fought the thickness of his own tongue. His vision was going dark at the edges and he shook his head to clear his mind. "They shot me, Sergeant."

"How bad is it?"

He tried to bring his hand up, but he was having a hard time fighting through the blackness. When he did manage to lift his hand, he saw that it was covered in blood as well. "Oh…" he muttered, holding it up in front of his eyes. He'd been shot through the back of his hand and his palm was a mass of destroyed flesh.

"I'm bad," Basir admitted.

He dropped his hand into the snow, allowing the icy coolness to seep into the wound. His head lolled to the side. Sergeant Dehkordi was hyperventilating behind the tire.

"Help me," Basir pleaded. "Need…bandage."

"I… I can't," Dehkordi said.

"I need help. Gonna bleed out."

The sergeant glanced at him, and then looked beyond him toward the open field on the opposite side of the road. There was nowhere to hide if he ran. There was no escape in the vast openness of the vacant fields they found themselves near.

"Help, Sergeant," Basir said once more. He could feel himself getting weaker and the darkness had returned.

"Okay," Dehkordi grunted. "I'm coming."

He dropped to the ground and began crawling toward Basir. The worm had overcome his fear, making the injured man smile. His sergeant would wrap the wounds and then they'd get into the truck and return to the airfield where a doctor could help him. That is what they should have done. They should have fled the moment they came under fire instead of trying to shoot back. Now Marzban and Piruz were dead, their lives wasted. Basir vowed to write their wives a letter once they returned to base.

Sergeant Dehkordi groaned loudly, making Basir focus his eyes. His squad leader was halfway to him, exposed along the vacant space underneath the large truck. As he watched, Dehkordi's head pushed back in the snow and a thick red mass flew from the new opening in his skull.

The sergeant stopped moving. Basir said a prayer to Allah for him and then remembered that he hadn't prayed for the others yet. He tried to do that as well, but he found that putting his thoughts into words was becoming increasingly more difficult.

Basir didn't know how long he lay there beside the truck in the snow. The sound of boots crunching on the frozen surface made him force his eyes open. He tried to turn his head, but the muscles were stiff and he found the action impossible. Several voices, including at least two women, drifted around the bulk of the vehicle.

An icy wetness hit him in the face as a white-clad form stomped up to him, flinging snow and causing his eyes to flutter.

"Hey, this one's alive," a boy's voice said in a language he didn't understand.

The sound of more boots assaulted his ears and the face of a woman appeared over him. He had a momentary hope that she was a nurse who'd been sent from the airfield to retrieve him so the doctors could operate.

Her features twisted into a sneer as she said, "Not anymore."

Basir saw the barrel of a rifle elevate toward his head. He started to beg for mercy, but the words never came and his life ended.

Sidney looked around at her small group with a smile. "Mark, disable the truck. We need to take what we can and get out of here before they send out reinforcements."

"Yes, ma'am," the youth said as he slid into the cab of the truck to release the hood latch.

While Mark worked his destructive magic on the engine, Sidney pulled a can of red spray paint from her pack. It was more than a bit cliché, but by God, she wanted their enemies to know who they were dealing with and for that knowledge to strike fear into their hearts.

In a nod to one of Lincoln Bannister's favorite movies about a group of teens fighting for freedom in their homeland after an invasion by the Russians, she'd adopted the local high school mascot as their own. Interestingly, she'd been offended by the name of the Redskins football team when she lived in DC, but when she learned that Liberal High School's mascot was also the Redskins, she took it as a sign.

She used the spray paint to graffiti a Native American war axe on the side of the truck. The red symbol stood out starkly against the green paint. There was no way that it'd be missed.

Sidney and Sally exchanged a grin. They were going to make these bastards wish they'd never set foot in America.

This is the end of the second installment of Sidney's Way. Want to read about the origins of the disease that swept the globe, and what happened to Grady Harper's team in Brazil? Look for Brian Parker's Five Roads to Texas prequel soon!

The Five Roads to Texas world is ever expanding. Look for more adventures from the minds of other Phalanx Press authors on the Five Roads' Amazon page.

OTHER AUTHORS UNDER THE SHIELD OF

Darren Wearmouth ~ Carl Sinclair

SIXTH CYCLE

Nuclear war has destroyed human civilization.

Captain Jake Phillips wakes into a dangerous new world, where he finds the remaining fragments of the population living in a series of strongholds, connected across the country. Uneasy alliances have maintained their safety, but things are about to change. -- Discovery leads to danger. -- Skye Reed, a tracker from the Omega stronghold, uncovers a threat that could spell the end for their fragile society. With friends and enemies revealing truths about the past, she will need to decide who to trust. -- **Sixth Cycle** is a gritty post-apocalyptic story of survival and adventure.

Darren Wearmouth

The Invasion Trilogy

Aliens have planned against us for centuries... And now the attack is ready.

Charlie Jackson's archaeological team find advanced technology in an undisturbed 16th Century graves. While investigating the discovery, giant sinkholes appear across planet, marking the start of Earth's colonization and the descent of civilization.

Charlie and the rest of humanity will have to fight for survival, sacrificing the life they've known to protect themselves from an ancient and previously dormant enemy. Even that might not be enough as aliens exact a plan that will change the course of history.

Allen Gamboa

DEAD ISLAND: Operation Zulu

Ten years after the world was nearly brought to its knees by a zombie Armageddon, there is a race for the antidote! On a remote Caribbean island, surrounded by a horde of hungry living dead, a team of American and Australian commandos must rescue the Antidotes' scientist. Filled with zombies, guns, Russian bad guys, shady government types, serial killers and elevator muzak. Dead Island is an action packed blood soaked horror adventure.

Dead Island: Dos and ***Dead Island: Ravenous*** are available now!

Owen Ballie

INVASION OF THE DEAD SERIES

This is the first book in a series of nine, about an ordinary bunch of friends, and their plight to survive an apocalypse in Australia. -- Deep beneath defense headquarters in the Australian Capital Territory, the last ranking Army chief and a brilliant scientist struggle with answers to the collapse of the world, and the aftermath of an unprecedented virus. Is it a natural mutation, or does the infection contain -- more sinister roots? -- One hundred and fifty miles away, five friends returning from a month-long camping trip slowly discover that death has swept through the country. What greets them in a gradual revelation is an enemy beyond compare. -- Armed with dwindling ammunition, the friends must overcome their disagreements, utilize their individual skills, and face unimaginable horrors as they battle to reach their hometown...

W.J. Lundy

Whiskey Tango Foxtrot

Alone in a foreign land. The radio goes quiet while on convoy in Afghanistan, a lost patrol alone in the desert. With his unit and his home base destroyed, Staff Sergeant Brad Thompson suddenly finds himself isolated and in command of a small group of men trying to survive in the Afghan wasteland. Every turn leads to danger.

The local population has been afflicted with an illness that turns them into rabid animals. They pursue him and his men at every corner and stop. Struggling to hold his team together and unite survivors, he must fight and evade his way to safety. A fast paced zombie war story like no other.

Joseph Hansen

ZOMBIE RUSH

New to the Hot Springs PD Lisa Reynolds was not all that welcomed by her coworkers especially those who were passed over for the position. It didn't matter, her thirty days probation ended on the same day of the Z-poc's arrival. Overnight the world goes from bad to worse as thousands die in the initial onslaught. National Guard and regular military unit deployed the day before to the north leaves the city in mayhem. All directions lead to death until one unlikely candidate steps forward with a plan. A plan that became an avalanche raging down the mountain culminating in the salvation or destruction of them all.

Rich Baker

ZED'S WORLD

BOOK ONE: THE GATHERING HORDE

The most ambitious terrorist plot ever undertaken is about to be put into motion, releasing an unstoppable force against humanity. Ordinary people – A group of students celebrating the end of the semester, suburban and rural families – are about to themselves in the center of something that threatens the survival of the human species. As they battle the dead – and the living – it's going to take every bit of skill, knowledge and luck for them to survive in Zed's World.

BOOK TWO: ROADS LESS TRAVELED

A terrible plague has been loosed upon the earth. In the course of one night, mankind teeters on the brink of extinction. Fighting through gathering hordes of undead, a group of friends brave military checkpoints, armed civilians, and forced allegiances in an attempt to reach loved ones. Thwarted at every turn, they press forward. But taking roads less traveled, could cost them everything.

BOOK THREE: NO WAY OUT

For Kyle Puckett, Earth has become a savage place. As the world continues to decay, the survivors of the viral plague have started choosing sides. With each encounter the stakes - and the body count - continue to rise. With the skies growing darker and the dead pressing in, both sides may soon find out that there is No Way Out.

<u>Brian Parker</u>

Grudge: Operation Highjump

The United States Navy led an expedition to Antarctica in December
1946, called Operation Highjump. Officially, the men were tasked with
evaluating the effect of cold weather on US equipment; secretly their
mission was to investigate reports of a hidden Nazi base buried beneath
the ice. After engaging unknown forces in aerial combat, weather
forced the Navy to abandon operations. Undeterred, the US returned
every Antarctic summer until finally the government detonated three
nuclear missiles over the atmosphere in 1958. Unfortunately, the
desperate gamble to rid the world of the Nazi scourge failed. The enemy
burrowed deeper into the ice, using alien technologies for cryogenic
freezing to amass a genetically superior army, indoctrinated from birth
to hate Americans. Now they've returned, intent on exacting revenge
for the destruction of their homeland and banishment to the icy wastes.

The Path of Ashes

Evil doesn't become extinct, it evolves. Our world is a violent place.
Murder, terrorism, racism and social inequality, these are some of the
forces that attempt to destroy our society while the State is forced to
increase its response to these actions. Our own annihilation is barely
held at bay by the belief that we've somehow evolved beyond our
ancestors' base desires.
From this cesspool of emotions emerges a madman, intent on leading
the world into anarchy. When his group of computer hackers infiltrate
the Department of Defense network, they initiate a nuclear war that will
irrevocably alter our world.
Aeric Gaines and his roommate, Tyler, survive the devastation of the
war, only to find that the politically correct world where they'd been
raised was a lie. All humans have basic needs such as food, water and
shelter…but we will fight for what we *desire*.
A Path of Ashes is a three-book series about life in post-apocalyptic
America, a nation devoid of leadership, electricity and human rights.
The world as we know it may have burned, but humanity found a way
to survive and this is their story.

Human Element

The Neuroweb began as the greatest invention since written language. A simple brain implant that allowed the user to access information, entertainment, and even pain relief. The Neuroweb was the beginning of a golden age for mankind...

Until it was compromised.

Everyone with the implant lost their most important commodity: their free will. The collective human consciousness was hacked, and now directed by artificial intelligence. Only those without the Neuroweb have a chance of resisting...If they dare.

Aaran has legitimate reason to believe he's the last free-thinking human alive. After his family was killed in the purge, he fled for his life. Now, he aimlessly wanders through the suburbs of Cincinnati alone, desperate to find a reason to live.

When he meets a girl like him - another free thinker - they search together for a cause worth fighting for. Worth dying for.

As the Ash Fell

Life in the frozen wastelands of Texas is anything but easy, but for Clay Whitaker there is always more at stake than mere survival.

It's been seven years since the ash billowed into the atmosphere, triggering some of the harshest winters in recorded history. Populations are thinning. Food is scarce. Despair overwhelming. With no way to sustain order, societies collapsed, leaving people to fend for themselves.

Clay and his sister Megan have taken a handful of orphaned children into their home--a home soaring sixteen stories into the sky. With roughly six short months a year to gather enough food and supplies to last the long, brutal winter, Clay must spend most of his time away from his family to scavenge, hunt, and barter.

When Clay rescues a young woman named Kelsey from a group of Screamers, his life is catapulted into a new direction, forcing him to make decisions he never thought he would have to make.

Now, with winter rolling in earlier than ever, Clay's divided attention is putting him, and his family, at risk.

54077454R10246

Made in the USA
San Bernardino,
CA